A Father's Daughter

Kat Rose

Copyright © 2015 Kat Rose
All right reserved.

Dedications

I would like to thank my family and friends. They have stood behind me every step of the way and never let me fall. A special shout out goes to Shannon Mayer. If it wasn't for you, my pages would still be locked in a closet. And to my editor Tina Winograd, thank you for taking a chance on an unknown. Your expert eyes dusted off the clumsy words and polished them beautifully. To everyone who is now reading this; it is because of you I can continue doing what I love.

I would like to dedicate this book to my Oma, Rose. Although she is no longer here with us, she was the very first person to read the words of this story. Reading was a passion of hers. She would often get lost amongst tales for days at a time. I wish she was here to see this day; the day my words came together and found an audience. Though you are gone, you are never forgotten. Your love and support still remains. We all love and miss you. This is for you.

"Here comes the hard part, for now it comes time to lay me down.
Please know that this isn't goodbye, for I have lived and I have loved.
Don't cry for me, my dear, for I am always near.
Please talk to me, my dear, for I will always hear your voice.
And don't forget to smile for me, my dear
For I will forever and always be right here."

To keep up to date check out my writing page!
https://www.facebook.com/Kat-Rose-Writing-997642216921062/

Preface: The Beginning

It all started when I was four years old. I remember hiding in the closet, which had become my "safe place." I hugged my knees gently and rocked back and forth. My parents were fighting again; I heard them screaming at each other from downstairs. My mom began to cry. I only heard bits and pieces, but it all revolved around a woman named Alison. My Dad sounded mad. I didn't understand what was going on, we used to be such a happy family but things had begun to change.

My mom and I had to move to a new house, a smaller house. It only had two bedrooms and a bathroom with faulty plumbing. It was a drastic change from our last house; which held large spacious bedrooms and two modern bathrooms. My mom said we had to downgrade because it was all she could afford on her own; I didn't know what that meant, but I knew it wasn't good. Our food took a hit as well. Instead of quality meats and fresh produce our menu now mainly consisted of cereal, crackers and meals that came out of frozen boxes.

My mom spent a lot of time crying and so did I. Often times I could hear her sob from my bedroom; it would keep me up at night and make me sad. I would crawl into her bed, where she would hug me tightly and promise me that everything would be alright. I was starting to get a strange and horrible feeling in the pit of my stomach; my dad didn't spend the night here anymore, so he couldn't check for the monsters under my bed, or read me my bedtime stories. But a part of me was glad. When my dad left, the screaming stopped. The yelling scared me, and it made my mom cry. I did not like it at all, and once, I even got mad at my dad and told him to leave because all he ever did was make mom cry.

Today, my dad had taken me out for ice cream. It did not feel the same. It seemed as though he were mad at me, he barely spoke, barely looked at me. It had scared me and I started to cry for my mom. My dad brought me home quickly after that and he promised he would see me again tomorrow; we were going to spend the day at the beach. When my dad had brought me home, I ran for my bedroom and forgot to give him a hug and kiss on the cheek. Once I was in my room, the screaming started downstairs. I jumped and hugged my teddy closer as the front door slammed shut. I heard my dads truck start, and then he was gone.

Footsteps sounded outside my closet, and my mom quietly peeked her head inside. "Hey, kiddo what are you doing in there?" My mom's voice was slow and sad, so I motioned for her to sit beside me.

She did. I gave her one of my favorite teddy bears. "Here mommy, Bear will make you feel better."

My mom nodded, and then she started to cry. I watched her wide eyed and crawled into her lap. She hugged me tightly, and we rocked back and forth until her tears stopped falling. I never saw my dad after that.

Chapter One: Responsibilities

I lay in bed and stared absently at the white ceiling; last night's troubled dream still played through my head. I turned onto my side and stared at my night table that was littered with pictures. Most of the photos were of my friends, and my mother and I. My eyes lingered onto a picture that was starting to fade; it was a picture of my father, Jack. In the photo he knelt down, laughing, and I was wrapped safely in his arms. A look of wonder spread across my features. My heart ached immediately. It was one of the few images I kept of my father; most of his photos were torn up in bitter disappointment. I sighed heavily, reached out, and lay the picture down so I could not see it anymore. As I groggily sat up and reached for my worn out jeans, somehow I knew things were going to change and I would soon find myself away from everything comforting and familiar.

Once I was dressed, I found my mom bustling around in the kitchen. A pan dropped and some words were muttered that were better left unsaid. I chuckled; my mother's strong points did not include her kitchen skills.

"Good morning, Mom," I said cheerfully.

"Good morning, Abby, did you sleep okay?" My mother's pretty face crumpled slightly as she glanced my way.

"My sleep was....err eventful so to speak."

"Nightmares; again?" This time my mother's big hazel eyes grew wide with concern.

A spasm of panic ignited within me. I had put my mother; Jenna, through some hard times without even meaning too. My parents divorce had been hard on me, though I tried not to show it, and without even realizing it, I had caused my mother to constantly worry about me. I stared at her now; her large hazel eyes showed her every thought; which suited her perfectly, my mom did not know the meaning of the world subtle. Today, her normally tidy auburn hair was askew and her eyes held a secret.

"No, not really, they were actually quite comical." I lied, and put on my most convincing smile.

"Well, okay then." With a quick nod, my mother went back to attempting to make something she thought would be considered tasty.

As I absently read a book, I was aware my mother stopped fussing, and she watched me intently. I couldn't quite read the look on her face. My heart raced slightly, what was that look? Worry? Doubt? Concern? Caution even?

"Mom," I said strangely. "What is it?"

My mother tidied her hair with a grace that I suddenly envied. Her eyes darted away as she fluttered her thick lashes and pursed her perfect lips. I knew she would tell me. My mother and I held an odd relationship. We were very close, more like friends, best friends even. She did not hold her authority above me, yet I respected it completely I was responsible, she was carefree, but somehow we always got by.

"Your father called." My mother's silky voice went on cautiously, "Alison left." My shoulder's relaxed and I pulled my long hair up in an unconscious effort. "Oh" I sighed, "Is that all?"

I felt a stab of guilt. I heard my usual kind voice turn frosty. Alison had left my father. Why should I feel guilty? He left us for her. I had no respect for the woman my father broke up our family for. He left us and he never looked back, he had made his choice. In my mind, the worst part was, she *knew* my father was married and had a child, but she wanted him, and she achieved her goal without a second thought.

"Abby, honey, I have moved on, I forgave him, you should too."

"Mom," I groaned. "Can we please let this conversation go? I can't have it again. I get it okay? Not all marriages work, sometimes two people are not meant to be, I know. You are with a great guy now, end of story."

"Honey, I forgave him. It was hard, but...."

I glanced at my mother and sighed. I knew how hard this conversation was for her. So, I bit my tongue, and let her go on.

"Abby...you never gave your father another chance. I have had it out with him; we have talked about what happened many times. I think you need to...to..." she circled her hands in the air absently "Have it out with him in your own way, ask questions, get answers." My mom nodded her head eagerly like she had achieved something.

"I don't know. Mom, I will think about it." I paused. "I'm not very hungry this morning. I can clean up the kitchen, you need to get ready for work." I nodded towards the clock as a silent reminder. I got up, and automatically started attending to the dishes. My mother sighed. "You are only seventeen years old, honey. When did you become the mother?"

I turned and saw the smirk upon my mother's face. "What can I say? You know how to raise a child well."

With that, she gave me a kiss on the forehead, and was polished for work in ten minutes flat. She floated out the door. Twenty minutes later I was ready for school and headed out to my old black Chevy pickup. My hair was still casually placed in a messy up-do, my jeans were torn in the knees, and my T-shirt was nothing that drew too much attention. *Unlike my mother.* I thought somewhat self-consciously. She always looked so put together, no matter what she wore.

I thought about my mother and I. We shared many of the same features. We each had long, thick hair, the same petite frame, soft voices, and large eyes. While my mother's eyes were hazel, mine were a deep blue. *Just like my father's.* I thought about that for a moment, and stared almost hesitantly into the truck's mirror. I may have had my mother's eyes and hair type, but my face was a mixture of both my parents, even I couldn't deny that. While I had my mother's small, button like nose and high cheek bones, I shared my father's lips, and defined, rounded jaw. I even had his hair color; golden brown. I sighed, tossed my school bag into the back of my truck, and fired up the engine. I couldn't hide from everything he gave me.

⌘

"Abby! Hey girl, I thought you were never going to show up!"

I chuckled, leave it to Sarah to brighten up anyone's day; that girl was on one permanent happy high.

"Hey, Sarah. Sorry, I know, I know. I'm late!"

"Yeah, but it won't kill us be a little late for Mrs. Hills daily lecture on proper…what is it this week? Lady-like behavior? Chivalry is dead?"

I rolled my eyes. "Something like that, yeah."

"Oh!" Sarah bounced excitedly up and down, sending her blond curls bouncing. "Guess who finally asked me out!"

It wasn't a hard guess, she had been flirting shamelessly with one guy almost the entire semester. "Greg?" I asked casually, hiding my smirk.

"Yes!" Sarah's voice hit an octave unknown to man.

"Congrats, you have been pursuing him for awhile now."

Sarah's green eyes widened, and she wore a shameless smile. "No. I have not been *pursuing* him; I have merely been giving him subtle hints."

"Ahh, okay, if that's what it's called." I grinned and rolled my eyes.

Leave it to Sarah, she could always make me smile. She linked her arm with mine, and began mindless chatter on what she should wear, and all the hopes she had pinned onto poor unsuspecting Greg.

"Late again girls!" Mrs. Hill's shrill voice rang out. Her eyes held no patience today. "Take your seats, now. This is the second time this week you have been late!"

Her eyes narrowed from Sarah to me, and her eyes held mine in disapproval. I broke the stare and began to scribble mindless doodles across my notebook. Mrs. Hill blamed Sarah for our tardiness. I knew that. She thought of Sarah as a wild uncontrollable girl, while she had labeled me as a student who should know better. I was one of her best students; English seemed to be my specialty. I was graceful with words in a way that lacked in other areas of my life, gravity being one of them.

Sarah groaned beside me as Mrs. Hill droned on and on about some upcoming essay, and for some strange reason, my mother's voice popped into my head. *Alison left your father.* What was left unsaid? What was wrong with our conversation this morning? *Cara.* What about Cara? Why was she never mentioned? Cara was Alison's and my father's little girl. What was she, about seven months old now? I made a mental note to ask my mother about her and ignored the stab of guilt that shot through my heart. I should know how old my sister was. I ignored the dull ache and tried to push Cara out of my head. It was hard for me to accept her; I had never met her in person. She existed only in photographs. I was never ready to meet her. That would make things too real. Apart of me was jealous; she got to see our father everyday, whereas I barely remembered the last time I saw him. The other part of me was hurt; Jack hadn't left her, but he had left me.

Sarah's elbow jabbed into me. "Hey, oww!" I squawked.

Sarah narrowed her eyes. "Shhh! You will never guess who is checking you out!"

Sarah cringed as Miss. Hill shot her a glare. "Never mind, here!" She hissed.

I stared down at the note she thrust my way. Here we go, into the inner high school working of Sarah Carver's mind.

I think I should wear a little black dress for our first date. Dinner and a movie, this Friday! Do you think that would be too much? Or—wait! Hello! Josh Brent is staring at you! He is fine! You know I thought Trish was going out with him? Or maybe, she got shot down? This is excellent news!

Josh Brent? I glanced up, and sure enough, he was staring. I looked away. He appeared way too smug. I gave him a condescending glare and turned my back towards him, hiding my face behind a curtain of hair. Sure, Josh was gorgeous, and on the football team. All the girls wanted a piece of him, but there was something about him that did not sit well with me. I decided not to tell Sarah exactly what I thought of Josh, for she wore that silly daydreaming look on her face again. I grabbed my pen, and began scribbling down a response for Sarah.

Don't wear the black dress, save it for a second date. Wear your good butt jeans, and a nice top. As for Josh Brent…it is not going to happen. Besides, I don't want to be on Trish's bad side! Let's leave it at that!

I pushed the note towards her. Sarah's smile brightened, then fell. Sarah glanced at me, curiosity heavy in her features. I shrugged my shoulders and shook my head.

She mouthed. "Whatever, you're crazy," putting extra emphasis on the word "crazy" until Mrs. Hill called on her. Saved by the teacher, and then the bell.

⌘

"I won the case today!"

"Oh, Mark that's incredible! I knew you could!"

I smiled politely. "That's great Mark, I knew you could do it."

Mark's grin would not be going away anytime soon. My mom leaned in to give him a quick kiss. I absent-mindedly pushed my food around on the plate. *Now or never.* I cleared my throat. "What about Cara?"

My mother stared back in shock. *Well what do you know*, I thought somewhat guilty, *Mark's grin disappeared after all*. His face fell into a puzzled expression. Concern flitted in his eyes.

My mother answered. "Abby, well….Alison, she…she, just left. Cara's with your father. He has been having a hard time with it, it's putting stress on his job and he's pretty upset about the whole situation."

I let my mother's words register. How could a mother leave her child? A seven month old child at that. "She just left?! How could she do that! And alone with Jack?" "Your father," my mother corrected me sternly.

I glared. "Fine, with my *father*. He has no clue about kids; he couldn't even deal with me!" As I said those words, the tears seeped forward. I closed my eyes. I would not let them fall now.

My mother's face looked pained and she softened her voice. "Oh baby, do you think that's why he left? That he couldn't deal with you? It's not that at all, it was never you. The issues your father and I had were just that, *ours*. We were young, we didn't always make the best decisions."

"Well, he didn't try very hard with me, Mom. It was what? Six years before he tried contacting me again? Doesn't say very much, does it? And I don't really think a Christmas card here and there really counts."

My mother's eyes filled with sadness, and then anger sparked up as she thought back to those dark days. "Your father doesn't always make the best choices…"

Mark shifted uncomfortably and I felt my sympathy go out to him. It wasn't fair to drag him into something so uncomfortable, especially on his special day. "I'm sorry Mark. Mom, can we discuss this later?"

My mother gave a quick nod and I turned back to Mark. "So Mark, tell us all the details!" Mark's face brightened as he chatted happily away, revealing a very detailed play by play.

A few hours later we found ourselves sitting in the living room staring down at an envelope stamped from the university of my choice. "Aren't you going to open it?" My mother exclaimed in what she thought was a calm voice, but anticipation rang thick. She squirmed excitedly. I, however, didn't feel the same emotion. I stared blankly at the envelope, my stomach in knots. How could one envelope, one piece of paper, make me feel ill?

I looked from my mother to Mark and placed a lopsided smile on my face. I glanced once more at the envelope with my name on it. All my hopes were pinned to what lay inside. "Well, here it goes…" I spoke in a shaky voice.

"Wait!" my mother interrupted. "Let me get the camera!"

I shot Mark a horrified look, and we both spoke in unison. "No!"

I ripped open the envelope, and hesitantly unfolded the paper. My eyes quickly scanned the first sentence. *Congratulations Abigail Taylor. We are pleased to….*

My jaw dropped; I didn't even finish reading it. "I got in! I GOT IN!!"

I jumped up and down, and embraced both Mark and my mother's warm hugs. As I stood back to glance at their faces, I suddenly knew what I was going to do. It was only a matter of time.

⌘

I closed my eyes and thought back to when I was eight years old. Things were bad. My mother tried her best to make things work. She had taken on two jobs, but that meant she barely saw me, and she ran herself ragged. My Grandmother had stepped in and taken us in into her picturesque two story white house, which was surrounded by a sea of colors from her garden. It was a welcoming sight. When it rained, the roof didn't leak, I remembered being surprised pots were actually used to cook meals, instead of acting as buckets. The shower had warm water, there was working heat, and the best part of all was the food; my Grandmother was an amazing cook. Things were starting to look up. My mother went back to school to get her Teaching Degree, and I was always well looked after. Still, something was missing in my life; my father. I felt so betrayed by him; I didn't understand how he could walk away so easily. I also felt remorse. It was something that I had never shared with my mom, but apart of me wondered if he had left because of me. I remembered back to when my parents fought, my name had come up a few times. Worry fell heavy over me; did I do something to drive my dad away? Did I not hug him hard enough? Did I forget to tell him that I loved him? Or, was it simply that he had stopped loving me?

While I snooped through my mother's things one afternoon I found my father's mailing address folded in an old book. I wrote him a letter every week for almost a year. I told him how bad things were. I begged and pleaded for him to come back. I apologized for yelling at him and forgetting to give him a hug and kiss on the last day I saw him; I apologized for everything I had ever done wrong in my young life. I told him how much I missed him, and how scared I was when he was not here. I must have checked the mail at least three times a day that year, waiting. I never received anything. The day I turned nine years old I made a silent promise to myself; if Jack would not come see me, I would go see him when the timing was right, whether he wanted me or not.

Eight years later, it looked like my day had finally arrived. I made a quick mental calculation before I spoke. I could easily transfer high schools. I was an honor student; I could catch on fast to the new curriculum. Besides, where I would be going was a small, cold, wintry town. I was pretty sure their academics would be well behind my current school. I would miss my friends terribly; I had always hoped to graduate with them but sometimes life throws you unexpected curveballs. This may turn out to be one of those moments I may look back on later on and regret; but for some reason, I felt a strong sense of obligation.

The university would only be a fifteen minute drive from my father's house. I had always planned on moving out that way when the time came to start my new academic journey. Living with Jack had never entered my mind, but if I could make this work, there was a chance I could escape the cost of rent. There would be no distractions. I could focus all my intentions strictly on school. I would treat my new home life like a job, I didn't need to necessarily like, or *love* anyone. I was responsible, I was confident in my abilities. I knew what it was like to grow up without a parent. I don't know why, but my heart ached for little Cara. I resented her, but I also loved her. She was after all, my half-sister. I was her big sister; surely I had some sort of a duty to her?

I opened my eyes and faced my parents. I took a shaky breath and dropped the bomb. "I'm going to move in with Jack. He needs help with Cara. I am doing this for her, not *him*. I'll talk to the principal tomorrow, and let them arrange it with the high school out there…" I sucked in a breath as I watched my mother's face pale.

"Abigail!" My mother's shrill voice stung.

"Mom, please don't. I don't know why, but I feel that I, well… I feel that it's my responsibility. I am going to move in with my father."

Chapter Two: The Move

It took two days for the shock of my news to settle in at home. Arrangements were made and the new school was eager for my arrival. As I packed up my bedroom, I thought back to the whirl wind of the week. I broke the news to my friends and their reactions were miserable, but they understood, or so they said. Their eyes told me otherwise. We all promised to keep in touch, but the promise lacked conviction. With college looming in the horizon, our lives were about to change whether we were ready or not. Deep, deep, down I knew I was making the right decision, or so I had hoped. I was not entirely sure where my decision had come from. It was so out of character for me, I liked routine. I was not a fly by the seat of my pants kind of girl. Was instinct kicking in? Did I need some sort of self-conscious change in my life? Or maybe, apart of me worried I was getting in the way of my mother and Mark's new marriage. I lingered on the last thought. Ridiculous. They both loved me; Mark was like a dad to me, and he thought of me as his own daughter.

    I looked around my empty room and shuddered. It was so eerie. I had made this my own safe place for the last twelve years, and I was about to upset that balance. The knot in the pit of my stomach twisted, growing tighter. I sat and put my head between my knees and took a deep breath. I was getting used to this feeling now. I had been feeling it ever since I had made this decision. I began to fight off a panic attack, but I didn't know how well I was achieving it. I thought back to the phone call with Jack. My mother left the room to give me privacy. I shakily dialed Jack's number, a number I had never dialed in my seventeen years.

A man's distracted voice filled my ear. "Hello? Wait, hold on, hello!"

I was taken aback by the sound of his voice. It sounded tired and stressed. A baby cried in the background. My heart ached slightly. "Jack? This is….Abigail…your daughter."

I added the last part just in case he had forgotten. It surprised me at how hard it was to say those words. I took a deep breath, this was going to be much, much harder than I thought.

"Abigail? Oh, hello. How are you? How's the weather? It's snowing here, and really cold, but they say the sun is supposed to make an appearance soon." He rambled on. *Good, he's nervous too.*

I didn't want to drag this out so I got straight to the point. "Listen. Jack, I heard about your situation. I'm headed down your way. I got transferred to the high school out there and the university has accepted me for next fall…"

I bit my lip, and continued, "The university is only fifteen minutes from your place and I heard you could use the help…" I trailed off, waiting for some sort of a sign.

Silence on the other end. What did that mean? Did he hang up on me? No, I heard him shuffle. I continued slowly. "I'm a great cook and a good student. I keep to myself quite well. Kind of like you….." My thoughts turned slightly hostile. *Keeps to himself all right; abandonment. No, Keep it civil.*

I lightened my tone and carried on. "I have quite a bit of experience with children, so I can help out with Cara. I have my own truck, so you don't need to worry about driving me anywhere."

Again, silence. I took a controlled breath as my anger began to stir. He had nothing to say? Not one thing, after all this time? "Listen, Jack, I'm just waiting on your approval now. Everything is set here on my end. Mom knows, the schools are aware…"

"I-I," he cleared his throat. "When will you arrive?" Jack's voice cracked.

"One week."

Jack's tone held no emotion. "I will see you then. Abigail?"

I stiffened at the sudden softness in his voice. "Yes?"

"Put chains on those tires. The roads are in bad shape." I sighed as he continued on about the roads; his voice hardened and became official. "Grab a pen and paper," he continued, "I'll give you directions."

⌘

Four days after the phone conversation with Jack, I was ready to leave. Technically, I had been ready to go three days ago, but I kept finding ways to put it off. My mother knew this, though she did not say a word; she knew this was something I would have to figure out on my own. I walked very slowly down the stairs, admiring the house I had loved so much. I took mental pictures of our cozy picture filled living room and regal stone fireplace. The images on the walls projected happy memories. Our tidy kitchen brimmed with flashbacks of my mother trying to make a decent meal. I stole one last glance around and stepped outside before shutting the door softly behind me. I instantly felt homesick. I stared at my mother, who fought back tears. Mark's arms were securely wrapped around her. He held a proud, sad smile. In that moment I knew how much he loved me. I also knew how much he cherished my mother, they would be okay without me. It was me who I was concerned about.

My mother was carefree, she never put much thought or preparation into anything, she loved to jump in headfirst. Mark was responsible. He was the man with a plan. They balanced each other perfectly. Mark calmed my mother while my mother helped loosen Mark up. On the bright side, he loved to cook, and he could actually make a decent meal. I was somewhere in the middle of the two of them. I was responsible, I liked to think things through, and I did not get rattled very easily. A quiet calmness surrounded me and I hoped it would stay with me during my new journey.

"Oh, honey, I am so proud of you." My mother's arms fell tightly around me.

"Thanks, Mom."

She let go and Mark squeezed my shoulders. "I'm really proud of you, kid. If you need anything at all, let us know."

I nodded silently, and gave him a tiny grin. My truck was loaded with all of my belongings. It was time.

"You make sure you call us when you get there, keep in touch honey, or I will be calling you non-stop, understood?"

I had to laugh. Whenever my mother tried to be authoritative, it always amused me. "Promise."

My mother nodded. I hopped into the truck and the engine clunked to life. Ready or not, here I come Jack. I reversed out of the driveway, gave a quick wave, and left the two people in the world that I loved more than anything standing alone in the driveway; that, and mild temperatures. The drive was agonizingly long. After driving five hours, I had to get some fresh air. I pulled over, hopped out, and began to shiver almost instantly. It was freezing. I rummaged through my bags, and found my winter jacket and put it on. I wouldn't have needed this back home for another month or so; a light jacket would have done the trick. I leaned against the hood of my truck and stared up at the blowing snow. The sky was a hazy pinkish gray. The cool wind nipped at my face and found it's way down my back. I shuddered and slowly stretched out my limbs, trying to wake them up. I couldn't delay much longer. With a heavy sigh to match my heart, I hopped in the driver's seat, turned the heat on high, and cranked up the music.

The sun started to set, and I was forced to slow my speed. I wasn't used to driving in snow. Back home, snow was a rarity. We usually got one or two good dumps each winter but the rain washed it clean the very next day. Just another thing I would have to get used to. The list in my head began to pile up. I blamed it all on Jack; which I knew was unfair. I had made this decision on my own. Heaven knows why, but here I was, driving in a blizzard out in the middle of nowhere on my way to a man I had no desire to be with. I shook my head, this was not a moment to hold on too.

After another two and a half hours of driving on icy, winding roads, I found the address I had half-heartedly been looking for; 6598 Lodge Street. I admired the cozy looking street from within the safety of my truck and gave Jack credit. It was a nice neighborhood; the houses were decently spread out from each other, it offered the perfect balance of having your own privacy; yet close enough to provide security from your neighbors. All of the houses had a welcoming "homey" look to them. For some reason it made me think of Christmas. I could almost picture children dancing around the tree, a blazing fire, smoke lazily floating from the chimney, and the smell of cookies wafting in the air.

I pulled into Jack's snow covered driveway, and turned off my headlights. I realized I held my breath; I wasn't sure how this was going to go down. Would Jack come out to greet me? I wasn't sure I really wanted him too. I had quietly hoped to sneak inside without drawing too much attention to myself, but that would be impossible. He would have heard me coming. My truck was anything but quiet, but then again, he wouldn't have known the sound belonged to me. My truck was everything that I was not; big, bold, and loud. It had been love at first sight when I saw it parked in someone's cluttered yard with a large 'For Sale' sign over the windshield.

I had a sudden worry, did my truck wake the baby? Would Jack be mad if it did? Rather than get myself worked up at the endless possibilities, I opened up my door, and stepped out. I didn't even have my other foot out of the truck when I felt myself go down. I reached out to steady myself with the truck door, but it was too late. My body hit the slick driveway with a loud thud and in that moment, I knew the ice and I were going to become quite familiar with each other. I lied on the snow-covered driveway for a moment, looking up towards the house. I gingerly got up, and gripped on to my truck for support. I decided to leave most of my belongings in the truck for the night. I took the bag that contained my daily necessities. I brushed myself off and gulped in anticipation; here goes nothing.

I tip toed my way to the door and hesitated. Should I knock? Maybe I should have called before I arrived. Before I had time to talk myself out of anything, my pale knuckles gave a light tap against the door. I held my breath and listened; muffled footsteps sounded. Almost instinctively, I jumped back from the door. It creaked open and I stared up at my father. He hadn't changed much over the years. He was a big man. He stood over six feet tall and was built like a quarterback. His eyes were a dark blue and he had sun lines around the corners. His hair had thinned a bit but all in all, he looked like the Jack I used to stare at in pictures when I was little, wishing with all my heart he would come home.

"Hi, Jack." I said in a quieter tone than I would have liked. He studied me with surprise, and what I thought could be pride.

"You look just like your mother" He nodded with approval. "Come in." His eyes narrowed at my truck. He nodded towards it as he grabbed my bag from my hands. I looked at him questionably as he continued. "That your truck?" He said with a laugh.

My eyes narrowed and I rolled my hands into fists, how dare he insult my truck. I was surprised at the protectiveness that seeped out of me over a vehicle. This was going to be hard. "Yes." I gritted through my teeth.

He must have sensed the reaction from me, for he chuckled. "A little big for you don't you think?" he sized me up. "What are you, 5'4, 5'5?"

"I took after Mom in the height department; as well as many other things." I sucked in a quick breath; I felt guilty for adding on the last part. I bit my lip and hoped he hadn't noticed my slip. Judging from his reaction; it appeared he did not notice.

Jack nodded. "Come on in, sorry for the mess. Make sure you keep quiet, I finally got Cara to sleep."

It was dark in the house, but I could see there was a mess to be cleaned. Shoes were scattered about, clothes slung over any spare piece of furniture. A quick glance in the kitchen made me cringe; dishes were littered on any open surface. I sniffed the air and hid back a groan; the garbage needed to be taken out. I was suddenly scared to see the conditions of the bathrooms.

Jack interrupted my horrified thought. "Want a tour now?"

I nodded quietly.

"Good," he gestured his hand lazily around. "To the left is the kitchen, through the sliding door is the living room, and across the hall the bathroom. I'll show you upstairs."

I paused at a closed door next to the bathroom. "What's in here?"

Jack narrowed his eyes. "You are not to go in that room."

I nodded quickly, slightly taken aback by his cold and brief tone. I watched Jack and noted he kept measured steps between us; every time he crossed some invisible boundary, he took a step back as though he had been struck.

"All right, here we have Cara's room, my bedroom is across the hall, another bathroom, and finally, we have your room here at the end of the hall." He quietly swung open the door, and gestured me in. He stood in the hallway.

"The room isn't much. The bed is new, and there's a desk over here for your homework. We have wireless Internet, so you can set up your lap top."

At least it was clean, I sighed a relief. The room had potential; it was cute. Large windows overlooked the snow-covered street, the closet was a decent size, and the walls had been freshly painted.

"Thanks, Jack." We each stood there silently staring at each other, each shifting uncomfortably. There was no more to be said and we both knew it.

He nodded gruffly. "Glad you made it here. Good night."

I watched Jack leave the room, quietly shutting the door behind him. I stretched out on the bed and was asleep before I could think of an excuse to go back home.

⌘

The sound of seagulls, and the gentle lull of waves crashing on the beach flitted behind closed eyes. I was five years old and I ran in my nightgown with tears streaming down my face. I called frantically for my father with my arms outstretched, ready to embrace him the moment I found him. A dark silhouette stood ahead. It slowly turned and called out my name. I quickened my pace but I felt myself begin to sink. The light sand below had turned into a goopy mess that quickly took me under. I awoke with a start and rested my head in my hands. This dream had been plaguing my slumber ever since I was a child. I hoped it wasn't a premonition of things to come.

Chapter Three: New Routine

I awoke the next morning, disoriented. I sat up quickly, and looked around in confusion. The sound of a baby crying echoed throughout the walls. *Oh. Right.* I had decided on my own free will to uproot my cozy, reliable life. Again, I shook my head and threw myself back on the bed and waited for Jack to tend to Cara. Five minutes had gone by and Cara still cried. I felt a surge of resentment toward her, which quickly turned to pity. I could not, no matter what, blame any of this on her. After all, she couldn't choose who her parents were. I quietly opened my door, and peeked down the hall. Jack didn't seem to be around anywhere. Cara's cries led me to her room. I opened the door quietly and peeked inside.

Her room was captivating. At some point, Jack and Alison must have been excited about having a baby; great care went into planning this room. The walls were painted in a soft pink and white marble. Her crib was dainty, yet sturdy, with cute little details engraved into the sides. A mobile of Disney princesses turned lazily above her. A rocking chair sat to the left of her crib, while to the right, held a generous changing table and matching dresser. A surge of loneliness washed over me. I walked over to Cara and peeked inside. She had grown since the last set of pictures I had received. She had a mop of dark brown hair and wide brilliant blue eyes. She was snuggled in a tiny pink sleeper, one look at me and I was sold. She was adorable.

"Hey there, baby; you're awake, aren't you?"

Cara stopped crying and studied me intently; it made me a little nervous.

I looked around, waiting for Jack to come in, but he never did. "All right, up we go. Time to start the morning. I bet you need your diaper changed don't you baby?"

Butterflies flitted in the pit of my stomach, every noise made me jump. I wasn't sure if I was allowed to be in here or not; somehow I felt like I was intruding. Cara didn't fuss as I gently strapped her to the changing table, nor did she squirm when I changed her diaper.

"Well, aren't you a sweetheart, you are making my job so easy!" I cooed.

I placed her in a tiny matching purple outfit, and was pleased with myself. "Let's find you some breakfast, baby." I balanced Cara on my hip and began to hum a tune. All the while, I was very aware of Cara's big blue eyes staring up at me.

When I got down stairs, I admired the furniture. Everything was modern and matching, yet to my dismay, the light revealed much more of a mess than I had hoped for. I settled Cara into her high chair and noticed a note posted on the fridge.

Abby: Went to work. Be home by 6. Cara's formula and bottles are in the cupboard.
Jack

I stared at the note, slightly horrified as my eyes settled on Cara. I didn't think Jack would leave me here on my first day alone, especially with a baby. I had hoped to shadow Jack for a day so I could mimic the daily routine. I had no idea what Cara's schedule was like. I looked around the kitchen for further instructions; but to my dismay, I found none. I glanced towards Cara who had begun to fuss. I looked through the cupboards and found everything I would need to keep her occupied. I checked the temperature of her formula on my wrist, making sure it wouldn't be too hot. I held the bottle for Cara and was pleasantly surprised when she grabbed onto her bottle securely. I let go cautiously, and she held it up herself, drinking thirstily. Her big blue eyes stared back at me. I looked at her with slight hesitation, wondering if she knew just how clueless I was. I gave Cara a handful of cheerios and watched carefully as she ate the first one. She still stared at me, chewing thoughtfully. *Good, that should keep her busy.* To my dismay, Jack didn't have a lot of food. I would need to go shopping. As I ate the stale cereal, I made a list of all the things I would need to pick up. I glanced at the clock; it was only 7:30 a.m. Today was going to be a very long day.

After breakfast, I placed Cara in the playpen in the living room, and made sure there was nothing she would choke on. I nodded with satisfaction and hopped in the shower. I changed into my sweats and a long sleeve shirt, casually braided my golden hair and headed downstairs. I glanced at Cara who made blowing noises and happily chewed on her toys. First things first, I found a laundry basket and began collecting stray clothes. With every item of clothing I found, my rage grew higher and higher. *Jack.* I took deep breaths and remembered my vow; treat this like a job, nothing more, nothing less. I had to live here too and I hoped for a peaceful environment. Maybe I would bring friends over to this place one day; it had to be presentable. I started the first of many loads of laundry, and got to work vacuuming, dusting, mopping floors, scrubbing bathrooms, cleaning out the sparse fridge, and finally the oven. Somewhere between dusting and mopping, Cara had gotten fussy. I fed her lunch, and placed her in her crib to sleep. I found the baby monitors, and turned them on.

Four hours later I was exhausted and plopped myself onto the couch. I took an admiring look around the place and sighed contentedly; finally, I was done. I took a deep breath, much better. The house smelled clean; it was a major improvement from the musty, old garbage smell that lingered when I first arrived. If Jack didn't help me keep this up, I would have to drag him down the street behind my truck. With that image in my head, I chuckled until I remembered I had left the rest of my bags in my truck. I groaned and found my jacket, stuffed my boots on and went outside. The cold left me breathless and gasping. This was going to take some getting used to. I grumbled the whole way to my truck, slipping and sliding, but I managed to bring three bags inside without falling. I was quite proud of myself. Two more bags to go and no wipe outs. I tossed the last bag over my shoulder and went to shut my door. My feet hit a patch of ice and slid from under me. An escaped "Oh!" escaped from my lips and I hit the ground hard. My bag landed with a thud four feet away.

"Hey, are you okay?" Crunching footsteps came toward me rapidly. I glanced up and was met by a pair of dark green eyes filled with concern. *Oh no, no, no. I do not need this.*

"You alright down there?" The eyebrows furrowed.

"Yes, I'm fine, I'm just…well, I'm not the most graceful person in the world." I sat up and smiled sheepishly.

The stranger smiled broadly, and offered me his hand. "Here, let's help you up before you permanently freeze to the ground."

I grasped his hand, and he yanked me up with ease. Yep, I definitely did not need this. The stranger stood at least 6'2", with broad shoulders and a nice lean frame. He had dark green eyes, a strong jaw, and dark brown hair which he wore a little longer, and mindlessly pushed it back from his eyes. His grin remained amused.

He held out his hand and shook mine. "My names Alex, I live across the street."

My cheeks grew hot as he casually gave me the once over. I looked down quickly and was horrified I was still in my sweats. I felt my hair as naturally as I could, and grimaced when I felt how out of place it was; this was so far from an alluring first impression.

"I haven't seen you around here before, how do you know Jack?" Alex piped up.

At the mention of Jack's name, my face turned over in disgust. Alex's eyes grew wide in surprise. I marched past him and went to retrieve my bag. "I'm his daughter, Abby."

I bent down to grab my bag and stumbled. "No!" I yelled, and steadied myself against the large tree that was within my grasp.

Alex chuckled and easily strode over toward me. He plucked up my bag, and offered his arm to me. "Do you need a hand?"

I contemplated accepting his offer until I saw the gleam in his eye. "No thanks, I think I can manage."

He nodded once. "All right, I'll carry your bag to the door at least," he eyed me over. "I don't like the idea of you multi-tasking in the snow."

My face grew hot, but I managed a smile.

"So, you must be Jack's older daughter…" Alex began hesitantly. He stopped talking when he saw my body stiffen. "Sorry," he began.

"No, it's alright. This is just new to me."

"Actually, he mentioned you were coming." He was interrupted by Cara's cry.

"Oh, she's up, I'll be right back, come on in." I kicked off my boots and ran up to Cara's room. Within minutes I had her changed and sucking on her bottle. Alex's eyes followed me and I realized I had let a stranger, a *perfect* stranger nonetheless into Jack's house.

He must have sensed the urgency on my face. He smiled, and set down my bag. "You have done an amazing job with the place, cleanliness wise."

I raised my eyebrows. "How would you know?"

Alex smiled ruefully. "I, uh, come over here sometimes."

"Oh?" Curiosity filled my voice momentarily. Again, I ran my hand through my hair and it reminded me of how un-kept I was at the moment. I shuffled uncomfortably. I shot Alex a silent plea to leave.

"Well, I guess I'll be off then."

I nodded. "Err, thanks for, you know, outside…" I gestured helplessly to the door.

Alex laughed lightly and stepped out. "By the way, that's a great truck. Impressive really."

Once again, his eyes lingered, and he smiled. A warm flush crept its way across my fair skin, and I smiled sheepishly.

"Oh," he said turning his back on me, "if you ever need a cup of sugar or anything like that, I'm just across the street." With that he winked and strode away.

Chapter Four: Missed Message

By 3:30 p.m. I grew restless. I flicked mindlessly through the channels on the flat screen TV, but nothing really caught my interest. Cara had been amazingly cooperative throughout the day and adapted to me quite easily. I desperately needed to go grocery shopping, but I couldn't find a car seat anywhere. I found Jack's work number posted on a corkboard above the phone and was tempted to call him. I sighed knowing I would never do that. Comparing the professional Jack to a father figure was night and day. He had done quite well for himself, financially at least. He had gone to a well respected university and was a talented surgeon. He was a very admired man, yet I felt no reason to hold him up on any pedestal.

Time passed slowly, and after e-mailing my loved ones back home, I settled for a sitcom on the television when Jack strode in. I sat up expectantly, hoping he would be pleased with my cleaning. He didn't seem to notice. He hung up his jacket, kicked of his shoes and then entered the living room.

His eyes looked around wearily, "Where's Cara? You didn't ignore her all day did you?"

"Ignore her!" My voice went shrill. "Jee, I don't know Jack, after changing diapers all day, putting her down for naps, and feeding her I don't think that falls under the category of ignoring her." I looked at Jack's face, nothing. No twitch of a smile, shock, guilt, nothing.

"Oh, and by the way," I continued "Thanks for just leaving us this morning, it would have been nice to have a heads up that you were just going to take off. I came down here to help you, but I would appreciate a little communication. For all you know I could have been starting school today! Then what would we have done with Cara?"

Jack shook his head. "But you didn't."

I glared up at him. "Didn't what?"

"Start school," he said pointedly.

I threw my hands in the air exasperated. "No, I did not start school today." I watched his face for some sort of a reaction. "I'm going to bed. You can be the *father* now."

My steps faltered, and I turned to face him, softening my voice. "Look, I'm sorry, this is all so new to me…"

I stopped talking. He wasn't even listening to me. Jack bent over Cara and spoke to her soothingly. Rejection shot through me like a bullet. "By the way, there's clean laundry outside your door." I said a little louder.

Jack looked up. "Laundry?"

I nodded, almost eagerly. "Yes, I cleaned the house today."

Jack looked at me blankly. "Okay."

My face fell at his reaction, I hoped for at least a smile, or a simple thank you. I continued on. "If you're going to be gone all day tomorrow, could you please leave the car seat?"

I almost hated myself at that moment. I felt like a lost and lonely puppy just waiting for approval, it unsettled me. I couldn't let myself soften like this. Jack turned his back to me and nodded wordlessly. I walked quietly up to my room and shut the door. I worried about leaving Cara alone with Jack. But then again, he had managed to take care of her on his own for two weeks now, so I had to give him some credit. I changed into my pajamas and stretched out onto my bed with a book. I was just settling into the story plot, when footsteps sounded outside my door. I froze, waiting.

"Keep walking man," I muttered under my breath. I was in no mood to speak to Jack. The footsteps shifted and continued down the hall.

I closed my book and tossed it on my pillow. I was too wound up to read, so instead I sat in the large bay window sill and looked out at the wintry world below. I stared at the streetlights, watching the snow fall silently. A figure caught my eye. He must have seen me first; a snowball hit my window that caused me to jump. Alex's laughter rang through the night. He waved a greeting and I waved back. He was with some of his buddies by the looks of things. They waved and began to nudge Alex playfully back and forth. They sauntered off to his front door, laughing. Exhaustion finally found me. My body hurt from today's fall and the night before. *I suppose I should get used to that,* I thought wryly. My feet, and arms ached from scrubbing every square inch of this place. At least I had gotten a lot done. Overall, it was a very productive day. There was also meeting Alex. I smiled and lingered on the last thought. It followed me into my dreams.

⌘

Cara's cry tore through my slumber. I shot awake, wondering why they were so loud. I glanced at the clock and groaned, 3:20 a.m. I sat up groggily. Something sounded off in her cries. They really were loud. I flicked my lamp on and saw why. The baby monitor sat on my night table. *What the….*then it dawned on me. The last one with the baby monitor was Jack. He must have entered my room at some point and placed it there. I thought back to my dream. Jack had been in it. He tiptoed through the clouds and left something behind before fading away. I looked at the monitor once more, maybe it hadn't been a dream after all. My thoughts turned vile. Names raced through my head that would horrify my mother. I quietly made my way to Cara's room. I checked her diaper, and it needed changing. I spent twenty minutes with her until she finally fell asleep. I walked past Jack's door, when I stopped. It was risky, I could wake Cara up again, but I could not resist. I pounded my fists on his door loudly and bluntly, than marched for my room. His snoring came to a halt, followed by confused mumbles. I smiled, and drifted off to sleep.

The sunshine awoke me bright and early. I glanced at my clock and it read 6:30 a.m. I turned over and groaned, I really should go back to sleep. In three days, I would start school, and I needed to be well rested. I closed my eyes and tried to concentrate. It was useless, I was up. I tiptoed past Cara's room, and she was still asleep. I stumbled into the kitchen and Jack sat at the table. I wanted to turn around and leave, but forced myself to continue on.

Jack looked up from his newspaper and eyed me silently. "Mornin.' You look like hell, you should go back and rest."

I answered with forced politeness. "Well, if someone watched Cara last night, maybe I would have had a better nights rest." *But I guess when you have to be a father for more than three weeks in a row it gets pretty tiresome.*

To my surprise, Jack smirked. "Sharp like your mother. Want some coffee?"

"No, thank you."

Jack nodded. "I set the car seat up in your truck."

I looked at him in surprise. "Oh, thank you."

I poured my cereal and contemplated eating outside in the snow. *The milk will probably freeze before I can get a bite in.* I sat down. Between the silent sips of Jack's coffee, and the crunching of my cereal, we avoided each other's eyes and shifted uncomfortably.

Jack loudly slid the chair back from the table. "Well, I'm off."

I looked in his direction. He stood a little longer than necessary, rubbing the back of his neck. "I saw you made a grocery list. I left some money on the counter."

Again, Jack surprised me. "Oh, thanks."

He nodded stiffly, and turned on his heel. "About last night," Jack called from the other room. "We need to work on respect."

My temper flared and I pushed back my chair to face him. "Yes, I think we do." He was already gone.

⌘

Cara and I had settled into a morning routine. As I went to her crib, she smiled, and my heart melted. She had begun to recognize me already. Breakfast was smooth sailing and the day was bright and sunny. The snowplow made its way through the neighborhood and uncovered the buried roads. I got ready to bundle Cara up for our outing. Once we were both dressed in layers, I carried her securely in my arms and carefully opened my truck door. I placed her in the car seat and buckled her in. I scurried to the drivers seat and quickly shut out the cold. With a flick of the key, the engine purred to life. For such a small town, I had a bit of trouble finding where I needed to go. Frustrated, but not surprised. After what felt like forever of driving in circles, I finally found the grocery store. I snuggled Cara against me, and placed her safely in the buggy seat. Confident that she was securely strapped in, I began to find my way through the store, stocking up on necessities and some comforts from home. As I shopped, I couldn't help but notice the stares from curious eyes and whispers. Of course, they would. Small town, new girl, with Jack's baby, oh the stories they must be coming up with.

I caught one particularly interested group of girls who were around my age. I glared at them. "You might consider taking a picture, it lasts a lot longer," I snapped. The girls gasped and turned away.

At the till, the girl behind the counter held an interested gaze between Cara and me. My patience ran thin and I was about to make a smart comment until recognition filled her features. "That's Jack's little girl isn't it?"

"Yes, it sure is."

"Ohh, so you must be his older daughter! Words been traveling about you! I'm sorry, I don't remember your name. People know that you two are slightly…well, not exactly close."

I nodded a little unnerved about how much people knew about us. "I'm Abby."

The girl smacked her forehead. "Of course, now I remember," she chuckled. "Everyone is dying to meet you. Looks like I'm the first one."

I smiled, already liking her. She was about my age, and reminded me of Sarah, personality wise. She was bubbly, chatty, and seemed to have trouble containing her energy. Her nametag read **LAURA**. While Sarah had green eyes and blond curls, Laura had jet black straight hair and hazel eyes.

"Wow, you sure are buying a lot of food!"

I laughed. "You are observant."

She smiled wider. "Yep, sometimes I really need to learn to keep my mouth shut," she shrugged her shoulders. "Man, you sure eat healthy." She made a disgusted face. I laughed even harder.

"Is it true, are you going to Mountain View High?"

I nodded. "Yep, I'm starting next Monday."

Laura's eyes lit up. "Great! I'm sure you will be in some of my classes. I can show you around. I think we're going to get along great!"

As I walked out of the store I felt slightly hopeful; at least I would know one person. Cara had fallen asleep on the drive home, so I decided to take advantage of the situation. I began to unload the groceries quickly and hoped she would remain asleep until the task was done. Once the last of the bags were unloaded and put away, I gingerly took Cara from the truck and tiptoed to her room. She remained deep in slumber as I lowered her into the crib. Feeling content and triumphant, I fixed myself a sandwich and noticed the answering machine blinked from a missed call. A pad of paper lay next to the phone for messages. I decided to have a listen and poised the pen, ready to scribble down notes.

Hello, I'm calling for Dr. Halett, this is Jeff Towns of the North General Hospital. I hope everything is all right with you, we were a little concerned when you didn't show up for work today. Please call back at 558-9687 and let us know when you will be in. Thanks.

I stopped writing the message after the first sentence. Jack left for work this morning, I saw him. I know he left. If he didn't make it in, where was he?

Chapter Five: Suspicions

Panic rose within me. It was a small town. The route in which Jack drove to the hospital was well traveled. If there was an accident, it would have been known. I found Jack's cell number and dialed. After two rings, it went to his voice mail. *What should I do now?* I was tempted to call the police, but a nagging feeling deep down said not too. Should I listen to it? I felt very out of place. Would I even care if something happened to Jack? I didn't even know the man. Still, I knew I couldn't sit here and do nothing, the simple fact that I felt panic and worry told me I had to do whatever I could. I decided to call the police.

I picked up the phone and went to dial. Awful static arose on the other end, I couldn't even make out a dial tone. I ran to look for my cell phone and stopped in mid-pursuit. It was as dead as a doornail; I had meant to charge it when I got back from grocery shopping, but I got distracted. Suddenly, I had an idea. I threw my jacket on, grabbed the baby monitor, and took off across the street. I ran to Alex's house, only managing to stumble once. I rang the doorbell repeatedly. It wasn't a cup of sugar I was after, but hopefully it fit the neighborhood code. Hurried footsteps raced toward the door followed by a voice, which held a hint of irritation. I stepped back from the door awkwardly. I really didn't know Alex very well, and at this moment, he didn't sound particularly pleased.

"What the hell! Jordan, if that's you pulling your crap on me…" He swung the door open and his anger turned to surprise when he saw me.

"Oh, hey there."His smile grew even broader and his voice turned teasing. "Did you come for that cup of sugar, or did you just miss me?"

My face grew hot. I must have interrupted his shower, for he stood in nothing more than a towel. A small puddle formed where he stood. "Actually, I came to use your phone. I would have used ours obviously, but they're not working." I was surprised by the tone of my voice. It actually sounded concerned.

Alex heard it too, and motioned me inside. "Yeah, come on in, I'll just get dressed, the phone's over there." He gave me one last look, furrowed his brows, and left the room.

Insecurity settled over me as I wondered how I must be coming across to Alex. His last glance made me feel uneasy. He looked at me as though I were a nuisance. I decided it didn't matter and I turned my focus back to Jack. Where was he? I clicked the phone on, and it too held a thick static. I let out a helpless cry, and plopped down on the couch, placing my head in my hands.

"Hey, what's wrong? I take it this isn't a shopping emergency."

I stared up at him, my mouth hung open.

He ran his hand threw his hair. "I'm sorry. That was supposed to make you smile."

"Your phones don't work either." I mumbled.

Alex grabbed the phone and listened. "Someone probably hit a power line somewhere. You would think people would learn to drive in the snow since it's almost always around these parts." He smiled weakly.

I looked at him slightly dumfounded. "You know Jack better than I do, has he ever missed work? Does he have any spots he goes to? Any friends I can contact?"

Alex held up a hand. "Whoa, slow down. What's all this about?"

I quickly filled Alex in and he looked apologetic. "I'm sorry, I don't have anything to say that's going to make you feel better." He shifted closer to me and took one of my hands and held it comfortingly. "Abby?"

I looked up in surprise, mesmerized by his green eyes.

He spoke seriously. "Can I offer you a bad joke?"

Laughter escaped my lips. Alex stared out the window toward Jack's place, and he squinted his eyes. "Hey, it looks like Jack's back."

I looked over at Jack's place quickly, then back to Alex. Something was off in his tone. I stood up to leave, when Alex grabbed my arm. "Wait for me, I'll go with you."

His voice held a quiet authority, and I didn't know him well enough to argue. I nodded and waited for him to get ready. I shuffled quietly from foot to foot, feeling rather anxious to see Jack.

Alex and I walked over to Jack's place. I couldn't help but study Alex curiously. He carried himself in a defiant matter; he seemed threatening and protective all at once. The sight of Jack safe and upright replaced my earlier fear and brought the rage out. "Jack, where have you been?"

Before Jack could answer, I noticed the man he was with. He appeared to be in his early forties and stood at six feet. He had short cropped dark hair, brown eyes, and he was built solid as a house. He moved slightly off balance and wore a strange smirk. The way he stared at me made me nervous. I immediately didn't like him and stepped backwards. The man noticed and gave a dark grin. He took a step closer. "Where ya goin', pretty lady?"

I shuddered at the intent way he looked at me. Alex glared at him, and the man backed off. Jack didn't even notice. Jack focused his gaze on me. "Where were you?"

I looked at Jack in surprise. I should be the one with the questions. "I was at Alex's, I needed to use the phone. Ours wasn't working and I got a message that you weren't at work…"

Jack looked at Alex as though he just realized he was there. His eyes narrowed from me to the strange staggering man. Jack suddenly looked frantic. "Where's Cara?" he bellowed.

I was taken aback by his tone. "She's sleeping, she's safe. I took the monitor with me."

Jack sighed. "All right, go inside."

I looked at Jack with a hint of impatience. That's it? That's all Jack was going to give me, a quiet dismissal? "I thought that you were dead Jack! Where were you? What happened? You didn't go to work. I saw you leave."

Jack rubbed his temples. "I called them, they know what's happening."

I was once again aware of the stranger's stare. I shot him a look of warning. Alex noticed as well and stepped between us, acting as a barrier.

"Your work may know what's happening, but *I* don't! Did you even think they may have called the house, and I would have heard that message? Do you have *any idea* how I felt today?" I stopped talking, my voice rose towards hysterics.

"I'm sorry Abigail, now go inside." Jack's tone held no sympathy. It was simply a command.

My heart ached; he couldn't even look at me. The tears began to well and Alex looked away. Jack shook his head. Maybe I was wrong to come here. It seemed Jack didn't want me here at all. I hadn't made much of an effort to patch up our relationship, but wouldn't, *shouldn't* a father want to at least try to get to know his daughter? Cara started to cry just then. I studied the men outside who appeared to be having their own silent conversation; one I wasn't intended to be included on.

Jack spoke first. "Can you please tend to Cara, Abby?"

I spoke quietly. "Is that all you're going to say?"

He nodded. I ran into the house and felt embarrassed. As I was about to shut the door, Jack silently spoke as if he were talking to himself. "I'm so sorry, Abby."

I changed Cara's diaper and she drifted to sleep. I wandered downstairs feeling disheartened, but also curious. Who was that man? Why was he here? I finished loading the dishwasher when heavy footsteps came from behind. I turned around and the strange man stood with a silly grin on his face. I immediately felt violated. Warning bells began to go off in my head.

"Get out of the house," I demanded.

I took a step backwards, anxiously looking for my escape. To my disappointment, he blocked it. I mentally calculated our height and weight comparisons. If this was to get physical, he almost had one hundred pounds on me, and the height to back it up. Still….I knew the weak spots in which I could hit him. He would go down surely and I would at least have a chance to run away.

The man took a step forward. "Hey there, honey. What's going on in that head of yours, huh?"

"Stay away from me." I glared threateningly at him.

"I like a challenge." He smiled and spoke in a husky voice.

I knew then and there that I had to get out and fast. He saw the sudden fear in my eyes and he took his chance. He lunged toward me and I jumped back with a yelp. I ran forward, but his iron grip pulled me against him. I smashed into his chest and started thrashing wildly, clawing at his face. I started to scream as I felt his grip tighten. Alex and Jack shot through the door. Both of their faces turned pale. Alex moved swiftly and ran to us, a shaken look on his face. As Alex neared us, he smacked the back of the man's head, and he released me with a painful yell. I took that moment to scurry away as Jack and Alex wrestled with the man. They dragged him out the door, kicking and screaming.

⌘

The few days that followed our incident left me with mixed emotions. I was shaken from my confrontation with the strange man, but it was quickly replaced by isolation from Jack's cold mannerisms toward me. I had called my mother afterwards and she tried her best to comfort me. Her words eased the initial blow, but I still felt like the odd one out. I was frustrated by how easily my emotions pulled me under. I had let myself cry in front of Jack, and he avoided me even more so afterwards. He never met my eyes, and if I entered a room, he would leave it almost immediately. It made me feel small, and alone. Was I that hard to love?

Despite it all, I was also curious. Who was that man Jack had brought home? He wasn't the type of person a surgeon would hang out with, even outside of Jack's work, he just wasn't the type of person *Jack* would be around. He was dangerous and dirty. My thoughts trickled to Alex. What did Alex know about the man? I thought back to the protective, almost threatening way Alex held himself; like he was expecting a fight, and he had definitely gotten one. The look in Alex's eyes had held a look of disgust and irritation towards the man. But when Alex had looked at me, a child-like fear stared back. Afterwards, he apologized profusely to Jack and I. Jack took him outside in the driveway, and after a quiet conversation, Alex had taken the stranger away. I tried my best to over hear them, but they kept their voices low; probably aware I would be listening. I was left with the impression this wasn't the first time the man had been here.

It was just after 10:30 p.m. I sat in my truck, I had nowhere to go, and no intention to go anywhere. I was simply sitting in my vehicle to get away from my thoughts. For some reason ever since arriving here, I felt safe in the confines of my truck. Perhaps it was because it was the one thing that was familiar to me, or maybe it was because it held a promise of an escape. My truck could take me anywhere I needed to go if I felt the need to run, and right now I needed a safe place to think. I closed my eyes and rested my forehead on the cool glass, reflecting on today's worries. A light tap on the cool window startled me. I opened my eyes hesitantly and was relieved to see it wasn't Jack staring back at me, but Alex.

I rolled down my window and gave a weak smile. "Hi."

Alex looked amused. "Hey, what are you doing? Are you going somewhere?"

I shook my head. "No, I'm just sitting."

He raised one brow. "I see. Aren't you cold?"

"A little."

"Uh-huh. Now, can you please explain why you're just sitting in your truck?"

I laughed quietly. "Well, you know how some people hyperventilate into brown paper bags?"

He nodded, waiting for me to continue. "Well, instead of that, I like to sit here. It calms me and allows me to see things a little clearer."

Alex's face fell. "Oh...are you sure that you're okay? I never thought..."

I held up my hand in quick protest. "Let me stop you right there, Alex. Yes, I am fine. Promise. What are you doing out here anyways?"

Alex drew a breath. "I couldn't sleep so I went for a walk."

"Makes sense," I glanced at my watch. "Hmm, I think I should head in and try to catch some sleep."

Alex nodded and stepped back. "Yeah, I should try too. Goodnight, Abby."

I hopped out carefully and shut my door. "Goodnight, Alex."

Chapter Six: School

Monday morning seemed to come just in the nick of time. Jack had the day off, so even in the middle of the night when Cara had started to cry, he took care of her. Even so, I had a very restless sleep. I was nervous about starting a new school and I couldn't help but wonder what Jack thought of me, his long absent daughter. Most of the time we practically ignored each other, a nod here, a small smile there. We managed to speak a whole sentence occasionally, but they were so few and far in between. Silence often fell heavy between us. After I showered, I decided on an outfit. I settled on a pair of dark wash jeans, and a long sleeve black V neck sweater. I left my hair down and it cascaded down the middle of my back with a healthy bounce. With a quick glance in the mirror, I was somewhat satisfied. I tiptoed past Jack and Cara's rooms; it had been a rough night. Cara was up almost every hour on the hour, and I knew they would need their sleep. I sat at the kitchen table and ate my cereal. From the corner of my eye, I noticed an envelope with my name on it. Curious, I opened it up.

Abby: Hope you had a good sleep. Good luck on your first day. I'm sure you will do great. I've left you some money, you can pick up a treat on your way home. Jack.

My stomach twisted into a knot. It was gestures like this that sent my head spinning and my heart aching. I wished I could see into Jack's head, even if it was for only a moment, just to see what was going on in there. I rinsed out my bowl and wrote a simple "thank-you" for Jack. I grabbed his note, folded it into a tiny square, and stuck it in my purse. I glanced outside. It was snowing again. I found my scarf and toque, bundled up, and was out the door. With a glance at my truck, I was glad I was up early. I spent close to ten minutes scraping the ice off my windshield. I grumbled the entire time.

The school was easy to find. I slowly pulled into the student parking lot, and finally found an empty spot large enough for my truck. Kids leaned against their cars, talking and laughing carelessly. I noticed most of them glanced in my direction. I grimaced, I would probably be the talk of the school today. For the first time in my life, I wished I had a vehicle that would blend in more. Gathering my courage, I grabbed my school bag and flung it over my shoulder. I had to shove my door open a little harder that necessary, the cold temperatures iced them shut. I walked carefully to the schools front entrance. I was determined not to fall in front of my peers.

A cheerful voice floated above the mindless chatter. "Abby! Hey, Abby!"

I stopped, and turned. Laura stood with a group of curious bystanders, and she waved with an eager grin. "Come over here!"

I nodded to her in acknowledgment and began to pick my way carefully toward the group. I arrived in one piece when one of Laura's friends went to playfully bump me.

I gasped. "No!" I said horrified, and that was all it took.

My feet were unsteady beneath me, and that gentle shove was enough to send me tumbling. My left foot went up and over as I landed on my side. I settled on the cold pavement with an unflattering grunt. Laughter surrounded me. I groaned in embarrassment and covered my face. This was the type of first impression I was so determined not to make, and here I was, lying in the middle of the parking lot for the whole student body to see.

"Aw, Abby, are you okay?" A muffled chuckle said above me.

I looked up slowly, and Laura's amused face stared back at me. I did my best to grin. She held out her hand and helped me up. I dusted off the seat of my jeans and looked at the four sets of eyes that watched me with such interest.

I gave a feeble wave. "You should see me with a pair of skates, that's truly where the magic happens." That was it. Laughter filled the air once more and

I had the acceptance of the group.

I spent most of the morning in the overheated office, filling in the last of my registration forms. The secretary cheerily handed me a map of the school and gave me a list of my classes. She gave me one last sympathetic smile before I left the stuffy office. My morning classes went smoothly. I had English and Biology, both of which Laura and I shared. She saved me a seat, and as I sat, I noticed students stared at me with such an interest; I wanted to disappear. I was the type of person who belonged in the background. I did not like the spotlight on me, especially when I felt incapable of walking safely across the classroom and remaining upright.

I immediately liked my English teacher, Mrs. James. She was a sweet woman with a smile that made you feel instantly welcome. Her voice was soft. She possessed warm green eyes and dark brown hair that was tossed in a messy bun. It was clear she loved what she taught. Her eyes gazed over like she was in a faraway land, and her voice would often sound dreamy. My Biology teacher, Mr. Smith was another story. He was a short, plucky slightly balding man with large glasses. He wore dark pants with a white shirt and a pair of oversized suspenders. He had a rather short temper, and had class rules he expected to be followed. I was glad when the lunch bell rang; I was eager to leave his class. He was the only teacher so far today who had made me stand in front of the class to introduce myself.

"You're going to love our lunch table. We have the best one!" Laura exclaimed cheerfully. I smiled to myself, wondering what could make a cafeteria table so special. They all looked alike to me. Laura continued chatting on happily about the days events as she linked her arm in mine. I felt grateful to know someone that I was at ease with; it made the curious glances easier to bear.

Laura's eyes caught mine and she gave me a sympathetic look. "Don't worry about the rest of them. This school is small, and you're the new big thing here. Anyways," she flicked her shiny hair over her shoulder. "Everyone is dying to meet you!"

I gave her a smile. "Let's stick to your friends for at least today."

Laura's nod was energetic. "They're all you'll need to know anyways, they are the best!"

As it turned out, I was right, all the tables looked the same. The only difference between Laura's table and the majority of the others was hers was settled under a large window that overlooked the outdoor track. Laura gestured proudly to the table.

"Aha, a window view." I tried my best to sound excited about it.

I sat next to Laura and she introduced me to her friends. The first was a quiet blond girl, Ali. She reminded me of a ballerina. She was slender and lithe. She smiled warmly. "Hi, Abby! If you need anything at all, let me know, I'll be glad to help you out."

The next two girls, Ann and Raye were very talkative brunettes and made it their mission to know all the gossip. They excitedly filled me in on the news about some hot new couple in the school. I had no idea who they were talking about. Then there were the boys, Mike, Dan, and Jay. They belonged to pretty much every sports team available and were quite attractive.

It turned out the only classes I had with Laura were my morning ones. Raye and Ali were in my Math class as well as Chemistry, along with Mike. Once lunch was over, Mike took over as my guide. He made it his mission to show me around, and he sat next to me in class. I was happy I had someone to sit with, but at the same time I felt a little uneasy. It was clear Mike was a favorite with the girls, for they spent most of the period staring at me with an awestruck look. Mike noticed the reactions of the other girls and he sat taller. I slid lower into my seat. Finally the school day was over. Mike walked me to my truck and began making small talk. He seemed to be digging into my plans for the weekend. I was relieved when one of his buddies stole his attention.

I hopped in my truck and took off slowly for Jack's house, wondering if I would ever be able to call it home. I pulled into the driveway and smiled at the day's events. School was definitely entertaining. I made a mental note to email Sarah all the details; I knew she would be dying to hear about everything. I wondered if she and Greg were still together. I felt slightly put out that I wouldn't be there to watch Sarah charm him.

As I slammed my truck door closed, I noticed Alex in his driveway. He must have just gotten home as well for he had a school bag slung lazily over his shoulder. He saw me, grinned, and gave a short wave. I gave him a feeble wave and almost ended up doing a face plant in the ice. I quickened my pace once I had steadied myself. He burst into laughter only he would enjoy. I scooted into Jack's house, and warmth surrounded me like a warm blanket fresh out of the dryer.

"Oh, hello, Cara!" I said surprised as Cara crawled to me with an ecstatic little grin on her face. I crouched down and held out my hands. Cara placed her tiny hands in mine, and forced herself to stand, looking at me with an awed look.

"She's been doing that all day on everything she can reach. She's going to be walking before we know it."

I glanced up at Jack, who casually leaned against the doorframe. I managed to smile. "Yeah, they grow up fast. Mom always said she only had to blink once and I was grown."

Jack's eyes held a hint of sadness. "Yes," he said quietly and he studied me. "Yes, yes they do. I think she's been looking for you most of the day."

I looked up, surprised. "Really, what makes you think that?"

Jack smiled a bit. "She's ignored me most of the day and has been on a hunt; she seemed to be on some sort of a mission. As soon as she heard the door open, she was there in no time."

I smiled and looked down at Cara. "That's cute."

Jack slowly shook his head and walked toward the living room. I gently picked up Cara and placed her in the living room with Jack. I noticed he set up baby gates up around the kitchen. It was strange to see Jack behave like a responsible parent. I stepped over the gate and automatically began preparing dinner. A few hours later, Cara happily ate her baby food with her hands. Chubby fists were busy at work. I smiled as she opened her mouth wide, and pulled her food in with determination. Jack and I ate silently. Nonetheless, I was proud of our progress, we were finally able to eat a meal together. It was usually in silence, but it was progress, at least we were in the same room.

Earlier in the week, I had noticed a quality that both my mother and Jack shared: they were horrible in the kitchen. I honestly don't know how they survived all those years together. Jack lived off of Kraft Dinner and frozen meals. Tonight I had made Chicken Cordon Bleu with garlic roasted potatoes. The delighted look on Jack's face as I set the food on the table made me feel like a hero.

"Mmm, this is delicious! I don't remember the last time I've had something this decadent! Jenna must miss this. I wonder how she's coping? I remember she wasn't exactly a star in the kitchen." He chuckled at some hidden memory.

I, on the other hand stood staring at Jack wide eyed. I had never heard him speak so much in one week, let alone in one day. "Umm…" I began. "Thanks for the compliment. Grandma taught me how to cook." I paused and tacked on one last comment carefully. "Mark's actually great in the kitchen."

Jack nodded. "Well, that's good. It sounds like she's happy."

I nodded. "She is. Mark's a great guy." I chose my words carefully, I didn't want to hurt his feelings. *Where is this coming from? The human mind will never be understood.*

"I'm glad Jenna's found someone like him. She deserves it." Jack nodded with satisfaction and went back to eating.

Jack had offered to help with the dishes, but I assigned him the task of wiping down Cara, she was covered in her mush. Jack grimaced as he glanced her way. He began mumbling some nonsense. I watched him for a moment. He handled Cara very gently. I turned my attention back to the dishes.

I was lost in thought until Jack's voice broke my ponderings. "I never did ask you, how was school?"

I spoke cheerfully. "It was great. I made new friends, and the classes are good. I'm quite surprised the curriculum isn't behind my old school at all."

Jack nodded. "Yep, the town may be small, but we take pride in keeping up appearances."

I nodded. "It's doing a good job."

I glanced back and Jack rubbed his neck and shifted restlessly. It must be a nervous habit. Jack took a deep breath and pulled out a kitchen chair, and then sat. He really was trying to make an effort. It took a toll on him, but he was trying. I took a deep breath and continued scrubbing the pan. Our communications seemed to go smoother if one of us was slightly preoccupied.

Jack continued. "You've really made things easier on me....with you being here and all. Cara adores you, and you're a natural with her." Jack furrowed his brows. "I have no clue what I'm doing half the time."

"You're welcome. And you're doing a better job than you think."

Jack cleared his throat. "It's a really nice night out. I sometimes take Cara for a walk around Willow Lake. It's only a ten minute drive from here. It's got a nice walking path that loops the water. There's a big playground there for when she gets older. It's got plenty of ducks and geese, Cara's taken in by them."

I stopped and turned to face Jack, it was too much too fast. He stood, and cleared his throat. "I'll leave you directions to the lake, if you ever want to take Cara out. Her stroller is in the garage. There's a cute coffee shop nearby if you're ever interested. I'm off to watch the news now, so…"

I smiled softly. "Goodnight is all it takes, Jack."

Chapter Seven: Janie

My alarm went off at 6:00 a.m. I wanted to crawl deeper under my quilt and sleep the day away. Cara was still asleep and Jack had left for work an hour before. I shuffled to the bathroom, hoping that a shower would wake me. Fifteen minutes later, I was showered, dressed, and eating my oatmeal when the phone rang. I glanced at the clock, six thirty-five, pretty early for a phone call.

I grabbed the phone and held it somewhat anxiously by my ear. "Hello? Um, Halett residence?"

"Abby, I'm sorry! I forgot you had school!"

"Jack? Is that you? What's wrong?" It was Tuesday. Of course I had school.

His voice almost sounded pained. "I forgot about Cara."

"What do you mean, you forgot about Cara? She's sleeping, here."

"That's just it! I tried, but I can't get off of work, I have an important surgery scheduled. Abby, I forgot to make *arrangements* for Cara today."

Then it hit me. My eyes went wide, and my voice rang high. "Jack! How could you forget? I can't miss school, it's only my second day."

"I know, I know." I heard the stress in Jack's voice clearly now, I imagined him rubbing his forehead.

"Listen, to me Abby. Go talk to Mary, she's been a real life saver for me. She'll know what to do."

"Jack," I said exasperated. "Who is Mary, and where does she live?"

"Oh, right, well you know her of course, Mrs. James."

"My English teacher?" I said clearly confused.

His voice struggled to stay polite. "Yes, yes, she lives across the street with Alex."

I raised an eyebrow. "Alex? As in the Alex I know?"

"Yes, Abby! He's Mrs. Jam—*Mary's* nephew."

That was news to me. I silently compared the two; they had the same eyes. "I don't know if she'll appreciate me barging in. I'd like to keep a good appearance at school…"

"She won't mind. She's helped me through worse, just *please!*" There was a desperation in his voice that I couldn't ignore.

"All right, Jack. I'll head over now."

"Thanks, Abby. Call me please and let me know what's going on."

"I will."

I bundled up quickly and stood outside. I stared across the street toward Mary and Alex's home in slight fear. How awkward was this going to be? Do I call her Mrs. James, or Mary? What should I say? I could see it now. "Hi, Mrs. James, I'm your new student. My father completely forgot about his child, and he told me that you would fix everything."

I sighed and started walking across the street; this was going to be pleasant. I hesitated before knocking, it was still dark out and I didn't see any lights on. *Here goes nothing.* I knocked twice and after a few minutes, I rang the doorbell. Footsteps sounded behind the closed door. They were slow and uneven, whoever it was, was not quite awake. Alex opened the door. His hair was tousled and he wore pajama pants and a T-shirt.

His tired eyes glinted, and he wore a side smirk. "You just can't stay away from me can you?"

I gave a nervous laugh. "Actually, I'm here to see your aunt."

He shivered. "It's damn cold out here, come on in." He opened the door wider, and motioned for me to come inside with a nod of his head.

"Thanks." I shuffled past him and stood uncomfortably.

Alex looked at me, slightly amused. "She's not here."

My eyes widened, and I took a menacing step closer and looked up at him. "What do you mean she's not here? Why did you invite me in then?"

"For your reaction, of course. I find them so pleasant."

"Ah, aren't you a peach."

Alex yawned. "It seems you only come over here when you're in trouble, and what guy doesn't like to feel like a Super Hero?"

I stared up at Alex dumbfounded. He chuckled again. "I think I know what this is about. Jack's come over before at odd hours with the same dilemma." He glanced over to make sure I still paid attention and then he continued. "Cara, right? Daycare?" He raised an eyebrow.

I nodded, and plopped onto a kitchen chair wearily. "Yes, Jack forgot to make arrangements, and I need to get to school." I glanced at the clock impatiently.

He stared at me with humor. "Would you like a cup of coffee or something? You seem to be quite comfy."

I sent him the death glare. He chuckled and then turned back to the phone book. "Aha, here we are." He dialed the number and leaned casually against the kitchen counter. "Hey, Janie, how are ya?"

He nodded his head. "That's good. Look, the reason why I'm calling is for Jack Halett. He's pulled another one." Alex chuckled. "Yep, his older daughter is staying with him, and she needs to get to school…..oh, yeah sure, she'll be there." He looked at me matter-of-factly. "Five minutes, she'll be ready."

Alex hung up and smirked. "Janie will be at your house in five minutes."

I looked at him with a puzzled expression. "Okay, that's great and all Alex, but who's Janie?"

"She's Mary's friend. She runs a day care. You better hurry, she'll be there soon."

I stared at him feeling unsure. "Jack's used her before?" I raised one eyebrow. I didn't feel comfortable handing Cara over to some stranger.

Alex smiled softly. "Janie's great. She's licensed, has a clean place, and great qualified staff. She's helped Jack out many, many times."

I sighed in recognition. "Okay. He did say Mary would know what to do."

"Technically, but today I'm the hero." Alex grinned and it went straight to his eyes.

I stepped outside and turned toward him. "Oh, and by the way, I knew a woman had to live with you."

He leaned against the doorframe curiously and crossed his arms. "Really? And why is that?"

"Because, this place is way too clean, and you Alex, do not strike me as a clean guy." With that, I smiled, and walked away.

I didn't even make it out of their driveway when Alex's voice called out. "Hey, Abby? Watch where you put those feet. I don't feel like trudging through the snow to pick you up."

I let the comment roll off my back. That was an easy shot. As I stepped into the warm house, Cara's cries filtered through the walls. I quickly changed her diaper, and got her dressed. I placed her in the high chair and fed her breakfast. While she ate, I ran upstairs to her room and packed a change of diapers, some of her favorite toys, and a clean change of clothes. I raced downstairs to add a few jars of baby food to the mix. I sat in the chair and my eyes fell to the phone. Jack! I quickly dialed the number Jack had left me, and ended up leaving a message with a nurse. Cara finished her breakfast so I grabbed a wash cloth and set to the task of uncovering her face behind the layers of baby food.

"There we go little one, I can see your cute face again."

Cara looked at me and gurgled happily. I grabbed her from the chair and balanced her upon my hip, and started to bundle her up for outside. A loud knock sounded at the door. I answered the door expectantly.

A smiling woman greeted me. "Hello! You must be Abigail. Hi, Cara! How are you sweetie?" Janie cooed and glanced at me quickly. "I'm Janie by the way."

Cara wriggled in my arms and giggled. That was a good sign; she seemed to like this woman.

"Hi, nice to meet you...it's Abby, actually."

"Of course, hun. Here, I can take her. I have a car seat in my car. Come, walk with me."

I was already bundled up for school, so I grabbed Cara's bag, and followed the cheery woman out the door. I studied the way Janie held Cara; she was experienced. She was a dainty, sleek woman with a stylish blond bob. Her blue eyes were merry and bright on her round face.

She turned to me. "Is this her bag?" Janie glanced through it. "Wonderful!" She muttered to herself.

She met my eyes to explain. "I usually have to pack Cara's bag as well," she chuckled. "Poor Jack, he really is a sweetie, but he's quite clueless! You, my dear, are much, much more prepared."

I smiled broadly, already liking this woman. "Thanks, I think it's a woman thing."

Janie laughed loudly. "You are so right, honey." Janie glanced at her watch. "Oh my, you better get going or you'll be late! Do you know where I live?"

"Yes, Alex gave me directions."

Janie smiled fondly. "He's such a good boy."

I wasn't sure I could agree with that statement entirely, so I just smiled politely.

Janie clapped her hands together. "All right, I will see you after school then. You're off around three thirty, correct?"

I nodded. "Thank you so much, Janie. You're a life saver."

Janie floated to her car. "Not a life saver, hun. Just a friend."

By the time I pulled into my parking space, I was ten minutes late. I was not off to a good start at the school that so generously accepted me. As I ran for my English class, I was thankful I had a good memory. I slid into the room, interrupting Mrs. James. A few sharp whispers arose from my classmates.

"So glad you could join us, Ms. Taylor." I winced as I met the eyes of my teacher, but to my surprise, she held a sympathetic smile. "After class, I'd like to have a quick word with you. Now please, sit down."

Mrs. James held such a polite authority. I had to admire that. I found my seat next to Laura. "Wow, second day and already staying after class. My, oh my, aren't we on a roll?" Laura bounced excitedly next to me.

"It was such a rushed morning, there were minor complications," I whispered.

Laura's eyes grew wide. "Is everything okay?" She studied me for injuries.

"Girls, please."

"Sorry, Mrs. James," Laura quietly whispered. "Pssst, fill me in with a note!"

Laura suddenly sat up straight, her full attention on the teacher. I raised my eyebrows, I think I had found Sarah's twin. I quietly tore a piece of paper out of my binder and scribbled down the morning's events.

After class I stood nervously as I waited for Mrs. James to address my morning tardiness. She finished up with her notes and then focused her attention on me. She motioned for me to sit next to the orderly desk. I gave her a helpless smile and hoped she would take pity on me.

"Alex called and told me what happened." Mrs. James's eyes were sympathetic as she continued. "The teachers and the principle are quite aware of your situation, and won't be criticizing your tardiness too harshly. We know you're a bright student, and have confidence that you will find your own routine."

I smiled a slightly pained grin. All this attention focused on my home life made me wary. It made me wonder just how many people were actually aware of my situation. "Thanks, Mrs. James."

She nodded. "However, with that being said, we do expect you to show up for class. I trust that you will settle in soon." Mrs. James must have seen the worry that crossed my face and she softened her tone. "Don't worry, Abby. If you talk to Janie, I'm sure the two of you will be able to work out a schedule that suits you, she has such a big heart."

I smiled. "Yes, she truly does."

Mrs. James looked thoughtful then, and her teacher mask fell. "As do you. I can't even imagine how hard this must be for you. I have known Jack for many years, if you ever need anything at all, don't be a stranger. You know where to find me, and Alex for that matter."

Yes, way too much attention was on 'my situation.' The red hotness began to fill my cheeks. I stood swiftly. "Thanks, Mrs. James, but I'd better be off to Biology now; I should try to make it on time for at least one class today."

⌘

I was glad when the final bell of the day rang. Laura and Ali walked with me to my truck. "Abby, are you busy today after school?" Ali wondered.

"Sort of. I have to pick Cara up from daycare, and watch her until Jack comes home."

"Oh, that's okay. Maybe this weekend we could all get together?"

I nodded. "I'd like that."

"Great!" Ali and Laura brightened.

I hopped in the driver seat. "See you guys tomorrow!" With a quick wave, I left the parking lot.

I found the daycare with only one wrong turn in the process; I was beginning to get to know this town. I pulled up front and walked up a long brick path that led to the large two story pale yellow house. I peeked in the fenced backyard and smiled. There was a spacious playground in the back with kids happily bouncing around with alert care takers nearby.

I knocked on the front door. Within seconds, Janie welcomed me. "Abby, you're early! Come in, come in!"

I walked into the warm house. The smell of chocolate chip cookies faintly lingered in the air. I glanced around. Everything was neat, tidy, and childproof. To the left, there was a large art room filled with easels, paintbrushes, markers, and paper. Attached to the art room, was the airy playroom filled with stuffed animals, a toy kitchen/tool center, boxes of Lego's, and general toys scattered about.

I was impressed. "Wow, you have quite the set up here."

"Thanks, I try. Come on and follow me to the toddler area."

We walked down the hall and made a right. Janie led me into a large room blocked off by baby gates. The room acted as one large playpen. I followed Janie as she led me into a separate room off to the left. "This is the nap room for the young ones," she whispered.

The room was decorated, as many nurseries are; bright and cheery. The drapes were drawn shut, with a single night light shining softly. There were three separate cribs, and a small row of child safe beds.

"She's sleeping soundly. She was an angel today. I really think she likes the other children."

I nodded. "She probably would. She's fascinated by people." I hesitated. "Before I grab her, could I speak to you about…an arrangement?"

"Of course."

"Well, I'm not too sure about Jack's schedule, but if I were to drop her off by seven forty in the morning, and pick her up after school, would that be okay?"

"That would work out just fine. We have some parents here by six thirty," she smiled warmly.

"Oh, that's perfect. If Jack has the day off, I will get one of us to call you so you don't worry." I looked at the friendly woman. "What about payment?"

"Don't you worry about that, Jack and I will discuss those minor details."

Cara slept the ride home, and I placed her gently in her crib. I decided to check my email and catch up on the news back at home. After catching up on the latest, I went downstairs to prepare dinner. Once dinner was set in the crock pot, I grew restless. With house chores caught up on, Cara sound asleep, and my homework done I had nothing to do. So, I decided to bake. From memories I remembered Jack loved chocolate. I decided to make brownies. I was half way through my preparations when I realized there was no sugar. *Oh no.* This could not be happening to me again, all in one day. I bundled myself up, grabbed the baby monitor, measuring cup, and trudged through the snow to Alex's. I straightened my shoulders and knocked on the door.

Alex answered, and a small but charming smile lit up his face. "Wait, let me guess. Is there a fire this time? Or no wait….hmmm, tree collapse on the roof perhaps?"

I rolled my eyes. "No, the toilets have backed up."

I burst out laughing as Alex's face fell, and his voice went low. "Really?" He glanced toward the house, looking slightly horrified.

I held up the measuring cup sheepishly. "Actually, I need a cup of sugar."

Alex's mouth dropped open and he let out a loud laugh. I didn't interrupt him, and within a few minutes, he caught his breath and waved me in, all the while, still chuckling. I cracked him a smile, and shook my head in disbelief. I really did not know how I got myself into these situations, it's not like I tried; misfortune followed me wherever I went. As he dug around the kitchen, he glanced back at me. "Did you make it to school okay?"

I nodded. "I was a little late, but apparently all the teachers know about my *situation*."

Alex studied me. "I find you fascinating." With that, he turned back to hunt for the sugar.

Fascinating? My heart raced slightly, how was I supposed to respond to that? My face grew red. If you were fascinated by something, you would want to watch it, keep an eye on it. I definitely didn't want any more focus drawn to me. I glanced around and fidgeted nervously.

"Aha, here we go, found it. A cup was all you needed, right?"

"Yes."

He looked curious. "What are you making?"

"Brownies."

"Brownies, huh? Sounds good."

"They're one of Jack's favorites…I think."

Alex walked up to me and tilted his head. "Here you go." I reached out and gently took the measuring cup, my fingers brushing his.

Alex softened his voice. "How are you and Jack getting along? When I, well…to be honest, when pretty much the whole town heard you were coming, I was prepared for drama. Living across the street from you guys and all, I expected a daily showdown. But I have to say, you're handling things very well."

My voice dropped. "I see. Thanks, I think." The blush was back. "We haven't exactly been seeing eye to eye." I sighed. I wanted to pour out all my frustrations to someone, anyone. One glance at Alex's sympathetic eyes was all it took. I sat down defeated. He quietly sat next to me, waiting.

"I'm not too sure if he wants me here," I began carefully. "It's honestly like I'm living alone over there most of the time. My mom's house was so, so, warm and full of life. Over here, it's…I don't know. I walk in, and my heart aches. Sometimes I think he wants me here. I think he's trying to get to know me. It makes me sad to think that I don't know him at all…" My voice trailed off.

Alex nodded. "Don't give up, keep trying to get to know him. He's really proud of you, you know."

I quickly looked up. "How would you know?"

"Jack's a good guy. He comes around here quite a bit. He and Mary are really good friends. Actually, he and Robbie, Mary's husband, my uncle, were best friends. When Uncle Robbie past four years ago, Jack stuck by us to make sure we were okay. We have game nights and dinners quite frequently. He spoke about you. I guess your mom sent him updates, and pictures over the years. He showed them to us."

Tears threatened, and I looked away. "I didn't know that." I stiffened my back. "He left home when I was four years old. We really haven't spoken since."

"Jack's a complicated guy. He-"

I cut him off. "Don't defend him, Alex. What he did….he never once tried to step back into my life. I don't know if I can ever forgive that. I spent so many years writing to him, crying for him… all the while I was left to wonder what I did wrong; wondering why I wasn't good enough…" I choked back a cry. I was startled to see that my hands trembled.

Alex softened his voice. "I'm so sorry. If I had known, I wouldn't have pressed the issue."

He took my hands in his and held on to them gently. I tore my hands back and stood. "Thanks for the sugar, I need to get back."

"Abby, wait."

I didn't look back. I kept walking, silently scolding myself for losing control like that, for letting myself become so vulnerable in front of a stranger. I needed to be stronger from now on. I couldn't let that happen again.

"Thanks!" I yelled over my shoulder as I gave a casual wave and ran back to the house.

Chapter Eight: An Evening Out

Jack walked into the house at 6:30 p.m. The smell of dinner welcomed him, and his grin widened. I lay on the couch, watching one of my favorite television shows. Cara was sprawled sleepily against my chest.

I looked up lazily. "Dinner's in the oven. I already ate."

"Thanks so much, Abby. It smells delicious."

As Jack settled down with his meal, he called out. "Janie called me. It seems you made quite the impression on her."

I mentally calculated if I had said or done anything to offend her, or if something came across as rude. "Oh yeah?" I called out casually.

"Yep, she says you're quite the responsible, bright young lady. Pretty as a picture, too." Jack continued speaking. "She told me that you two have worked out a schedule, thanks. I appreciate it."

"No problem."

The dishes clanked in the sink before Jack walked in. He sat down, sighed, and put his feet up on the wooden table.

"Hard day?" I inquired.

"Nothing I couldn't handle. On my way home I ran into Mary."

"Mm-hmm?"

"She invited us over for dinner Friday night. It should give you a nice break from kitchen duty."

My thoughts flitted back to the conversation earlier with Alex. I cringed. I wasn't sure I wanted to be in the same house with him so soon. "That's a nice thought," I said politely.

Jack's eyes flickered to me. "Do you have other plans?" The look on his face resembled disappointment.

I spoke quickly. "No, I'll be there."

Jack smiled and nodded. "Good, they're a nice family. It will be fun."

⌘

The school week flew by. Friday came faster than I was ready for. On the bright side, I had been on time for the rest of the week and on Saturday, Ali, Laura and I were going to a movie. I was excited; I needed some time to unwind with friends.

"Do you think it's going to be that bad?" Ali sympathized.

It was after school, and we leaned against my truck. I filled Ali and Laura in on everything that had happened during the week. After my latest conversation with Alex, it stirred up some old feelings and I was more upset than I realized. When I got to school, Ali and Laura had noticed right away something was wrong. They took me away from the rest of the group and I found myself venting. After I had gotten things off my chest, we had all decided that a movie night was in order.

I thought back to tonight's unforeseen events, and pondered over what was to come. "It will be awkward at the very least."

Laura piped up. "Don't worry. I take my phone everywhere with me. If you need to get out of there, call me. I will come and get you with some horrible girl emergency or something along the lines of brilliant."

Ali rolled her eyes and smirked. I would have burst out laughing, but Laura looked dead serious. So I nodded instead. "All right, sounds good….wish me luck."

"Hey, Abby!" Laura called. "Wear something that will knock his socks off anyway!"

A few hours later I stood in my bathrobe, staring at my closet. Laura's words were still in my head. I didn't really own anything that would "knock his socks off." I decided that fancy casual would be the way to go. I planned to settle for my nice pair of jeans, but at the last minute I threw on a pair of my favorite worn in blue jeans with holes in the knees. I grabbed a pretty dark blue V-neck shirt and looked in the mirror. It would do, casual on the bottom, pretty on the top. I pinned back my hair away from my face, and I was happy with how it fell. I nodded in satisfaction. Appearance wise, I was all ready to go; emotionally, well, that was on another playing field. I made it downstairs before Jack. Cara played happily in her playpen and I curled up with a book until it was time to go. I had finished an entire chapter before Jack came down.

"Wow, Jack, you look nice." And he did. He wore a pair of jeans, with a pressed shirt.

"Thanks." He studied me, and smiled. "You look good, too."

I grinned back. "I'll get Cara ready."

Within a few minutes, we were warmly greeted by Mary. I was slightly taken aback by her appearance. At school she always wore her hair up with polished suits. Tonight, her dark hair fell to her shoulders in a silky wave, she wore a beautiful flowy skirt, and a silky jade green top that accented her warm green eyes.

"Come in, come in! It's so nice to see you all." Mary's eyes drifted to me. "Abby, you look beautiful, and Jack, as always, you look dashing."

I thanked her politely and commented on her outfit. Jack thanked her warmly, like a close friend would.

"Mary?" I interrupted. "Is there somewhere I can put Cara?"

"Yes of course, in the living room. I have a play area set up for her."

I glanced at the kitchen table, a high chair was all ready to go. Mary was definitely prepared. Jack must have spent a lot of time here. The thought comforted me, I was glad Jack had good friends who offered to give him things that no one else could. As I made my way to the living room, I was very aware that I had not seen Alex yet. Maybe he wasn't coming. I sighed in relief. I sat on one of the comfy leather couches and listened to all the stories Mary and Jack reminisced about. I found myself quite intrigued until Jack changed the subject. "Where's Alex tonight?" I stiffened.

Mary tossed her hand in the air. "He's just finishing a paper. He should be up soon."

Great, so he was here. Jack settled deeper into the seat. "I can't believe he's in university already, I still remember him as a boy."

Mary looked thoughtful. "They grow up so fast, you better be ready for it!"

"Is there somewhere I could use the washroom?" I interrupted quietly.

"Yes, of course. Unfortunately, the upstairs one is out of sorts. You'll have to go downstairs. Follow the hall, it will branch off, go to the right, it will be the third door."

"Thanks Mrs.—err, Mary."

Mary chuckled. "It's always difficult for students to relate to us teachers outside the classroom. We're not aliens you know."

I was about to respond, but Jack beat me to it with a grin. "I know. When I run into my patients occasionally, they never call me anything but Dr. Halett." The two of them broke into a lively conversation as I left the room.

Downstairs was just as warm and bright as the upstairs. I found my way to the washroom with ease. I slightly adjusted my hair, walked out, and took my time. I admired pictures on the wall when a sound caught my attention. I turned as one of the doors opened. I stopped dead in my tracks and my heart began to race. Alex had stepped outside, his hair slightly tousled. He hadn't gone into the lengths of effort his aunt clearly put in with her appearance. He wore worn jeans, and a dark shirt. Alex's eyes took me in with male approval, and his face softened slightly. I tried to slip past him, but the hall was too narrow. He held his arm out against the wall blocking my escape.

"Abby, I think we should talk about-"

I held up my hand to stop him. "There is nothing to say, Alex," I said slightly irritated. "You didn't know. I shouldn't have told you all of those things anyways," I said quickly.

His eyes narrowed. "Do you regret telling me?"

"Yes."

He took a step back. "I see. Well, you shouldn't. There's nothing to be ashamed of. It's not good to keep things like that bottled inside anyway."

I met his eyes for the first time in awhile. "I'm not ashamed, now can you please stop prying into my business?"

He looked thoughtful. "You do this a lot, don't you?"

I threw my hands up. "Do what?"

"Close yourself off when you talk about personal things, push people away."

"Stop trying to analyze me." I stormed past him and shoulder checked him roughly. He let me slip by with a frustrated sigh. He knew he wouldn't get anywhere.

I was very aware of Alex walking behind me up the stairs. It made me skittish. I hurried my pace, but the tip of my right foot caught on a stair. "Whoa, ooof!" I landed flat onto my stomach with my arms sprawled out. My face went bright red as I heard Alex chuckle. He yanked me up, and I scurried up the stairs as though my life depended on it, cursing silently at my lack of grace.

⌘

"This is delicious, Mary!" Jack happily crowed as he helped himself to another large bite.

Mary beamed proudly. "Why thank you, Jack!"

I politely joined the conversation. "You shouldn't have gone to all this trouble."

I was vaguely aware Alex had watched me intently the entire night. I kept my back turned to him as best as I could. He spoke up before Mary could. "It was no trouble at all, this is what Mary loves to do. Also, I hear that it gives you a nice break."

I avoided his gaze completely, and smiled sweetly at Mary. "It sure is delicious, thank you."

Alex continued to study me out the corner of his eye. I stiffened and sent him a dark glare. Mary rose an eyebrow and I shot her a quick reassuring smile. Jack didn't even notice, his eyes were still lit up like a Christmas tree at the large spread of food before him. As I watched Jack, I wondered how my mother captured his heart. It seemed the easiest way to please Jack was with food, and my mother never would have achieved that feat.

Cara started to cry and I got up to tend to her immediately. Mary grabbed my arm gently. "Take the night off. I can deal with the little sweetheart."

"No, it's okay," I propped Cara neatly on my hip. "I think she just needs a diaper change. Is there somewhere I can change her?"

Alex stood. "Here, let me lead the way."

I stared at him blankly, and he smiled smugly. He knew when to pick his moments. There was no way I would make a scene in front of the adults and he knew it. I followed Alex stiffly into a spare bedroom. A solid oak table stood in the corner. I gently placed Cara down and set to the task ahead of me. Alex didn't say a word. He propped himself carelessly against a wall and stood silently.

"There we go, baby! All clean." Cara played with her feet, and she giggled up at me. The warmth from my smile radiated to her. I had definitely fallen in love with this little girl.

"You're a natural." Alex's smooth voice cut into my moment.

"Thanks."

Cara interrupted as she started to fuss. Between her sniffles and cries she wearily rubbed her eyes. I sighed, picked her up, and began bouncing her gently until her tired head collapsed against my shoulder.

"Wait here," Alex whispered. "I know where she can sleep without being disturbed." He tried to be helpful, so I gave him a slight nod. Within a few moments, Alex came in carrying a playpen. "There," he said proudly. "She won't be disturbed in here. Jack and Mary like to visit after dinner, then have coffee and dessert."

"Okay." I gently tucked Cara in. "Snug as a bug in a rug," I whispered.

"You can trust me you know." Alex quickly held up his hand to interrupt me from objecting. "I'm not trying to pull anything, Abby. I'm really a pretty decent guy. I can see that you're hurt, and I'm just letting you know I am here if you ever need someone to talk too, or just get away for awhile."

I was about to object when he cut me off. "You're what, seventeen?"

I nodded. "Eighteen in a few months."

"Right, see, there's your problem. You act as though you're at thirty. You need to remember to have fun. You have plenty of time to worry in the future. For now, try to enjoy life. Kick back, let loose."

What was he doing? Why did he notice all of these things about me? Why did he care? No one had ever noticed so much about in me in such little time. It made me apprehensive.

"Alex, stop this right now, please." My voice sounded strange to me. I pictured a wild animal trapped by its prey, and I didn't like it one bit.

Alex's face fell ever so slightly. "I'm sorry, I don't want to scare you."

He stepped closer. I slammed myself against the wall. Alex stopped dead in his tracks and took two deliberate steps back. I fled the room.

Jack looked up expectantly as he heard my footsteps. "Is Cara sleeping?"

"Yep, she went down quickly."

Alex strode into the room and sat on the empty couch. He kept his gaze low. Mary stirred her coffee, looking thoughtfully between us. "Have a seat, Abby. Make yourself at home."

I looked around; the only empty seat was next to Alex. I shot Mary a look. *Traitor.* I collected myself and sat next to Alex, bringing my legs into a neat tuck "Would you like some coffee, Abby?" Mary asked.

"No, thanks…actually," I shifted. "I'm not feeling too well. I think I should lie down."

Jack looked concerned. "Are you all right?"

"Yes, just a slight headache. Will you be okay with Cara, Jack?"

He nodded. I stood and turned to Mary. "Thank you for the dinner. It was great."

Mary smiled. "I'm glad you enjoyed it. It was nice to see you again, Abby. I will send Jack home with leftovers and a piece of dessert for you." Mary's eyes shifted from mine to Alex.

"Alex, how about you walk Abby home?"

My mouth opened in disbelief. Couldn't I do anything without the boy? Alex got up and gestured for me to follow. He didn't say a word. We bundled up quietly and strolled down the driveway in silence when he finally spoke. "So, we're already at the point where you're faking an illness?"

I said nothing. He nodded and sighed as he walked me to my door.

"Thanks, Alex. Have a good night."

"Abby, wait for just a second, please."

I stopped and turned to him. I kept my eyes on his boots. Alex leaned in, and with his finger, he tilted my chin upwards. I was too startled to respond.

"In case you haven't noticed, I find myself drawn to you. I don't know why since you seem so dead set on pushing me away."

Alex raised one eyebrow and continued. "I told you Jack used to show us pictures of you, and I had always hoped to meet you someday." Alex bit his lip and continued. "I'm not too sure how to act around you. I seem to scare you, I'm not used to that."

Alex tilted his head thoughtfully to one side and added. "Girls usually find me charming." He grinned a harmless smile.

I slowly smiled back. Why did I push him away? A part of me wanted him around, I felt safe with him. But then again, there was also a part of me that wanted to run from him as fast as I could. I didn't want to get attached to someone who would most likely leave anyways. Besides, my life was a mess right now, what guy in his right mind would even want to step into it? I highly doubted I was worth all the trouble, and he would see that soon enough.

"Alex…I am sorry. I'm just not good at these things." I started rubbing my temples. "I'm not scared of you. You make me uneasy. You notice even the smallest of details."

Alex smiled. "I guess now is a bad time to tell you I have X-ray vision?"

I laughed. "Goodnight, Alex."

"Abby?"

I turned to face him. "Yes?"

Alex ran a hand through his hair and sighed. "You should let Jack in, he's trying."

"Excuse me?" My anger flared. "Why should it always be up to me?"

I stepped closer to Alex. "Do you have *any* idea how *hard* this was for me to come here? I have been trying. Did you ever think that maybe it's too late? That maybe I am not good enough?" I stopped to take a breath. "And how is it that I'm made out to be the bad guy?"

As soon as the words were out, I regretted them. I let something slip that

I had never wanted to say out loud. Alex's remorseful look only made things worse. I held up my hands in defeat. "Don't say anything, Alex. Just don't." I turned in the house, and slammed the door.

⌘

Ali's face fell. "Aw Abby, I'm so sorry last night turned out that way." Ali frowned thoughtfully. "But, you know, he really does seem to like you." Ali said the last sentence carefully, watching my reaction closely.

Laura piped up. "Are we talking about Alex James here?"

"Yep, that would be him," I forced out.

"Hmm, well that would explain it then." Laura said matter-of-factly.

I glanced at her curiously. "Explain what?"

Ali and Laura glanced at me. "Oh, you don't know what happened, do you?"

"No." She had my full attention now.

"Hey, are you guys buying a ticket or what?" An annoyed ticket holder tapped her fingernails impatiently.

"Oh, right. Three for '*Left in LA.*'"

We quickly paid for our tickets and headed for the theatre. An athletic looking male stepped purposefully into our path. His eyes lit up in recognition. "Hey, you're the girl with the truck!" He stared at me with a wide grin.

I glanced at Ali and Laura who watched me with a new intrigue. I spoke questioningly. "I'm sorry, do I know you?"

His smile faded in disappointment. "Oh, you don't remember me? Ah that's alright, we've only met in passing. I won't take it personally. Oh wait, you'll know him." The guy jerked his thumb back. "Hey, Alex! Over here."

Recognition struck me. I met him briefly the day I found my way to the grocery store. Alex had friends over, and they had called out teasing remarks as I unloaded my haul. Alex turned as his friend called out. He sauntered over with a tall fit blond guy who I faintly recalled as well. Ali and Laura were sold. College boys, and good looking ones at that.

"What movie are you guys here to see?" Laura asked bright eyed.

"*Left in LA*, it's supposed to be awesome!" the blonde haired guy remarked.

Laura's grin widened. "We're here to see that one, too! Do you want to join us?"

Ali wore a small grin but it quickly faded as she looked toward me; concern clouded her features. I knew she wanted to sit with them, but loyalty was something she took very seriously.

"Yeah, why don't you guys join us?" I did my best to sound enthused.

Ali and Laura brightened, so did the guys. Alex studied me carefully and followed the group to the theatre. We found empty seats, and Alex cautiously sat next to me. He acted unusual. Every movement was carefully measured and I immediately felt guilty. I knew he was doing that for my benefit. I tried to relax my posture and settled deeper into my seat. I sighed contentedly, hoping he would loosen up. His eyes watched me, and he relaxed ever so slightly.

Alex spoke up suddenly. "Hey, sorry, I guess I should introduce you all. Guys this is Laura, Ali, and Abby."

The guys nodded our way and exchanged muffled greetings. "This guy over here," Alex nodded to the blond settled next to Laura, "is Dave, and that's Jordan." He nodded to the tall one with a mop of dark brown curls who seemed to be infatuated with Ali.

"All right, it seems everyone's introduced themselves." Alex muttered almost to himself. I grinned, and studied Alex with new curiosity. I wondered what Ali and Laura began to tell me about him.

"Hopefully it doesn't snow too much while we're in here," Dave muttered. "The weather forecast is calling for a lot."

Laura's eyes twinkled. "I guess we would be snowed in here." She looked thrilled by the thought.

The movie started, and we all settled. I wasn't a huge fan of horror movies, but I was quite entertained as Laura and Ali used the boys as their props; squeezing onto them at the scary parts. I grinned as Jordan and Dave sat taller. I jumped a few times during the more frightening scenes. Alex's hand reached instinctively for mine, but he quickly pulled it back.

The movie was half way through when Alex abruptly got up and left. I didn't think too much of it, until Jordan leaned over to me. "Where'd Alex go?"

"I don't know, he just left."

"Oh....did you talk to him?"

I turned to face him. "No, why?"

Jordan shrugged. "I've known Alex forever and he really seems to like you. I just thought that…" His voice trailed off as he searched my face. "You don't know…" He shook his head, and then focused back on the big screen.

"Excuse me for a minute." I got up and left the theatre and stepped into the lobby.

I wandered around aimlessly until I found Alex sitting at an empty table. He looked upset and rested his forehead against his hand. I stood there for a moment before cautiously approaching him. "Alex?" I said weakly

He looked up surprised. "Abby? What are you doing out here?"

"I just needed to….I thought you might want some company?" I bit my lip, and sat across from him.

He nodded absently. "Oh." He looked away and focused on something I couldn't see.

"Alex, are you okay?"

"Yeah," he sighed. "Just some family stuff."

I sighed, secretly relieved I hadn't been the one to cause this sudden change in his personality. I began to shift uneasily, unsure what to say next. I didn't know how Alex would take to my prying. He knew my private matters fairly well, and he always seemed to speak his mind on the subject, even though it upset me.

"Abby, go watch the movie. This isn't any of your concern."

I shivered at the tone of his voice and slowly got up. I hesitated, deciding he was being a little unfair. "Expectations are a two way street, Alex. If you need me…you know where I am."

I sauntered off and went to find my seat in the theatre. The rest of the movie passed by in a blur. Alex never did come back inside. After the movie ended, we all went our separate ways. Laura and Ali were ecstatic as I drove them home. For the duration of the drive they chatted eagerly about how the boys looked at them, if there was any hidden meanings behind their smiles. I kept a smile posted to my face, telling them what they wanted to hear. It wasn't until after I had dropped them off and was on my back home I realized I had forgotten to ask about Alex James.

⌘

I walked into the house quietly just after 10:30 p.m. Jack watched the late night news. As I shut the door, he glanced my way with a slight nod, before turning his attention back to the television screen. Just for fun, and my own curiosity I decided to start a conversation. "My night was fun. The movie was pretty scary."

Jack looked away from the television and gazed at me briefly. He didn't say anything, and his attention was pulled back to the screen just as quickly. It was just the reaction I expected, nonetheless, it was a little disappointing. I quickly showered and put on my favorite pair of pajamas. I tiptoed into Cara's room and said a quiet goodnight, even though she was already fast asleep. I snuggled under my quilt and tried to fall asleep.

I began to enter a pleasant dream when something startled me awake. I heard men's soft, but rough voices followed by a loud clang come from downstairs. Disoriented footsteps followed. I sat up abruptly and glanced at my clock, it read 2:44 a.m. I slipped out of bed, and opened my door. I hesitated in the hall. Jack's door was shut, and Cara's was securely closed. I peeked inside her room, and she slept, undisturbed. Again, I heard the harsh whispers from downstairs, followed by another loud crash. I pounded on Jack's door. There was no answer. I opened it and stepped inside. His room was empty. I didn't know what to do. I assumed Jack was downstairs as well, but was he in trouble? Should I join him? Something loud fell from below, followed by a curse. Whoever it was must have knocked over the end table. I ran to my bedroom, grabbed my baseball bat, and slipped downstairs. I turned the corner when someone grabbed onto my arms in a tight grasp. The baseball bat fell with a thud on the floor as I let go from surprise. Panic gripped me. It was dark, I couldn't see who it was, and I started thrashing wildly.

I was about to scream when the voice spoke. "Abby, calm down, it's okay. It's me."

"Alex?" my voice was shrill. "What the hell! What are you doing here? Are you trying to scare me to death?"

Before he could answer, a man stumbled into the room and he was angry. His dark eyes tore into mine threateningly. I winced and took a step back. The man came at me cursing and stumbling all the while. Alex gave a sharp breath and grabbed the man roughly, and half dragged him toward the room Jack told me to stay out of when I first arrived here. They left me standing there all alone, bewildered. What was going on here? Should I be scared? Who was that man, and why was Alex here? A warning settled over me as the man's harsh voice cut through the silence of the night. Jack suddenly appeared and he and Alex grabbed a hold of the wild man. It was utter chaos, but somehow it seemed to be an organized chaos; like this was nothing new. I quietly followed from a safe distance and tried to sneak a peek of what was going on. The door slammed shut with all the men inside. I was too wound up and curious to go to bed, so I paced silently and pressed my ear to the door. I heard Jack's soothing tone, a rough angry voice, followed by Alex snapping harsh words impatiently. Within a few moments, the door opened, and a very tired looking Alex stepped out. I stepped back and felt like a deer caught in the headlights. I shouldn't have been trying to eavesdrop, but I did have a right to know what was going on, didn't I?

"Alex, what's happening? Please tell me." I stepped in front of him and gripped onto his forearms.

Alex sighed wearily. "I brought Billy here, he caused another disturbance at home."

"Billy?" Then it clicked. My mind brought me back to that horrible day when I thought Jack had died. He had brought a man home that day; this was the same man, the one who had attacked me.

"Yes, Billy….he's my…well, my uncle. Not much of one at that." Alex's tone turned sharp and he continued, wearily. "Whenever Billy gets drunk like this, Jack has offered to give him a place to stay until he calms down. It saves my aunt and me from a bit of the heartache."

"Heartache? I...don't understand."

Alex rubbed his forehead absently. "He killed my uncle Robbie, Mary's husband. He was drunk and angry one night, but that's nothing new. My uncle Robbie tried to calm him down. Billy hopped into his car, and Robbie tried to get him out of the vehicle. Billy resisted and tried to drive away. He must have thought he was in reverse, but he was still in drive. That was it; that was all it took."

Alex's face twisted in pain, and his tone turned cold. "My uncle Robbie had a good heart; he was the only person in the world who looked out for Billy, not that he deserved it." Alex stopped and took a slow, shuddery breath. "My father died when I was just a baby and my uncle Robbie stepped in to help my mom out. He was like a father to me."

Again his voice turned hard. "The only reason why I put up with Billy is because I know Robbie would have wanted me to. He tried so hard to raise me to be forgiving. But I just can't. I will never be able to forgive Billy. So, out of guilt I figure the least I can do is give him a safe place when he acts like this. I won't let him hurt anyone else."

I sat there, staring at Alex. He looked so vulnerable and frail in this moment. I reached out and wrapped my arms around him. "I'm so sorry for your family's loss."

Alex stepped back, running his hands through his hair. "I won't have to deal with this for much longer. Billy's used up his last chance. He's going to an institution where they can deal with him. He's leaving tomorrow morning. My nightmare will end."

I walked beside him, following him to the front door. "Are you sure you're okay? If you ever need to talk, you know where to find me." I gave him a small grin.

He didn't smile back. "Thanks, Abby, but I don't think so. Just remember, hold on to what you have. Things can change so fast."

He opened the door and stepped out into the cold swirling snow. I watched him. I felt the sadness and pain that lingered around him. Alex crossed the street and faded like a ghost in the night.

Chapter Nine: You're on Your Own Kid

True to Alex's word, Billy was picked up shortly after 7:30 a.m. I was up to see the departure. After he left, the house felt lighter. I hoped Alex would feel the same. Cara woke up shortly after five thirty in the morning, and I had taken care of her. I decided to let Jack sleep in after last night's ordeal. I had a newfound respect growing for the man, as much as I hated to admit it. I settled Cara into her high chair when the doorbell rang.

To my surprise, Alex stood at the door. He looked tired and worn, but he managed a small smile. "Can I come in?"

"Of course." I stepped back and motioned him inside.

"Thanks."

I glanced his way. "Are you hungry?"

"No….but do you have coffee on?"

"Sorry, I don't. But I can make a pot."

Alex slumped into a chair and his eyes followed me as I bustled to prepare the coffee. Cara started to sob unhappily, and I realized that I hadn't gotten around to giving her breakfast. "I'm sorry, little girl; hold on just a minute…where is it? Oh, here we go."

I found a baby safe bowl and mashed a banana for the hungry child. "Here we are." I gently set the bowl in front of her, and quickly strapped on her bib.

Alex watched admiringly. "You sure are good with her."

I smiled. "Thanks. She's easy to fall in love with. One look from those big eyes and I was sold."

Alex chuckled. "You two have the same eyes. They have a powerful effect on people. One look and you're completely mesmerized."

A warm heat crept across my cheeks. "The coffee's done," I said with quick relief. I brought Alex a mug and let him prepare his drink, his face growing more serious with each stir.

"Were you up to see Billy leave?" he asked quietly

"Yes."

"How did it go?"

"It was easy. He was still tired from last night so he didn't fight them. To tell you the truth, I'm not sure he was aware of what was happening."

Alex nodded quickly. "Good." His eyes flew to mine. "How are you and Jack getting along?"

"Fine, I guess. We don't talk much. He works a lot, and when he gets home he says a quick hi to Cara, has dinner, and then settles down with the TV."

Alex sighed. "I suppose I know a different Jack. He's been like a hero to my aunt and me with the whole Billy ordeal."

A stab tore at my heart. "I've never known that side of Jack. I guess it's easier for him to be that way around others instead of with me."

"I'm sorry, Abby. I'm sure things will work out with the two of you. He says you've been a real life saver to him." Alex continued on. "Thanks for last night by the way."

My brows furrowed in confusion. "Thanks? For what?"

"For just being there for me. I'm sorry I snapped at you. I just needed to be alone, it was a long night."

"Anytime. I know the feeling, sometimes you just need to be by yourself."

Footsteps sounded and Jack walked into the kitchen. He stopped in surprise as he saw Alex at the table. "Good morning, you two." His eyes drifted to Alex. "How are you?"

"I'm doing better. He's finally out of my life. I never thought I would see the day."

"You and Mary can sleep easy now. He's in a safe place. He will get the help he needs, when, and if he's ready." Jack's eyes drifted to the coffee pot and he grinned. He poured himself a cup and settled into a chair next to Alex. He took a sip and smiled. "This is good."

Alex nodded. "Yep, it sure is. Abby made it."

Jack's eyebrows rose. "Well done." He gave me a brief nod, and settled his gaze out the window.

I didn't even bother to smile. He wouldn't have seen it anyways. I ignored Alex's studious gaze, and made my way over to Cara. After tidying her up, I set her gently in her jumper. From the living room, I heard Alex thank Jack for all of his help with Billy. I glanced around the room and decided to head back to the kitchen; it would be too obvious I was hiding out if I didn't come back and I wouldn't give Jack the satisfaction. I quietly settled into an empty chair. The silence hung heavy and Alex looked uncomfortable. The phone rang and I was thankful for the interruption. I launched from my chair to answer it.

"Hello?" Silence on the other end. "Hello? Hello?" I continued on.

"H—Hello…is Jack there?" A sharp female voice barked out.

Taken aback for a moment, I answered. "Yes, hold on a moment please. Jack, the phone is for you."

Jack strode over, and took the receiver. He looked up with a strange expression on his face and walked out of the kitchen with the phone pressed against his ear.

Alex cleared his throat. "I could cut the tension with a knife."

I had forgotten Alex was in the room. I looked his way and started to laugh. He was clearly uncomfortable. "Is it like that between the two of you all the time?" he asked in disbelief.

I choked out a laugh. "Picture perfect family." I said sarcastically.

"Yeah, I can see that. You two would actually look good in a picture by the way. Photogenic bone structure."

I rolled my eyes. "Alex, you are something else."

Before Alex could respond, Jack marched into the kitchen, and slammed the phone back into its cradle.

I jumped in surprise. "Jack? Are you okay?"

He shot me a look of frustration. "What did you say to her?" He demanded.

Alex stood to make his way next to me; I shot him a look and motioned him to stay where he was. "You were standing next to me when I answered the phone. All I said was hello."

"I'm going out, I need to get out." Jack grabbed at his hair. "Watch Cara." With that, Jack stomped out of the house, and slammed the door behind him. I silently walked into the living room and sat down on the couch, wondering what just happened.

Alex sat beside me, watching me with concern. "Are you okay?"

I nodded. "Alex, can you please go. I'd like to call my mom."

He sighed. "Sure, you know where to find me."

After Alex left, I dialed the familiar number and waited. Finally, after what had seemed like forever, my mother's kind voice filled the other end. "Hello?"

"Mom!"

"Abby! Oh, Abby, I miss hearing your voice! How are you, sweetie? Wait, what's wrong? I can hear the tone."

I had to smile, my mother knew me so well. "I don't know, Mom. Everything."

"Start from the beginning."

I filled my mother in on almost everything, from my thoughts, some of the events that happened, and Jack's distant reactions toward me; everything that mattered. I listened in silence as my mother voiced her thoughts, making me more homesick than I had ever been. By the end of the phone conversation, it was all I could do to keep myself from not hopping in my truck, and driving back to the home I missed so much.

Jack didn't return home until nearly 11:30 p.m. I was still up, waiting. I met Jack in the hallway, hoping for an explanation. He gave me nothing. He looked at me wearily, then went into his bedroom and shut the door. I stood staring angrily at his door, debating whether or not I could knock it down. With a frustrated sigh, I went to my bedroom to settle in for the night.

The next morning dawned bright and clear. I stretched out happily from under the covers as I felt the sun warm my skin. It felt like a piece of home. Through the baby monitor, happy gurgles and coos sounded from Cara. I smiled, and quickly went to get her ready for another day. I ate breakfast when Jack came downstairs. I was quite surprised to see him in the same room as me. He avoided my eyes as he went over to say good morning to Cara.

Jack stared down at the happy little girl when he spoke to me very hesitantly. "I'm sorry about yesterday. There were a lot of things going on."

I stared blankly at him. "Anything I should be included on?"

"No."

I shrugged and focused my attention back to my cereal, hoping my pain wasn't obvious. Would he ever be able to share his life with me? Would he ever want me in it?

"Abby, I don't want to fight. Today's a beautiful day. I was thinking of taking Cara to the lake. Would you like to join her? Uh, us. Would you like to join us?"

I stared at Jack as he began to rub the back of his neck, focusing his gaze out the window. My eyes flitted to Cara. She caught my stare and happily threw her hands in the air with a squeal, sending mashed banana's flying.

I smiled. "Sure."

"Good. Be ready to leave in twenty minutes."

I got dressed, and noticed Jack had left me to dress Cara. With a shake of my head, I grabbed the little munchkin who happily played with her toys. With an angry grunt, she allowed herself to be carried away with minimal protest. Jack and I, along with Cara, walked out of the house together in a group. It was the first time since being here that we walked out together, almost like a real family. Alex was outside shoveling the driveway. When Jack's attention was focused on locking up the house, Alex shot me a grin with a thumbs up. I fought back a laugh and settled Cara into her car seat. Within minutes, we were on our way to the lake. The car ride was awkward. It felt stuffy and hard to breathe. Jack's back was rod straight and his knuckles were white from grasping the steering wheel tightly. To my disappointment, his radio didn't work. The only sounds came from the wheels crushing ice, the scraping of snow, and Cara's gurgles. She was completely oblivious to the tension around her.

"You will like the lake." Jack broke the silence.

I nodded. "I'm sure I will. It sounds quaint."

I braved a glance at him, he focused on the road ahead. I turned my attention out the window, settling my chin onto my hand. We finally arrived after what felt like forever. We pulled into a parking lot in front of a small but picturesque lake. The mountains were clear in the distance and the trees were freshly dusted with snow. I stepped out of the car and took a deep breath. The air was so crisp and clear it almost burned. Jack pulled out the stroller, and I grabbed Cara from her seat. I settled her into the stroller, adjusted her toque, and wrapped the blanket around her snugly. Jack went ahead, already walking to the path leaving us behind. I lengthened my strides to catch up. As we strolled side by side, Jack loosened up and almost looked content. He even started a conversation, and as I listened, I realized he could be almost funny. I smiled warmly at him, and was delighted when we actually made eye contact.

"So, do you think you would like to do that again?" Jack inquired as we drove for home.

I brightened. "Definitely, that was a lot of fun."

"I thought you would like that." Jack grinned. "What do you say about grabbing some hot chocolate for the way home?"

"That sounds good. While we're here, do you want to stop and rent a movie?" I held my breath for his response, hoping that I hadn't pushed him too far.

Jack's eyes twinkled a bit. "Now, that's something I haven't done in awhile. Sure, why not."

Hours later, it was time to call it a day. For the first time in a long time, I felt like we could salvage something of our relationship, and it sent me afire with hope. And for some reason, I couldn't wait to tell Alex about the day's events. I imagined the grin he would surely give me.

"Goodnight, Jack. Thanks for today, I had fun."

"You're welcome. I had fun too. See you in the morning."

I snuggled in bed, and for the first time since arriving, I fell asleep with a genuine smile on my face and looked forward to what tomorrow would bring. I awoke bright and early the next morning, and decided to make a nice breakfast. It was Jack's last day off and I hoped we would spend it together like the day before. I set the coffee maker and prepared blueberry pancakes. We had kept Cara up later than usual and she was still asleep. A soft knock at the door took me away from the kitchen. I jogged to the door to answer it.

"Alex!" I squealed. "Hi!"

Alex wore an eager expression on his face. "Hey! Well, aren't you little miss sunshine this morning."

I rolled my eyes and yanked him inside. "I had the best day with Jack yesterday!"

I happily filled him in on yesterday's events as I automatically served him pancakes and coffee. Alex's grin made my own smile even wider, he sported the crooked grin I had pictured yesterday.

Jack entered the kitchen with a pleased smile on his face. "Are those blueberry pancakes I smell?"

"They sure are, and they're delicious!" Alex said with a mouthful.

Jack settled in his chair and smiled. "Thanks, Abby. I haven't had these in years."

His eyes went to Alex. "What brings you here this morning?"

Alex swallowed and then spoke. "Mary mentioned that your truck was acting up, so I came to take a look at it."

Jack nodded. "Right, I completely forgot."

While the boys chatted on about the truck, Cara woke up. I slipped away to get her ready. I heard the phone ring from downstairs. I almost bounced into the kitchen while placing Cara into her chair. I hadn't felt this light in a long time. I glanced around and Jack spoke quietly on the phone from the living room. I mashed a banana and Jack nearly hopped into the kitchen. His face looked bright and happy. "Alex, can we do the truck another day?"

"Sure, no problem."

"Great. Thanks for breakfast, Abby. I'm going to get ready. I'll see you in a few hours."

My face fell slightly. "Oh, okay. See you later."

Alex watched Jack leave. "I wonder what's gotten into him. He looks like a kid in a candy store."

I shrugged my shoulders. "I have no idea. Do you know who just called?"

Alex shrugged. "Not a clue."

After Alex left, it was just Cara and me. I decided to go to the lake again; it was the one place that offered me hope. I took my time walking around the paved path and on the way home I stopped to pick up groceries. It was nearing 4:00 p.m. when I finally got back. I was slightly disappointed when I noticed Jack's truck was still gone. After hauling in the groceries, I checked the answering machines for missed calls. I pressed play and started unpacking the food.

"Hey, Abby, it's Jack. Don't worry about cooking dinner, I've got plans. I won't be home until late."

I shrugged and decided I would settle on a sandwich for myself tonight. The next morning I woke to the sound of my alarm. *No, not yet!* My body ached and my eyes felt heavy. I sat up wearily and hit the sleep button. I trudged to the shower and started my morning. Cara had kept me up most of the night. Jack hadn't come home, but he called once to tell me that he was okay. I figured that was progress, at least I knew he was okay, unlike the last time. I glanced at the clock, 7:10 a.m. Jack's shift at the hospital would be starting.

I threw my school bags into the truck and quietly crept into Cara's room. I lifted her gently, and without waking her, I carefully placed her in the truck. I held my breath as I started the engine, and stole a glance back at her. To my relief, she slept soundly. I drove to Janie's and she met me warmly at her door. "Come inside, you must be freezing."

I mumbled a thanks and placed Cara into one of the cribs. Janie walked me to the front door, and I wearily handed her Cara's bag. Janie looked concerned. "Are you all right, Abby? You look exhausted."

I waved a hand carelessly. "I'm fine, just tired. Cara was being really fussy, so she had me up most of the night."

"Oh, you poor girl. Try and have a good day at school!"

⌘

"Psst, Abby? Abby! Wake up!"

I faintly heard someone call my name, and the voice poked me repeatedly. I groaned and mumbled. "Leave me alone. I'm sleeping."

Ali hissed. "Abby, class is over!"

I opened my eyes. "Huh, oh, okay, good." I walked out with Ali, and ignored the teachers disapproving glance.

"Abby, are you sure you're okay? Maybe you should go get some sleep."

"No, I'll be okay. I just need some food I think."

Ali looked unconvinced. "Uh-huh, sure."

I glanced at Ali, and gave her a sly grin. "You look pretty tired yourself, late night?"

Ali blushed. "Yeah, me and Jordan were out a little late."

I clapped my hands together. "That's great! I'm glad the two of you have hit it off, you make a really cute couple."

Ali blushed even more deeply. "Thanks."

The rest of the school day crawled by and I had fallen asleep several times. When the final bell of the day rang, I was so tired, my body felt like it weighed a thousand pounds. Mike helped me to my truck, not that I needed any help, but he insisted.

"Are you sure you're okay to drive?" he asked with worry.

"Yeah, I'm fine. Thanks, Mike, the cold air woke me up."

"All right. I guess I'll see you tomorrow. If you can't make it in, just call my cell. I'll swing by your place with your homework after school."

I nodded, and gave him a small smile. "Thanks, Mike."

All day long, Mike had been my shadow. At first it was flattering; but now, six hours later I needed a break. I picked up Cara, and was out of there in two minutes flat. I was not in the mood to chat. By the time I pulled into the driveway, I wanted nothing more than to crawl into bed and go to sleep, but Cara had other ideas. I groaned; would this day never end? I tried feeding her but she put up a fuss and refused anything I gave her, or should I say, tried to give her. Most of the food had ended up on me, or the floor. I picked her up, feeling a little irritated until I noticed that she felt hotter than usual.

I didn't have the energy to make dinner, so I settled for cereal. As I ate even my teeth felt tired, and I doubted that could be possible. Cara had worn herself out in the jolly jumper and was finally asleep. I was too tired to carry her up the stairs, so I left her as she was. I curled up on the couch, and found one of my favorite TV shows. I fell asleep within the first few minutes. A sudden knock at the door woke me up. I sat up bewildered. For a moment I had forgotten where I was. I shuffled to the door, and glanced at the clock, 8:30 p.m. and there was no sign of Jack being home yet.

I answered the door and Mary stood outside. She took in my appearance and pursed her lips in disapproval. "I'm sorry to wake you. May I come in?"

"Sure. Come on in. Would you like a cup of tea?" I secretly hoped she would say no. I was just trying to be polite.

"I'm okay, I don't want to trouble you."

I noticed Mary's eyes had lit up slightly at the offer. I couldn't back out now, especially since I had been the one to bring up the idea. I forced to keep my voice even. "No, it's no trouble, I was about to make myself a cup."

Mary glanced at me somewhat skeptically. "Thank you, that sounds good."

I showed her into the kitchen and began to boil water before excusing myself for a minute. When I glanced in the bathroom mirror, I groaned. It wouldn't have taken a scientist to know I had been asleep; my hair was a mess, it stuck out in almost every direction and pillow lines were marred onto my face. I quickly ran a brush through my hair and splashed cool water against my skin. I didn't have time to work miracle, this would have to be good enough. I entered the kitchen just as the kettle started to whistle.

"Here, I hope it's not too hot for you." I gently handed Mary a steaming mug.

Mary gripped the cup. "It's perfect." I noticed Mary's eyes took in the place with an expression that mimicked surprise. "You have done a wonderful job with organizing things here. I have never seen it so clean before!"

I smiled. "Thanks, it was definitely a big job."

"Is Jack working late?"

"I...I'm not too sure actually."

Mary almost looked disappointed. "I guess you know why I'm here. Today in school you fell asleep in almost all of your classes."

I sighed. "I know, sorry. I tried to stay awake…"

"If you're sick, you don't need to come to school."

"I know. I wasn't sick, just tired. Cara kept me up all night, I think she's coming down with a cold."

Mary nodded sympathetically. "Ahh yes, they sure do get fussy then." Her eyebrows pulled together. "Jack didn't help you?"

"He wasn't home." Another disapproving look crossed Mary's friendly face.

"It's okay, Mary. I can manage the house by myself." I reminded her gently.

"I know you can, you're quite capable. But on a school night, Jack should know you need your rest. I'm sure he has a good reason." She pursed her lips. I nodded absently, my eyes were drifting closed again.

"I'll let you be now. Thanks for the tea." She paused by the door. "If you need anything, anything at all, you give myself or Alex a holler."

I smiled tiredly. "I will. See you tomorrow."

⌘

"Please go to sleep, Cara!" I whined.

It was 2:45 a.m. and Cara had kept me up for almost two hours. Her cold was in full swing now, she was miserable, and I was exhausted. It wasn't until 4:30 a.m. that Jack walked in. I was practically sleepwalking to my room, bouncing off the walls, when Jack found me. He was the complete opposite of me; chipper and lively.

"You!" I glowered up at him. "Where have you been?"

Jack stopped and looked surprised. "Out. What are you still doing up?"

I could have throttled him right then and there, and wouldn't have cared. "Cara's sick," I growled. "And since I've been the only one home for almost two days now, I have had to deal with it!"

He looked concerned immediately. "Sick? How sick? Why didn't you call me?"

"She just has a cold. I made an appointment for her tomorrow a one o'clock, and I tried calling you, but you never answered your phone." I shot back.

"Oh, right. Sorry, I will next time. I promise."

"There better not be a next time Jack, not on a school day. I am exhausted, I fell asleep at school today."

Jack rubbed his chin. "That's not good. You get some rest. I have the day off, I will take care of Cara in the morning and take her to her appointment."

I almost toppled over in relief. "You promise?"

"Promise. You can sleep in a little bit, it looks like you could use it." Jack looked at me in disapproval. I didn't bother with an answer, I was already heading for my room, dreaming of a decent night's sleep.

My alarm went off at 7:30 a.m., instead of the usual 6:00 a.m. It wasn't much of a sleep in, but it made a world of a difference. Until I sat up. My head was so heavy, and exhaustion hit me like a ton of bricks. I groaned, and decided to skip the shower this morning. I managed to pull on a pair of black plants and a purple sweater. I walked sleepily down the hall and noticed Jack's door was open. I glanced in his room. It was empty. I peeked in Cara's room where she was fast asleep. I trudged downstairs into the kitchen only to find that it too was vacant. That was odd, I thought Jack would have slept in. I was too tired to eat, so I skipped breakfast and threw my lunch together. I stepped outside into the brisk morning air when I stopped. Jack's truck was gone. I ran back into the house, glancing around for a note, finding none. I placed my head in my hands. *How could he?* I couldn't just leave Cara alone. We had already called Janie telling her we wouldn't be bringing Cara in because she was sick. I called Jack's cell.

"Hello?" Jack's voice was happy and wide-awake.

"Jack, where are you? I have to leave for school, what about Cara?"

"Cara?" he sounded confused for a moment. "Oh, shoot. I completely forgot! I'm actually out of town."

My mouth dropped, out of town? Did he really say he was out of town? "What do you mean you're out of town?" I yelled. "You were just here!"

"I'm sorry, Abby. It slipped my mind. Something urgent came up."

"How could you do this to me, Jack? I was counting on you."

"Look, Abby…"

"No, never mind. That was my first mistake, counting on you." I hung up the phone infuriated. He was starting again, slowly, but he was beginning to forget about Cara.

Chapter Ten: New Addition

Cara awoke abruptly and she was not happy. I sighed with slight impatience and went to her room. "Good morning, baby. You're not feeling too good are you? Let's get you changed."

Cara sniffled and cried nosily as I changed her diaper and got her dressed into a clean pink jumper. I stood her up. "There you go, all clean!"

She started crying again. I balanced her on my hip and opened the blinds. I stared out without really seeing anything, until I noticed the lights were on in Mary's basement. Alex was up. I glanced at the time, 7:45 a.m.. I would be late. School started at 8:15. I briefly remembered Alex had mentioned he was off school for two weeks, he might be my only chance. I grabbed the nearest phone and dialed his number.

Alex's sleepy voice crackled on the other end. "Hullo?"

I skipped the hellos and got straight to the point. "Alex, are you busy today?"

A faint smile lit his voice. "No," he said slowly, "but shouldn't you be?"

"I'm sort of in trouble."

"Trouble? What kind of trouble?"

I quickly explained my situation with forced patience. I was proud of myself for keeping my voice low and steady.

Alex didn't hesitate. "I'll be right over."

My voice went thick in relief. "Thank you."

Within two minutes Alex walked in, rubbing his hands together. "All right, I'm here, tell me what I need to know."

I glanced at his outstretched arms; they looked too rough to hold Cara. I glanced wearily down at her, then to him. I released her with slowed reluctance. Alex held her close to his chest delicately, but securely.

I couldn't hide the surprise in my voice. "You have experience with this, don't you?"

He smiled proudly. "Older sister, she's got a few little ones. I have babysat many, many times for the little monsters."

I smiled back. "Great! I will give you a quick tour of all her things, follow me."

I headed for the door moments later, when I stopped to face him, "I will be back around twelve-thirty to take her to the doctor's." I softened my tone. "Oh, and Alex? Thank you. You have no idea what this means to me."

Alex shook his head. "Don't worry about it. I will think of a way you can thank me later." A wide grin slowly spread across his face.

I rolled my eyes as I quickly ran for my truck. I hopped in and fired up the cold engine when I realized I had left my school bag in the house. I jumped out, ran into the house, gave Alex a quick wave, and yanked up my book bag. I leapt off the stairs and high tailed it to my truck when one of my knees hit the ground. "Ouch!"

My anger swelled as my bag hit the ground hard, sending my pens and pencils scattering across the driveway. I groaned loudly and hurried for them, picking up as many as I could at a time. Once I had everything, I shoved my bag into the truck with more force than necessary. I reversed out of the driveway, and glanced up quickly only to catch a very amused Alex watching through the window.

Once I arrived at school, I grabbed my late slip, and slipped into Biology as quietly as I could. "Late again, Miss. Taylor. Let's hope you can stay awake today."

I avoided the gazes burning into me, and slipped into my seat. "Jeez, Abby. You look awful."

I glared at Mike. "You know that's not really a compliment."

Mike stared back. "I wasn't trying to give you one."

I placed my head in my hands and told myself to take a deep breath. I needed to stay on Mike's good side, I would need a favor from him. "Hey, Mike, could you do me a favor today?" I asked in my sweetest tone. For an added measure, I leaned in closer, and casually flicked my hair over my shoulder.

His face brightened. "Sure, what do you need?"

"Can you go to the office after school? I've already arranged the details with them. I have to leave early today, and I was wondering if you could pick up my homework and bring it to my place?"

"Yeah, that's not a problem." Mike beamed.

"Thanks." For the final touch, I squeezed his shoulder lightly. Guys were so easy. For the rest of the period I fought myself to stay awake. After this morning's madness had calmed down, my body realized how tired it was. Finally, the bell rang. I gathered up my books and hurried to the parking lot.

I parked in the driveway and stepped into the warm house. Alex greeted me. "Abby, you look terrible."

"So I've been told," I snapped. "How's Cara been for you?" I set to work bundling up Cara. I waited for his response but wasn't really listening.

"We had our moments. I think she's getting a fever though."

I nodded. "So I noticed." I looked at Cara's flushed face and sighed. "Poor girl." I stood, and Alex tore the keys out of my hand.

"What are you doing?" I looked at him incredulously.

"I'm driving, you need to relax. Besides, I don't want you behind the wheel when you look like you do. We'd probably get pulled over and dragged down to the police station." I was too tired to argue, so I just nodded.

The appointment told me everything that I already knew. Cara had a fever. The doctor recommended children's Tylenol. On the way home we picked up a bottle from the drug store. Cara had finally fallen asleep, and I settled deeper into my seat, watching the road blur by. I opened my eyes slowly as I heard the engine quiet. I looked up wearily, and realized we were home. I lifted my head and couldn't recall dozing off.

"Go back to sleep. I've got Cara."

Alex gently carried Cara into the house. I grabbed what was left of my strength and hopped out of the truck. It did me no good. I slipped and landed on my back. The snow pierced it's way down my shirt and cold stabs of snow began to melt and trickle down my skin. I was too tired to move, so I lied there staring as the lightest of snowflakes began to fall. My mind drifted toward sleep, and I wondered if Jack would ever come back and what he would have to say. Footsteps sounded, and Alex cursed lightly. I was to tired to open my eyes or speak, but I thought of what I would say to him, and it made me smile.

A sea of warmth enveloped me. I sighed contently and snuggled closer. The world began to move and my eyes opened briefly. I found myself in Alex's arms. I looked up and he gave me a crooked grin. "Go back to sleep, I've got you."

I nodded once. "You know, Alex you have become my life saver." My eyes grew heavy and then I was gone.

⌘

I didn't know how much time had passed. It felt like days. I woke up feeling disoriented as I gazed around. I was in my room with an extra blanket placed over me. I glanced at the clock, 3:40 p.m. Was it the same day? If so, I had only been asleep for two hours, yet it felt like so much longer. I remembered taking Cara to the doctors, falling, and Alex carrying me inside. Self-consciously I glanced at my clothes. Relief washed over me, I was in the same ones that I wore earlier. I slowly sat up, and began walking down the stairs. Mike's voice floated toward me.

"Well, is she here?" he sounded annoyed.

"Hey, Mike." I let out a yawn.

Mike smiled self-righteously and shot Alex a look as he stepped in closer. "Hey, Abby, how are you feeling?"

"I don't really know honestly."

Alex looked at me with concern. "You should lie down, I think you've caught what Cara has. It's no wonder, when's the last time you have slept? You're completely run down."

"Yeah, and who's fault is that?" I mumbled angrily.

Mike looked unsure as he shot Alex an evil look. Alex saw it and smiled before leaving the room.

Mike stepped closer. "Here's your homework. It doesn't look like a lot."

"Thanks, Mike." I stood there waiting for Mike to leave. He didn't move. He looked at me, waiting to be offered more.

I sighed in frustration. "Drive safe, it's snowing again." I said pointedly.

Mike's face slightly crumpled. "Yeah, I'll see you whenever you get back then." Mike headed for the front door. It closed with more force than necessary.

Alex walked back in the room and handed me a cup of tea. "Thanks." I sighed as the warmth from the cup spread.

He nodded and leaned himself against the doorframe. "So, is that your boyfriend?"

I shot Alex a look of disbelief. "No, not even close."

He chuckled. "Well, he sure thinks he's something."

I leaned back into the comfort of the couch. "He's sadly mistaken."

Alex's smile fell. "I called Jack."

"Did you get a hold of him?" I asked dryly.

Alex let out a surprised noise. "That's it? I was expecting you to rip my head off."

I sat deeper in my seat. "Too tired."

"Yeah, I got a hold of him."

I studied Alex, I didn't like the tone of his voice. I could tell he knew something and it made him uncomfortable. "What do you know? You know something, don't you?"

Alex held up his hands. "I just told him what was going on. I'm not on his side for this one."

"He's not coming back, is he?"

"Of course he is." Alex stared at me in shock.

"That's a first," I mumbled. I put down the mug of tea and curled up with the pillow. Alex picked up the remote to turn off the TV.

"No, leave it on, please. I like the sound." I pleaded.

Alex did as asked. I closed my eyes, listening to the background noise and found I began to drift off into dreamland, it felt safe. After some time, my sleep became disturbed. As I rose into consciousness, two low voices began to argue.

Jack spoke first. "I'm grateful for everything you have done for my girls today, but this is none of your concern."

"She's just a kid, Jack. You can't put all of this on her, it's not fair." Alex sounded upset.

Jack's voice went hard. "That's right, Alex. She is just a kid, you remember that."

Alex's voice went cold. "She needs a father; it would be nice if you would actually be there when she needs you. She has a lot of mixed feelings, Jack. This isn't going to help. You can't spend one day with her and think that's going to fix everything."

Jack's voice held no room for argument. "Go home, Alex."

"I'm leaving."

I lied on the couch unmoving, trying to make sense of their conversation. Jack entered the room and I sat up. As soon as I was upright my head began to spin, and my stomach twisted. Jack saw the look on my face, and he got out of the way as I ran past him for the washroom. This was going to be a long night. I had the flu. I was in bed for three days before I even attempted to get up and think about food. Mike had stopped by with my homework, and I tried not to think about how far behind I fell in school. Jack stuck around, but he had begun to grow restless. Again, I wondered what was going on with him. It would have to wait just a little longer. I didn't have the strength to get into it yet, I knew there would be an argument somewhere in between.

As I stretched out, my stomach twisted in hunger or so I hoped it was hunger. I made my way to the kitchen and stopped in surprise. "Oh…hello." I self-consciously smoothed my hair. I wasn't expecting company.

The sleek, polished woman smiled at me and began studying me intently. I cringed back automatically. The woman was tall and sleek like a model. Her platinum hair fell into a polished wave around her face. Her large brown eyes burned into me. I glanced down at my worn pajamas and looked over the woman's put together slacks and polished blouse.

She smiled a slow smile. "Hello, Abigail. You've grown. You sure look like your mother."

I stood back and stared wordlessly at her. I suddenly placed her face in my head and I wanted to hit her with a frying pan. "Alison?" I blurted out.

"We meet at last."

"What are you doing here?" I asked horrified.

Alison raised a manicured eyebrow. "This is my house. I think the real question is, what are you doing here?"

I filed through my head for a polite response but couldn't find one. "Cleaning up after your mess."

Jack walked in at that moment with a rather large smile set in his features. "Good morning, sweetheart," he leaned in and gave Alison a quick kiss. "It's nice to see you up and about, Abby." He nodded in my general direction.

I stared back in horror, so this must have been why he was so busy and preoccupied lately; her. "Where's Cara?" I almost whispered.

"Oh, my poor darling is still sleeping. I can't believe she got the flu." Alison drawled smoothly.

"I'm going to have a shower." I stormed out, this was not going to be fun. This wasn't part of the deal.

After I freshened up and was in clean clothes, I spent half an hour pacing, arguing with myself on whether or not I should go downstairs. A lot was to be said and it was going to get ugly. I walked down the stairs with purpose. Jack and Alison sat at the table laughing away at something.

"Well, you look more presentable, slightly," Alison laughed, and then pursed her lips as she studied me intently. "I should take you shopping. It could be fun, a girl's day out."

I stared at her, and Jack smiled adoringly. He gazed at her like she was the greatest thing on Earth. How could he look at her with such admiration? Alison left him alone with their baby, could that have been forgiven so fast? Or was he just that desperate to not be alone with me?

"I like my clothes." I said lamely.

Jack scolded me with a look, but Alison laughed it aside. "If you say so.

When you're ready, you let me know and we'll dress you up nicely."

"Will you actually be sticking around this time?" I spat out.

Jack glared at me. "Careful, Abigail."

I glared back. "Well, I'm sorry, but do you honestly expect me to be polite after everything that has happened lately?"

Jack looked dumbfounded. "You're not even going to apologize are you, Jack?" I shook my head in disbelief. "Unbelievable, you don't think you have done anything wrong, do you?"

Jack straightened his shoulders. "Abby," he continued slowly. "I'm grateful for all your help, really I am. You have done a wonderful job, but you can't blame a man for trying to make his family work."

His words felt like a slap in the face. "*I* am your family."

At that moment, Cara started to cry. I took that as a cue, and hoped someone else would take care of her. I slammed my boots on and tore my jacket off the hanger. I quickly grabbed my keys and shut the door behind me. I stood outside in the swirling snow and shoved my toque over my damp hair. I stared at the keys that hung lifelessly from my hand and realized I had no place to go. I leaned against the side of my truck and gave a sidelong glance at the house I suddenly feared.

Alison opened the front door. "Abby, could you park that big truck on the side of the road? I want my car to be in the driveway next to Jack's."

She shot me a sickly sweet smile, and slammed the front door. I looked over at the shiny red car parked next to the curb, it left me with an empty feeling. I suddenly wondered why I ever thought I could belong in Jack's world. I collapsed lifelessly against my truck when I heard familiar voices laughing. The careless sounds of their laughter made me feel even more alone in the world. I had left all of that behind me. It took me a moment to place the faces that belonged with the voices; Ali, Jordan, and Alex. I stole a glance in my truck's side view mirror and saw the three walking in a row, laughing, and throwing the occasional snowball at one another. Ali saw me first, and started waving. At that moment Alison came out of the house.

"Abby! What in god's name are you doing? Look, I asked you to move that thing," she pointed out in disgust at my truck. "I don't want my car to be on the street. Your truck is in my spot, so move it."

I stepped back in slight surprise. Her mood had changed extremely fast. I glared at her, and heard Ali exclaim in horror. "Who is *that?*"

Alison must have heard as well, for she shot Ali a dark look. Her eyes narrowed to me. "Did you hear me girl? I want that truck moved, now!"

I took another step back instinctively. There was something about her tone and the way she moved that began to frighten me. Jack stepped outside and stood next to her. "Is everything all right?"

Alison smoothed her shirt. "Yes, we were just having a little girl chat." She flashed me a dazzling smile and I stared back with wide eyes.

Jack smiled. "Okay then." He focused on Alison. "Do you want to come back inside?"

Alison smiled. "I would love to."

She shot me a warning look and I hurried backwards. I turned around and saw the mouths gaped upon my friends faces. I hopped into my truck and revved the engine. I reversed as quickly as I could and began driving down the street. With a quick glance in my rear view mirror, I saw that Alison had already claimed her spot back on the driveway.

Chapter Eleven: The Party

I didn't really have anywhere to go. I supposed I could have gone to a friend's house, but I didn't want to talk about it. I wasn't even sure I knew how I felt yet, everything had changed again, and so suddenly. Only this time, I didn't see any chance for a happy ending on my end. What I needed in this moment was some comfort, a hope to hold on too. And so, I drove to the lake. I pulled into an empty parking stall, cut the engine, and stared outside. Loneliness settled over me like a wet blanket. My heart ached, and my stomach twisted. I remembered the last time I had come here; it was the one day I dared to dream Jack loved me. He almost felt like a Dad. Tears slowly escaped my eyes. My stomach dropped as I knew 'that day' would be nothing more than a memory from now on. I sat in my truck until a light layer of snow began to settle over the world outside. I delicately hopped out and began to walk around the lake. I glanced at the time on my cell phone. I had been gone for almost two and a half hours now. I slipped the phone back into my pocket, and sat on a bench facing the lake. I hugged my knees for warmth, and stared out at the glistening icy water. I felt cold despite the beauty around me. The frigid breeze grabbed at my hair and sent shivers down my spine. The buzzing of my phone snapped me out of my mindless daydream. I stared at my phone hesitantly, and wished I had purchased caller ID.

"Hello?" I said unenthusiastically.

"Abby, are you okay?" A worried female voice was on the other end.

"Ali?"

"Yes, it's me. Jordan, and Alex are here too."

I smiled a little as I heard their upbeat hellos in the background. "Abby, where are you?"

"I'm at the lake."

"Come meet us for coffee, please?"

I closed my eyes. They were so happy before. Now I could picture their faces heavy with concern. If I said no to meeting up with them, they would only worry more. "Sure. I can be there in ten minutes."

"Great, see you soon!"

I sat on the bench for a few more minutes, watching the geese lazily float about. I wondered if I would still be able to take Cara out on our day trips. Alison and I clearly felt the same way about each other, and I knew she would try to prove that she was the "head" of the household in every way possible. I slowly stood, stretched, and dusted myself off. I headed for my truck and drove to the coffee shop. I pulled into a vacant space awhile later and found my friends easily. They were huddled together at an outside table under a large space heater. Ali saw me first and waved excitedly. I forced a grin and made my way to them.

"Here you go." Ali handed me a warm drink. "Hazelnut hot chocolate. Your favorite!"

I smiled. "Thanks for remembering."

I sat down and a twinge of nerves followed. My friends gave me warm smiles, but their eyes held a genuine concern. I fidgeted, and wished that their attention would be focused elsewhere. I took a quick breath, and decided to get to the point. "So, who wants to ask first?"

Their smiles faded and they sat back in surprise. "Well," I continued. "How much do you know?"

They shifted gazes from one to another and Ali finally spoke. "That was Alison, wasn't it?"

I nodded. "Yeah, she's a cheery bundle." I sighed loudly. "It seems she's made her way back home, and apparently isn't going anywhere."

Ali spoke suddenly. "I don't like the way she talks to you. What was her problem anyways?"

I shrugged my shoulders. "Things are going to get interesting."

"What about Jack? Does he let her speak to you that way?" Alex asked quietly.

My gaze fell to the table. I was strangely embarrassed by Jack's apparent lack of concern. "He's trying to make his family work. He doesn't want to upset her. Besides, so far she's been decent to me when Jack is by her side."

Alex gave a disgusted snort and Jordan piped up. "He does remember that you are his daughter, right? How many times have you saved his ass? And after everything that you've done for him…"

I stopped him from saying anything more. It was fine for me to bash Jack, but I wasn't sure I could hear it from anyone else…it would make my worries all the more real. "I know, just let it go, please. I haven't exactly absorbed everything that's happened as of yet."

Jordan chuckled. "Yeah, I'd like to see your reaction when you have absorbed everything."

Ali smacked him on the arm and he gave me a sly grin. I stared vacantly at the parking lot until my phone rang. I answered it. "Hello?"

"Abby!"

My heart felt warm. "Mom!" A mixture of reactions appeared on my friend's faces; relief, worry, and doubt.

My mother's warm voice distracted me. "I called Jack's house looking for you, and Alison answered the phone. What's going on?"

"The prodigal wife has returned…apparently." I said dully.

My mother's soft voice sharpened. "Oh, has she now? Is she being nice to you?"

"Well…we're not exactly seeing eye to eye."

"Oh, Abby. I'm so sorry. You listen to me, okay? When it comes to that woman…don't you let her talk to you like you are nothing. Do you hear me? You stand your ground. If she's anything like I remember…"

My mother's voice cut off quickly. I knew she would never get over the hurt that Alison had caused. Especially since Alison didn't even seem to care her actions had consequences. She simply brushed it off as though it was none of her concern, a mere wrinkle in her smooth clothing.

"Are you coming home?"

My mother's question caught me off guard. "Home? Oh...I don't know, Mom. I hadn't thought of that..."

Ali's face twisted. Alex's expression matched hers and I looked away. Home. The thought felt safe. To see my mom and Mark again, to feel wanted, included, loved. Yet, the thought of going home also made me feel weak, like I would be running away from my responsibilities, a hidden challenge. I thought of tiny helpless Cara, my new friends, all of which held me here in a strange way. I also realized Jack wasn't on my list of reasons to stay. Maybe that was a sign that my time was in fact up here. I sighed and rested my forehead against my hand.

"It's your decision, Abby. I just don't want to see you get hurt." My mother's voice prodded.

"I know, Mom...I'll think about it."

"That's all I ask. You know you will always be welcome here...always."

Tears began to well up, and I fought them back. There was no way I would cry in front of an audience. "Thanks, Mom. Love you."

"I love you too, honey." The warmth of my mother's voice split me in two as I hung up the phone. I met the gazes of my friends cautiously.

Ali spoke, and she looked a little shaken. "Are you leaving, Abby?"

"I honestly don't know."

Ali nodded and spoke quietly. "Okay, I guess that's fair."

Ali and I were a lot alike. We were both fairly quiet and preferred to be in the background. She would be going to the same university I would be attending next fall. We were already enrolled in a lot of the same courses. If worst came to worst, I could probably stay with her for my college years if I was no longer welcome at Jack's.

I gave her a reassuring smile. "Don't worry, Ali. If I leave, you will be the first to know so you can throw me an awesome going away party." I grinned, trying to make things light. "I will be back for college..." I whispered.

Ali brightened up a bit. "Yeah, okay. I guess it wouldn't be forever." She gave me a weak grin.

I stood. "Well....I guess I should head home." My smile fell as soon as I said the words. *Home.* What a joke.

The group nodded. "Good luck." Alex suddenly got up. "Let me walk you out."

Alex and I strode side by side until we reached my truck. My memory flashed to the night I got sick and overheard Alex and Jack arguing; it made sense to me now. They had been arguing about Alison.

I tried to keep my voice light, but it came out in an accusing tone. "You knew she was coming back, didn't you?"

Alex winced like I had thrown cold water in his face. "I had an idea. I didn't know for sure what was going on…"

"You should have told me."

"I didn't want to upset you. If she wasn't coming, then I would have caused you to worry over nothing. You already had so much going on."

"Forget it, Alex." I opened my door and got in and drove for home.

I parked my truck on the side of the road, like I was told. I wandered inside, and Cara's cries were the first thing I heard. I looked around, and there was no sign of Jack or Alison anywhere. I headed for Cara and realized she must have been crying for awhile; her face was red, and her voice hoarse. I picked her up, and her cries slowly eased as I gently bounced her up and down.

"Poor baby, let's get you changed." I murmured to Cara as I gently laid her on the changing table. I gave her a toy to keep her preoccupied as I set to work.

"There we go, all clean! Now, when's the last time you were fed?"

Cara and I both settled in the kitchen, eating lunch, when Alison walked in. "Oh, you're home are you? Where have you been?"

I kept my eyes focused on my plate. "Out."

"I see." Alison raised an eyebrow. "Why isn't Cara in her pen?"

"She needed to be changed and she was hungry. Didn't you hear her crying?"

Alison grabbed a drink out of the refrigerator. "Sure I did." Her eyes flew to mine, "Why did *you* get her?"

My tone was bitter. "Someone had too. I couldn't just ignore my little sister."

Alison spun around, clearly horrified. "Your sist—"

"Hello ladies." Jack walked in, clearly oblivious to the feud. "Mary invited us over for dinner tonight. She's throwing a small neighborhood get together."

Alison clapped her hands together. "Wonderful that should be fun!" Alison's face looked deep in thought. "I wonder what I should wear? Hmm, Abby, I hope you don't have any plans tonight. Someone will need to stay home and watch Cara."

I stood there, looking at her in disbelief.

Jack spoke. "Well, Cara's more than welcome to come over as well."

Alison smiled warmly. "Of course, but Abby and I were chatting and she mentioned she's behind on her homework."

Jack nodded, and glanced at me. "Oh, I suppose you would be. Got to keep on top of those grades."

I glared at Alison. She was good, and sneaky. I looked at Jack's sparkling face and decided not to press the issue. I would indeed lose. "I can watch Cara tonight. Excuse me."

I placed my plate on the counter and went upstairs into my room, and pulled out my pile of homework. For the first time in my life, I was actually glad to be behind in my school work. It offered a great distraction. Hours later I headed downstairs, holding Cara as I watched Jack and Alison leave for Mary's. I stole a glance out the window. The house was lit up and cars lined the streets. Music lingered in the still night and the aroma of food wafted amongst the breeze. It seemed Mary knew how to throw a party. I switched Cara to my other hip and headed for the kitchen. I rummaged through the cupboards looking for something to eat. I didn't feel like much, so I settled for crackers. I let Cara loose in the living room and I watched her carefully as she crawled around. She was experimenting with trying to stand on her own. I smiled softly at her determined little expression as she continued to try to pull herself upright after every failed attempt.

I glanced at the clock it was only seven thirty. I placed Cara in her pen and stretched on the couch with my homework. I had spent the majority of my afternoon completing homework, and there wasn't much left. Forty minutes later, I set down my last book. I was finally done. I glanced at the clock yet again, eight ten. I tapped my fingers on the side of the couch and decided to change. I wandered into my closet and grabbed one of my favorite outfits; my worn jeans, a pretty flowy white camisole, and a black pullover sweater. I pinned back some of my hair and decided to head over next door. I packed a bag of necessities for Cara before bundling her up. We stepped into the winter wonderland and I did my best to hurry across the street and keep us upright all at once.

I gave a light knock on the door and Mary answered shortly after. "Abby! Cara! I'm so glad you could make it over, come on in!" I smiled warmly at Mary and was greeted by many happy faces.

"Is the music too loud for Cara?" Mary's face looked thoughtful.

I listened, then shook my head. "No, it's perfect."

"Good! Here, let me take your jacket."

I stepped into the busy living room with Cara, who was wide eyed, intrigued by all the faces around her. I didn't know many of the people here, but they all seemed to know who I was, and were extremely friendly in return.

"She's here!" I turned to see Laura towing through the crowd of people. Ali followed behind her and looked relieved when she saw me. "Abby! I'm so glad you're here! We thought she had you locked away in your room or something."

Laura's face fell. "Yeah…I met your stepmother. She's quite a treat."

I burst out laughing. "Yeah, she's something all right. I'm so glad you two are here!" I looked around. "Where's Jordan?"

"He's with Alex and some of the guys. They were helping set up the music or something like that."

"Gotcha." My eyes trickled to Laura, who seemed to bounce in place. I raised my eyebrows. "What's up, Laura?"

"He asked me out!" she blurted.

My eyes wandered to Ali's for help and she gave me a mysterious smile. "Okay, great! Who exactly asked you out?"

"Dan!" her face looked surprised when she could see I had no idea who she spoke about. She continued slowly this time. "Dan, from school. He's on the football team, he's number 14!"

"Oh, Dan. Of course. Congrats, Laura!" I smiled at how easily she recovered from last week's heartbreak when Alex's friend, Dave, wasn't that interested in her.

"I know right!" Laura crowed. "Come on, let's go find the guys."

I allowed myself to be dragged away by Laura. When the boys were in view, she gave a little squeal and hurried off to meet them.

Ali rolled her eyes. "Way to keep it cool, Laura," she mumbled

I laughed quietly. "Laura can't do anything muted."

"I know. I think it's physically impossible for her." Ali's eyes settled on Cara, and she held out her hand, at which Cara grasped eagerly.

"She really is adorable." Ali's eyes looked from mine to Cara. "You two really look a lot alike. That must drive Alison mad."

"Huh, I never really noticed actually." I looked down at Cara with new curiosity. Jordan saw Ali, and his face lit up. He gently made his way to her and he placed one arm securely around her waist. She smiled, and comfortably leaned into him. A few of the guys I wasn't familiar with glanced at me with intrigue, but also with some reservation. "Cute kid."

I grinned. "Thanks. I think my sister's pretty cute, too."

The faces relaxed. "Oh yeah. I see the resemblance now."

"I'm sure you do." I said wryly.

I noticed an empty seat next to the group, so I sat down, and placed Cara on my bouncing knee. She squealed with delight. I listened contently to the conversations around me, wondering where Alex had gone. I hadn't seen him all evening.

"I was about to go over to your place and drag you here myself." A voice directly behind caused me to jump in surprise.

I turned my head and Alex's playful smile greeted me. A loud, deliberate cough came from the corner and I turned to see Laura giving me a smile and thumbs up. I stared at her horrified, until Ali yanked her out of my eye sight. Alex chuckled, and took a seat next to me. He held out his hand automatically, and Cara gripped his thumb with a great deal of concentration.

"So, how are you holding up?"

"I'm all right…do they know I'm here?" I asked nervously.

Alex frowned. "I don't think so."

"Good."

Alex tilted his head slightly. "You're allowed to be here. You were invited."

"Yeah, I know."

A conversation out of my eyesight caught my attention. I heard Alison speak in a serious tone to someone. "She's a handful, that's for sure. She's going to need some work. Jack's been letting her run wild. We have been discussing our options with her."

A voice that was unfamiliar to my ears answered. "Oh my, that bad? I have only heard wonderful things about the girl; good in school, responsible, and she's so good with that little girl of yours."

I glanced at Alex horrified. So this was her plan, to get rid of me. I turned my attention back to the conversation.

Alison responded smoothly. "Well, yes, she has been a help, but lately she's been causing a lot of stress in the household. Jack's not too sure it's working anymore and I have to agree. Apparently her mother had a wild streak, and this may be the case of like mother, like daughter."

Alex suddenly gripped my arm. "Abby…"

I turned to face him. "Here, hold Cara, please."

He shook his head. "No. I won't let you do this to yourself."

"Fine." I stepped forward and made my way to Alison with Cara in tow. I stepped into Alison's view, and she stopped mid-sentence. "Abby, what are you doing here?"

"I'm done my homework, so I thought I would join in the fun. I was invited as well, afterall."

Alison glanced at Cara. "This is no place for a baby."

"As the mother, would you like to take her home?" Alison glared at me. I smiled innocently.

Jack's voice rose from behind. "Abby, I thought you weren't going to come over."

I turned around to face him. "I finished all my homework, so I thought I would stop by."

"Oh, all right then." His eyes looked from mine to Alison, and he looked concerned. "How about you girls come with me for a moment," he spoke quietly.

Alison nodded, and I hesitantly followed them into a back room. "Would someone like to fill me in on what's going on here?" he demanded.

"Your daughter is being extremely disrespectful!" Alison shot out.

Jack sighed. "Abby?"

I threw Alison a glare. "Don't put words in my mouth."I turned to address Jack. "Is it true? Am I becoming a burden?" I spat out.

Jack looked surprised. "What are you talking about?"

"I overheard Alison talking about me, and—"

"Abby, stop. Alison wouldn't do that. Why do you have to cause so much trouble? Maybe this wasn't a good idea...."

I closed my eyes and took in his words. I had imagined him thinking them, but when they were finally out, they hurt more than I could have ever imagined.

"Do you not want me here, Jack?"

Jack's face was unreadable. "We will not do this here, Abby."

"If we don't do it now, you know as well as I do that the conversation will be placed on the back burner."

Alison took Cara from my arms and she and Jack left the room without another word. I followed them out into the hall where Alex and Ali waited. "Jack, don't keep walking away from me, please. Just look at me!"

Jack turned around and waited for Alison to catch up to him. He spoke darkly. "Don't do this to yourself, Abby."

Alison shoulder checked me slightly, my body shuffled but I was too weary to make with a smart comeback. My heart ached with a vice like grip, it was so hard to breathe. I pressed my body against the wall, and gently slid down, resting my head against my knees, willing myself to take slow and steady breath's. Again, Jack hadn't been able look at me. What did he see when he looked my way?

Arms embraced me suddenly. I looked up and Ali sat herself next to me. "I'm so sorry, Abby. I had no idea you were going through so much."

Alex slid down and drew his arm around my waist, pulling me closer. He let out a deep breath, and I envied the carefree way in which he breathed.

"How about you stay here tonight?" he said quietly.

"No, thanks. I think I'll head home now. I could use the sleep anyways."

Alex tightened his grip around me slightly. "I'll walk with you."

"No, Alex, it's not really necessary."

He ignored me. "Come on, let's go." Alex grabbed me by the arm, and gently led the way through the crowd.

As I put on my jacket, I saw Jack holding Cara. Alison leaned in, and adjusted one of Cara's pant legs. They laughed and looked like a perfect family. A perfect family that had no room for anyone else. Alex followed my gaze and gently took my hand, leading me away from the scene. Once we were outside, the breathing became easier.

"How are you doing?" he asked softly.

"I'm okay."

"Really?"

"Cross my heart."

He nodded and walked me into the house silently. As I took off my coat, I couldn't help but notice he seemed nervous.

"Alex? You okay?"

His gaze settled on my face, and he took a step closer. "Yeah, I'm okay."

"Are you sure?" I raised my eyebrows in question.

My feet were glued to the ground as Alex took another step closer. He leaned down and gently swept the hair out of my face. My heart beat so loudly; I thought for sure Alex would hear it. He didn't seem to notice. His eyes focused intently on my face.

He smiled at me softly and mumbled. "You're beautiful." I looked at him in surprise, and his lips brushed mine. He pulled away slowly, but his hand remained gently placed upon my cheek.

"Are you okay?" He asked softly.

I nodded, wide eyed. "Y—Yes."

He bit his lip thoughtfully. "Not everyone you let in is going to hurt you, Abby."

I continued staring up at him, eyes wide. My heart still raced. This was Alex I was talking to. I forced myself to remain calm. Alex had saved me many times, he was always there when I needed him. I had told him things I had never meant to say out loud, nor wanted to share with anyone. Yet, he was still here, looking at me with such tender affection. This look was not new, he had been looking at me that way for quite some time now.

I moved closer to him, and circled my arms around his waist. His arms wrapped securely around me and I sighed. "Thank you" I said quietly.

"Let's get you to bed."

I nodded slowly and he took my hand gently in his. I got changed quickly and sat on the edge of the bed. Alex sat down next to me. "What's going through your head?" he asked curiously.

I smiled at him. "I don't know, so much has happened in the past few days…"

"Yeah. You should get some sleep. Come on lie down."

I rolled my eyes. "I'm not a child, Alex." Even as I protested, I found myself doing as he asked. I shifted onto my side, clutching a pillow.

He stared down at me thoughtfully and covered me with my quilt. "I should go."

I nodded. "Thanks for everything, Alex. It's nice to know someone is on my side."

Alex smiled softly, gently brushing the hair out of my eyes. "I'll always have your back. Sweet dreams."

He left the room quietly, and gently shut the door behind him. I smiled contently. I had found the silver lining amongst a day of heartbreak.

Chapter Twelve: A Night Away

Despite recent events, I awoke with a smile on my face. I pressed my fingers lightly to my lips and grew warm at the memory. I followed my usual morning routine, got showered and dressed. I reluctantly made my way to the kitchen. It was ridiculous that I felt ready to bolt at the slightest sound in this house. This was a place I was supposed to feel safe. A shiver ran down my spine as I heard the sound I feared; dragging footsteps coming my way. Alison slumped in with her housecoat securely wrapped around her waist. Her hair was disheveled and her face looked ordinarily plain without her makeup on. I smiled to myself; Mom was a million times prettier.

Alison raised an eyebrow. "Did you have a good night?"

I glanced her way. "Mm-hmm." My smile grew wider, as I realized what I said was indeed true.

"I see. Well, Jack and I have some things to do today, we will be taking Cara with us."

"Okay."

I decided the best way to deal with Alison was to pretend she didn't bother me. I hoped it would make me look like the bigger person in front of Jack. I had also hoped that I could control my temper around her. We both sat silently at the kitchen table. She drank her coffee, and peered at me from behind the magazine she read. While I waited for my oatmeal to be done, I stared dreamily out the window with a small smile on my lips.

Jack walked in and greeted Alison. He stopped and stared at me curiously.

"This isn't the reaction I expected from you this morning."

"Mmm," I continued staring.

Jack turned to Alison questionably. "What's going on with her?"

Alison threw one hand in the air. "Don't ask me. I can't even get her to say a single sentence."

I went to prepare the final touches on my oatmeal, and I happily took the warm porridge upstairs. I curled up in my bay window, watching the street. My eyes drifted to Alex's house and I wondered if he was up yet. Once my breakfast was done, I felt the need to stretch my legs.

I hopped downstairs and was almost done bundling up, when Alison walked in, and crossed her arms. "Where are you off to?"

"Nowhere in particular."

"I see. So you have absolutely no reason to go for a walk, alone?"

"Nope, none at all." I shot her a genuine smile, and bounced out the door.

A smile was still plastered to my face as I stepped into the bitter cold. There was a café just around the corner, and I decided to grab a warm drink to kill some time. After I got myself a treat, I began walking home slowly. The excitement from last night's events started to die down and nerves began to form. What did this mean for Alex and I? Would it be awkward between us now? Was the kiss just in the heat of the moment, or did he want more? I was pretty clueless on the whole subject. I knew I would have to ask him. And there he was. Dressed in jeans and a warm jacket, he determinedly scraped ice off his windshield. A lock of dark hair fell across his eyes, and he gently pushed it backwards. My eyes lingered on him for a moment. What did someone like him see in me? I tore my eyes away and kept my pace steady. My heart began to thump louder the closer I got. In all the time I had known him, I had never been the one to start a conversation, not really anyways. I took a sharp breath and crossed the street. At the sound of my footsteps, he looked up.

"Morning." I said and quickly flashed him an uncertain smile.

He was much surer of himself. He set down his window scraper and wrapped me up in a one armed hug. "Good morning." He whispered in my ear. He pulled back and grinned down at me. A warm blush crept across my face and I smiled, feeling a little dazed.

"What do you have planned this morning?" he asked thoughtfully.

I furrowed my brows. "Nothing that I can think of, why?"

"Well, I was wondering if you would like to grab breakfast with me?"

"Oh, actually I already ate." *I should have lied.*

Alex grinned. "Yeah, I did too. It was just my way of asking if you wanted to do something with me today."

I laughed at the disappointed look on his face. "What's up with you?"

He shot me a pathetic look. "I think I've lost my touch. I'm normally so charming."

I looked up at him. "Trust me, you are plenty charming," I mumbled.

A door slammed shut, and Alex stiffened. He released me from his embrace. I turned to see what pulled his attention, and my smile fell. Jack stood next to Alison's car, and his gaze focused on us. I couldn't quite read the look on his face, but it looked close to disappointment.

"Hmm, I guess I might be a problem from the looks of things." Alex mumbled.

Alison finished placing Cara into the car when she strode over to Jack. They had a low conversation before she sauntered across the street to meet us. She flashed a blinding smile and Alex pulled me closer.

"So, I see why you wanted to go for a walk." Her eyes lingered on Alex with amusement. Alex looked away.

"Anyways," she drawled on. "Abby, we have some errands to run, and you should come along with us."

"I thought I wasn't invited."

Alison looked bored. "Plans change."

"I'm sorry, but I can't. I have plans of my own," I said quickly.

Alison pursed her lips. "Fine with me." As Alison walked away, Jack's rage was clearly visible now.

"How you holding up?" Alex asked me quietly.

I nodded silently. "Fine." I watched Jack and Alison, and relief fell over me as they drove away. For once, I was glad to be out of the picture.

"Hey, listen. Mary won't be home this evening, how about you come over for dinner and a movie?"

I blinked in surprise. "You can cook?"

"No, not really," he gave a sheepish grin. "But the 'defrost' button and I are very close."

"Hmm, how about we head out to the grocery store? I can make us dinner tonight?"

"I can't argue with that. Come on, hop in the car."

After Alex and I picked up groceries, I headed home, and promised I would be over later for our evening plans. I tidied up the house and made a batch of Jack's favorite cookies. I found myself growing uneasy at the thought of seeing Jack; I had no idea what he was going to say, or do. I was upstairs in my room when I heard them enter the house.

"Well, well, well. Smell that, Jack? Fresh baked cookies, and a clean house. It looks like someone's trying to please you."

I frowned at Alison's disapproving tone. I strained my ears to hear Jack's comment, but I couldn't make out anything concrete. I sat on the bed while my stomach twisted in knots. I lost count of how many times I had started heading down the stairs, only to turn back and head back to the safety of my bedroom once more. I was perched in the window sill when I saw Mary pack up her car and leave. I wanted so desperately to be able to walk downstairs, say a casual greeting, and head over next door.

I didn't know why I felt so guilty. I had done nothing wrong. Alex was a great friend, more than a friend lately. Jack had no right to step into my life now and take that away from me. I glanced at the clock, it read 4:22 p.m. I took a deep breath and decided to head over next door. Before I left the room, I quickly looked out my window and pondered an alternate route. It didn't look that high; I could shimmy down the drain pipe...*no*. That would be a bad idea. I had once broken my ankle just by taking a hike in the woods. There was no way I would add falling from a distance to test out my luck. I stepped down the stairs in what I hoped was a confident matter. I heard the adults talking in the kitchen and I tiptoed to the coat room. Carefully and quietly I put my boots on, grabbed my jacket off the rack, and opened the door. I was on edge, I felt like I was going to get caught at any moment.

I shut the door behind me and set a brisk pace down the driveway. Jack's voice rang out firmly. "Where are you going?"

My heart almost jumped out of my chest. "Jack! Hi. I have dinner plans." I smiled meekly.

"I see, and you felt the need to sneak out did you?"

"I wouldn't call it sneaking really." I offered lamely.

"What's going on between you and the James kid?"

I glared at Jack's cold face. "His name is Alex and nothing is going on between us. Besides, I thought you liked him?"

"He stuck his nose where it didn't belong."

I thought back to the day I was sick, and remembered the two of them arguing. I figured that was what Jack referred too. "He's one of my best friends these days, Jack. He has been there for me whenever I needed him….that's something I'm not used too."

I could see this conversation wasn't going to end well. "Goodnight Jack, I'll be home later. I hope you enjoy the cookies."

"I'm sure I will. Alison and I are going out tonight, Cara will join us." His voice turned hard. "I hope he's a real good friend like you say. I don't know when we will be home, and I gave Alison the extra house key. So you can either wait out in the cold until we come back or hope he lets you stay there."

Jack turned and walked inside. I was puzzled, now how did that make sense? He wanted me to stay away from Alex, but now he almost gave me an excuse to spend the night alone with him. The thought made me blush. As I crossed the street, I left my worries behind, or at least I tried too.

Alex greeted me eagerly at the door. "Come on in, it's freezing out here."

I smiled somewhat shyly and stepped inside. Alex took my coat and his eyes held a mysterious twinkle.

"What are you up too?" I asked curiously.

Alex held his hands up. "Absolutely nothing." His facial expression changed ever so slightly. "At the risk of ruining a great evening, how did things go at home?"

I shrugged. "Not too bad. Jack doesn't seem to be very fond of you." I turned around to face Alex. "What happened between the two of you anyway?"

Alex shrugged. "Let's not get into this now."

I nodded. "Yeah, you're right. Shall we start dinner?"

"Definitely."

Alex was certainly not a star in the kitchen. I attempted to teach him a few quick tips but it didn't do much to help the poor guy out. The kitchen was alive with clanging pots, pans, and laughter. Half way through preparing the meal, Alex excused himself.

Just as I set the chicken in the oven, Alex popped his head back in. "Is it all done?"

"It has to cook now. Why, what's up?"

"Close your eyes and give me your hands."

I lifted an eyebrow, but I obeyed, and allowed Alex to lead me away.

"Okay, open your eyes."

I slowly opened my eyes and stood in the dining room. A wide smile stretched across my face as I took in my surroundings. "Alex, it's beautiful."

Alex had the lights down low, and placed a tablecloth over the dining room table, accented by a vase of flowers. On the mantle above the fireplace, a row of candles flickered, sending the shadows dancing and glittering off the walls.

My voice grew heavy with emotion. "Alex, you shouldn't have done all of this. It's perfect."

"I thought you could use something special." He smiled sheepishly.

Alex leaned into me, and I wrapped my arms around his neck, pulling him close. "Thank you so much."

"You're welcome. You know, this actually works out quite well." He shot me a sly look. "You're a pretty cheap date, and easy to please. A little bit of candles, some flowers…hell, you even cooked the meal."

"Hey!" I released my grip and playfully tossed him a punch. "Alex James, you're terrible."

After dinner wrapped up we settled on the couch for a movie. I glanced at the time. It was 10:45 p.m. I quickly peeked at the house and saw no sign that Jack had come home. My evening had been amazing, and just what I needed, carefree, comfortable, and safe. Over dinner, I told Alex that I no longer had a key to the house, and he assured me I could stay here as long as needed. Despite his reassurance, I began to feel antsy. I didn't want to wear out my welcome. Alex gripped me and cradled me in his arms, where I settled neatly against him.

"Are you getting tired?" he asked quietly.

"No, I'm okay." I lied.

"You're a bad liar."

I made a face. "Yeah, I know."

"I told you that you can stay here for as long as you need."

"I know you did. I just don't want to over stay my welcome."

"That's not possible, come on." Alex stood, pulling me with him.

"Where are we going?"

"I'm putting you to bed. It seems to be becoming a habit these days."

I laughed tiredly. "So it would seem." I followed wearily expecting to be led to the upstairs guest room. I hesitated when he led me downstairs. "Err, Alex, where are we going?"

"To my room."

I planted my feet. "Alex, I don't think I'm-"

He held up one hand. "I know, but my bed's a lot comfier than the other one, and you need a good night's sleep."

He opened up his door. "See, I cleaned my room just for you."

I smiled up at him, glancing around. There wasn't much to his room. A large bed sat next to a small matching night table, and a shelf that proudly displayed some photos and books. In another corner, a stereo and TV sat on a pine shelf, and a small computer desk was set to the right.

Alex interrupted. "I'm going to be down the hall if you need me."

I bit my lip feeling slightly out of place. "Okay. Goodnight."

"Sweet dreams."

He moved in slowly and cautiously, giving me time to move away. I didn't. His lips brushed against mine, and my eyes fell closed. He slowly pulled back and muttered. "Sweet dreams indeed."

Crawling into Alex's bed felt a little daunting, yet it also felt welcoming. His blanket smelled of his cologne and I wrapped it around myself tightly. Falling asleep was going to be easy tonight.

⌘

In my dream, I was asleep in my bed. The color was off, but I recognized the bare walls and my empty dresser. I slept peacefully until loud thumping footsteps began to boom. The closer they got, the louder they became. I sat up in fear and my door burst open. Alison stormed into the room and shot me a horrible look which sent chills down my spine.

"You!" she bellowed. "Should not be here. You don't belong here!"

Before I could move, Alison threw me down on the bed and took a pillow and held it against my face. I thrashed under her wildly, trying to catch my breath. My muffled screams desperately called out for help. My arms were outstretched as far as they could go, desperately trying to wriggle away. But the darkness overtook me. Out of the corner of my eye, I saw Jack. He leaned one shoulder against the bedroom frame, smiling softly.

"Abby! Abby! Wake up. It's okay. You're dreaming. Wake up, Abby!"

I woke up gasping and coughing for air. I quickly sat up and my eyes fell into Alex's worried gaze. He held my shoulders, and spoke soothing words. I trembled beneath his touch.

"Speak to me please," he pleaded.

I found his face in the dark. "It was only a dream?"

"Yes, I could hear you screaming from down the hall. Are you okay?"

I bit my lip and nodded. "Mm-hmm."

He wrapped his arms around me, pulling me in. "You really are a terrible liar."

I tried to laugh but nothing came out. I gripped onto the back of his shirt, and placed my head against his shoulder. "I'm sorry I woke you, what time is it?"

"Just after three, and don't be sorry. Do you have nightmares often?"

I bit my lip and thought about it. I had been plagued with nightmares most of my life, but they had never felt this real before. "Yes. I haven't had them in awhile though…they started back up when I moved here."

"Do you want some water or anything?"

"No, I'll be okay."

A shiver tore through me. Alex released me and grabbed the blanket, draping it around me. "Crawl under, get warm, you're freezing." His eyes deepened with concern.

I nodded wearily and closed my eyes. Again, I could see the vision. I felt the pillow held against my face, and it became hard to breathe. I opened my eyes in panic and looked around wildly. My heart began to beat rapidly. It felt much too real.

"Alex?" I called frantically.

"Yes?"

"Can you stay with me tonight?"

"Of course." Alex made his way to the other side of the bed and crawled under the covers. He lied on his side, gently looking my way. "Are you okay? Do you want me to leave when you fall asleep?"

"No." I found myself moving against him. His arms found me and held on tight. "I want to wake up next to you." I murmured.

My eyes began to drift close and I let them fall heavily. As the warm sunlight crept it's way across my face, my eyes flickered open. I turned over quietly and Alex lied beside me. A sleepy smile lit up my face.

Alex's eyes blinked open. "Morning," he smiled.

"Good morning," I said cheerfully. My eyes grew wide. "Oh, it's morning!" I sat up quickly.

Alex groaned. "Yes, morning generally comes after night. What's wrong?"

I scrambled out of the bed and stretched quickly. "Jack might be worried…"

Alex sat up, a little confused. "He could be…but he was also the one who took the key away from you. What did he expect? For you to wait up all night until he got home? It's ridiculous. Have breakfast with me."

I sighed. "I would love to, but I don't think I should. I've got to go. Thank you for everything last night. You should go back to bed, sleep in."

Alex shot me a dubious look. "You should be the one to sleep in." He took one look at my stubborn face and sighed. "Fine, I'll see you later?"

"Without a doubt."

I ran up the stairs and quietly bundled up. I stepped outside the front door when I nearly collided into Mary. "Oh!" I said shocked. "You scared me."

"Well, isn't this a surprise to see you here, Abby." Mary's eyes took in my appearance suspiciously. My cheeks flared. This could not look good. Pillow lines were pressed into my face, my clothes were slightly rumpled, and my hair was a mess.

I smiled weakly. "I better get going. Have a good day!" I ran home before she could say another word. I was mortified; I may never be able to show my face there again.

I quickly slipped inside the house. There was no noise. I hoped everyone was still asleep. I decided to slip into my room and get some more sleep but Cara began to fuss. I groaned and got up to tend to her. I stepped inside her room and gently plucked her out of her crib. I wrinkled my face. "You could use a diaper change little one, oh, uck, and a change of clothes."

After Cara was freshened up, I wandered into the kitchen to give her breakfast. Hunger had not yet found me, so I made myself a cup of tea. My mind drifted to next door. I hoped Mary wouldn't give Alex a hard time.

Footsteps sounded behind me and I glanced up. "Morning, Jack."

He stopped in his tracks and raised an eyebrow. "So, is he a good friend?"

My anger flared a little. "Yes, he is." I answered crisply.

Jack's eyes took in my appearance, his face paled slightly. Again I wished that I had at least tidied my hair.

"Good sleep?" he forced out.

"The best." Again, a smile spread across my lips.

"Have you eaten breakfast?" Jack asked carefully.

"No."

"Would you like to go out for breakfast, with me?"

I looked up in shock. This was not the reaction I had pictured. I stared up at him, and shook my head in slight frustration. I had officially given up trying to make sense of his moods, there were just so many, and they didn't fit together. While I pictured one reaction, he would often surprise me with something I would never expect.

"I would love too." I responded. "What about Alison?" At the mention of her name, last nights terror raced through my head. I shook it off abruptly.

"She needs to sleep in today, late night. You better go get freshened up, I'll get Cara ready."

"Sure thing." I raced upstairs, tossed on some fresh clothes, and finally ran a brush through my tangled golden hair. I threw it up in a loose ponytail and went to meet Jack downstairs.

We arrived and got a table easily at the charming country diner. Cara's eyes grew extra wide as she took in the hustle and bustle of the morning crowd. I sat across from Jack and couldn't think of a way to start the conversation. Luckily the waitress came and asked for our order. I listened quietly as Jack ordered his meal and I quickly put in an order of strawberry waffles and a hot chocolate.

Jack's eyes looked over me softly. "That was your mother's favorite."

I looked at him in surprise, he remembered. "It still is."

Jack smiled at some fond memory only he could see.

"Do you miss her?" I covered my mouth with my hand; I hadn't meant to say that out loud, it slipped out.

To my surprise, Jack looked thoughtful. "At times, yes. Abby, what I did to your mother and you, it is not my proudest moment. Your mother and I were never right for each other. She was never as happy with me as she is with Mark. I don't regret my decision one bit. It led me to Alison, and I got Cara."

I listened to his speech quietly and wondered where I fit in. The waitress arrived with our meals. I stared down at my waffles, and watched the fresh fruit muddle into the whipped cream. I had lost my appetite. Jack happily dove into his breakfast, so I took a few experimental bites to please him.

As we walked to Jack's truck he spoke. "There is a reason why I took you out this morning."

My heart dropped. "What is it?"

"I have to leave for three weeks, for work."

Oh no. Alone with Alison for three weeks? That wasn't such a good idea in my books. At least when Jack was there, he acted as somewhat of a barrier; Alison never made her snide remarks when he was in earshot. I fought to remain calm.

"When do you leave?" I asked disheartened.

"Tonight." I shot Jack a horrified look, and he laughed. "It won't be so bad, Abby. The two of you need time to bond anyways."

Bond? I didn't see that happening anytime soon. As far as I was concerned, Alison wanted me gone.

The rest of the ride was filled with a heavy silence. One hour later Alison, Cara, and I all stood on the front porch as we said our goodbyes to Jack. Neither of us was happy to see him leave. I glanced toward Alison, and thought I saw a flicker of uncertainty cross her features. I wondered if she was as nervous as I was to be without his presence. As Jack drove away, I envisioned myself running behind his car begging him to reconsider leaving me alone with her.

Once he was out of eyesight, Alison turned to me with a small smile. "Well, Abby, it's just us girls. I think we're going to have lot's of fun."

The tone in which she spoke sent a cold shiver down my spine and into my boots.

Chapter Thirteen: Face Off

"All right, I'm going to bed." Alison announced.

I looked up from my book. "Okay, night."

"Abby? Put Cara to sleep when she's ready."

I set my book down. "You said you would do that tonight. I have to get up early for school and you're not working tomorrow."

Alison waved her hand. "Please, I'm exhausted." With that, she sauntered off.

I gritted my teeth and clenched my fists. Alison had decided to throw a small dinner party earlier, so I got stuck cleaning the house for her guests, prepared the meal, made awful small talk to a group of stuck up people, and after all that, she left me to clean up the mess. The only reason I went along with any of it was for Jack. Alison had lingered the threat in the air that I could make things easy, or hard. If I made them hard, she would tell Jack and that would put my future living arrangements in jeopardy.

It was now ten in the evening and I hadn't managed to see Alex today. I marched downstairs to get Cara. Alison had kept her up all day, so she missed her nap. As luck would have it, she was on the verge of falling asleep. It didn't take much coaxing for her to be out for the night. I gently covered Cara with her blanket, and shut the door gently. It was only 10:05 p.m. and I decided to fit in a quick face to face hello with Alex. I bundled up and took the baby monitor with me; I didn't trust Alison to check on Cara if she started to cry. Once I was at Alex's, I decided against knocking on the front door. I was in no hurry to see Mary after our latest encounter. I was already dreading seeing her tomorrow at school. I wandered over to Alex's window, and saw the faint glow of his lamp through the curtains. I knelt down and tapped on it lightly. He opened the curtains with a confused look before a smile crossed his lips.

He slid open the window. "Is something wrong with the door now?"

"I wanted to spice things up," I grinned unsurely. "I wasn't sure who would answer the door." I confided.

"Ah, I see, come on in." He grabbed my hands, and helped me climb through the window.

I looked at Alex cautiously. "Was Mary upset?"

"She was surprised," he rubbed the back of his neck. "Yeah, she's not exactly

thrilled. She's a little suspicious. The candles and the flowers didn't help my case, and then, uh, the way you looked when you ran into her this morning." Alex laughed suddenly. "She thinks I'm corrupting one of her most promising students."

I groaned. "Sorry."

"Don't be, I'm not." He leaned in and gave me a kiss. "So, what's kept you so busy today?"

He sat down on his bed, and pulled me with him. I made a face. "Jack left for three weeks, so it seems I've become Alison's personal maid."

He shook his head in disgust. "Abby, you shouldn't let her treat you like that." His eyes settled on the baby monitor. "What's that doing here? She can't take care of her own kid now?"

I sighed. "It's much easier to do what she asks, that way she can't tell Jack I have been a royal pain. We all know whose side he'll take…if I get kicked out I have no place to go. As for Cara, she is my sister. I can't just leave her alone with them."

Alex ran his fingers through my hair softly. "They don't deserve you, and you will always have a place here."

I looked at him, smiling warmly. "I should go, early morning tomorrow."

He released me reluctantly. "All right."

He helped me out of the window and yelled softly. "Hey! I like this whole sneaking through the window thing."

I looked at him and rolled my eyes. "You would. Goodnight."

Once I crawled into bed, I drifted off to sleep in no time. The nightmares found me again. This time Jack was downstairs sitting on the couch, nonchalantly looking at the stairs. Alison stood at the foot of the stairs, where she let out an ear splitting scream. She stared wide-eyed as Cara was pulled by an invisible force. I ran after her, desperately trying to catch her. No matter how fast I ran, she remained just out of my grasp. I almost had Cara in my arms, when the unseen force threw me against the wall. I lay stunned and horrified as Cara got dragged down the stairs and landed with a sickening thud.

I woke up abruptly drenched in a cold sweat. I ran to Cara's room to check on her. She slept soundly. My knees buckled in relief. I grasped onto her crib as I regained my strength. I walked back into my room, and made a note to buy a baby gate for the top of the stairs. I couldn't fall back asleep; I read until 4:30 a.m. when my eyes finally drifted shut. I was in the midst of one of those dreams where I wasn't sure whether or not I wanted to wake up. I suppose it wasn't much of a dream, it was more of a memory. My hair was in pigtails, and I sat in the corner of the living room crying.

Jack walked in and sat in front of me, tilting my chin upwards. "What's the matter, kiddo?"

I sniffled. "Sad."

Jack looked at me seriously. "Well, that won't do, will it."

The next thing I knew I was up so high, I thought I could fly. I giggled hysterically as Jack caught me and held me securely. I looked into his warm blue eyes and felt safe. Jack walked to the CD player to put on one of his favorite songs. As the music started to play, Jack danced around the room with me as my giggles filled the air. All at once the image faded as my alarm began to buzz. I rolled over sleepily and smacked the 'off' button. I felt dazed and didn't put much effort into getting dressed. I settled on sweat pants and a blue long sleeve shirt. I lazily brushed my hair and left it down. Alison had taken three weeks off of work, so I left the house praying that Alison could take of her own daughter.

"So," Laura said in a taunting voice. "Words going around that you and Alex had a sleep over."

My eyes grew wide, and I turned to her and hissed. "Keep it down! And where did you hear that?"

Laura laughed. "So, it is true! You're turning so red!"

I buried my face in my hands and moaned. It was lunchtime and the chatter went on endlessly around me. Raye put in dryly. "I guess when you have one of the most sought after guys in town, you can come to school in sweats, hey, Abby?"

I glared at Raye and chose to ignore her. How was I supposed to know that she had been after Alex for some time now?

Ali shot her a dark glare. "Hush, Raye. It's none of your business."

I shot Ali a grateful look and addressed Laura's earlier question. "It's not how it sounds, nothing happened."

Laura grinned and rested her head behind her hands. "All right, if you say so." A large smile spread across her face. "English should be awesome!"

I moaned again, this time I dropped my head to the table. The rest of the day passed by quite quickly, Mrs. James was a professional and left personal matters alone. Her gaze lingered on me quite a few times, and to my dismay Laura had noticed as well. She however, seemed quite thrilled by the whole thing. I wanted to fade away. Once classes were done, I headed home like it was any other day, and tried to ignore the twisting in my stomach. I pulled into the driveway with a wry grin. With Jack gone, at least I had my spot back. Alex was outside, leaning on his car along with Jordan and Dave. I gave a casual wave and headed to the front door.

Before I even turned the handle, the door swung up. I gasped, Alison looked terrible. Exhaustion was heavy in her features as she held an upset Cara on one hip. Alison's hair was askew, her clothes were smeared with baby food, and her face looked downright annoyed.

"Take her now." Alison roughly handed Cara over, and I took her gently. Alison threw her jacket on and marched past me.

"Where are you going?" I called in disbelief.

Alison turned toward me. "I am going out! I have been home all day with that child! She's impossible, I don't know what you did to her, but I need a break! You practically abandoned us this morning!"

I wanted to cover my ears. Alison's shrill words could have been heard down the street. Cara's cries grew louder. I spoke as soothingly as I could. "Alison, I went to school. I didn't abandon anyone. Isn't that why you took time off of work? To be with your daughter, who is a baby by the way. They cry. They need to be looked after."

I winced as Cara's cries grew close to hysterics, I had never heard her cry that way before. Through her clothes, I could feel she needed a change.

Alison glared. "Don't give me that." She hopped in her car, and sped away. She left us standing, bewildered, in the driveway.

Gazes burned into me. Alex and his buddies stared wide-eyed. Jordan's voice rose above the rest. "That woman is crazy!"

I focused back on Cara. "It's okay, little one. Let's get you cleaned up."

I began to step inside when footsteps sounded from behind. The sudden loudness of them startled Cara, and she stopped crying for a moment.

"Hey, what's going on?" Alex asked breathlessly.

"Beats me, but by the look of things she had a hard day with Cara."

I opened the door and groaned. Alex sucked in a breath. "Wow, it looks like a hurricane hit."

"I don't believe this." I muttered. The house was filthy. Clothes were scattered everywhere. I glanced in the kitchen. Food was left on the counters, dirty dishes were littered about, and the TV blared in the background.

"Get Cara changed. I'll try and sort things out down here."

I looked at Alex like he was a godsend. "Really?"

"Of course, go on, your sister needs you."

I turned and began to head upstairs. I stopped abruptly and walked up to Alex purposefully. He stood there, watching me curiously. I went up on my tiptoes and pressed my lips against his firmly. "Thank you."

Alex smirked. "You're welcome. Now, come here." He reached behind me and pulled me in once more.

⌘

"Oh gross, this is so beyond a diaper change, Cara." I wrinkled my nose. It looked like the diaper hadn't been changed all day.

"You need a bath and it looks like I need to do a load of laundry." I grabbed a clean pair of clothes for Cara and drew a bath.

"I did the best I could down there." Alex walked into the bathroom and leaned his tall frame against the door.

"Thanks, she's almost done, aren't you, pretty girl?" Cara squealed and threw her rubber duck excitedly. It landed with a splash, which brought on an excited giggle.

I chuckled. "All right, little one, out of the tub we go. You're a clean girl again." After drying her off and getting her dressed into a clean sleeper, I decided to feed her. "I wonder if she's even been fed today." I grumbled.

"Has Alison ever done this alone before?"

I thought about it for a moment. "I honestly don't know. Now that I think about it, she's never really had to deal with Cara on her own before. Jack has always been there."

I set Cara in her chair and gave her food. She gurgled and ate happily. I watched Cara with something close to admiration. She was a strong little one. "Well, at least she's happy now. I can't leave her alone tomorrow, I think I'll take her to Janie's." I mused to myself.

"That sounds like a good plan. I would offer to watch her but classes starts up again tomorrow."

I turned to Alex. "Are you looking forward to going back?"

Alex sighed. "Oh yeah, I was going a little crazy being homebound."

I looked out the window, and Jordan and Dave were still in Alex's driveway waiting for him. "I'll be okay here. It looks like your friends are waiting for ya."

"Yeah, I know." He grinned and planted a kiss on the top of my head. "Let me know if you need anything."

"I will. Thank you."

With Cara happily eating away, I decided now would be as good as a time as any to vacuum. I really hoped Alison hadn't let Cara crawl around on the carpet, it was filthy. I was fuming angry as I set to work, it really didn't take much to keep a baby happy, especially an easygoing girl like Cara. A clean diaper, food and naptime was all it took. It was nearing 5:30 p.m. and Cara happily jumped her heart out in the jolly jumper, squealing in excitement every once in awhile. I decided to make myself a sandwich for dinner, nothing that required a lot of effort. I called Janie earlier, and arranged for Cara to come back this week. She was thrilled. I put Cara down for the night at nine o'clock and was relieved when she fell asleep easily. I began to get myself ready for the night and wondered if I should be worried that Alison hadn't come back yet. I decided I didn't care. I drifted off to sleep, when the phone awoke me. I grumbled and ran for the phone, thankful that Jack had set one up in the hall.

"Hullo?" I answered groggily.

"Hey there Sleeping Beauty, did I wake you?"

"Yes, you did. What time is it?"

"Nine forty-five."

"Are you kidding me?"

Laughter filled on the other end. "No, I am quite serious. I am sorry to wake you, I just wanted to say good night and see if things were okay over there."

"Mm-hmm, things are nice and quiet."

"That's what I like to hear…all right, I will talk to you tomorrow."

"Sounds good, hey have fun tomorrow at school."

"Yeah, I will. Sweet dreams okay?"

I smiled. "I shall try."

After hanging up, I shuffled into my room and crashed onto my bed. I was asleep before my head even hit the pillow.

⌘

"Good morning Cara, don't you look as cute as a bundle!" Janie was busy having her own conversation with Cara as I brought in her bag.

"Thank you so much Janie." I interrupted.

Janie shooed the idea with her hand. "It's no problem, dear, and this little girl is so easy."

I smiled brightly. "She really is. Well I better get going, see you later."

I drove to school in a relaxed manner. Before I made my way into the parking lot, I dialed Jack's home number one more time. I got the machine and left a message for Alison, letting her know where Cara was in case she didn't see my note. She never did come home last night. I had no idea where she went and I honestly did not care.

School was out early in preparation for exams. I picked up Cara when my cell phone rang. "Hello?"

"You know what? I think I miss you."

I smiled at the sound of Alex's voice. "You think you miss me? Wow, do I feel honored. Aren't those college girls keeping you busy?"

Alex's tone turned teasing. "Hey now, let's not go there. You know how I worry about those high school guys."

I laughed. "Uh-huh. I'm sure you lose sleep over it."

"What are you doing right now?"

"Nothing really. I just picked up Cara, and was thinking of heading to the lake."

"Oh, that sounds like fun. I wish I could join you but my breaks almost over. What are you doing tonight?"

"Well, after my date with Mike, I have this fabulous party to go to…"

"Hey, that's not funny!" he paused. "I don't like that guy," he mumbled in a low voice.

I laughed. "I think it's rather amusing myself." I cleared my throat. "I don't have much going on tonight, why?"

"I was thinking about that last dinner we had…."

"Which part? The meal or waking up next to me?"

I smiled as I heard the grin in his voice. "Both. But I thought we could start with dinner. I'll be at your place by six?"

"I'll be there."

Alison still wasn't home. I furrowed my brows as I played the messages back, there was nothing from her, or the authorities, which had to be good, right?

Shortly before six, the doorbell rang. I answered it cheerfully, and motioned Alex to come in. He stood dressed in jeans, and a button down shirt. "Are you ready to go?" he asked.

I looked around puzzled. "Go? I thought we were having dinner here?"

He smiled proudly. "Actually, I wanted to treat you to a nice dinner. I made reservations at the little Italian place you mentioned you liked."

My mouth fell. "You did?" I raised one eyebrow. "How did I get so lucky?"

Alex looked thoughtful. "I don't know," he said slowly. "You don't seem to have much luck, do you?"

"Hey!" I lightly shoved him. "Oh, you do know that I have Cara though, right?"

"I know. I made the reservation for three."

I shot him a wry smile. "You think of everything, don't you. I'll be ready in five minutes."

Alex, Cara, and I followed the hostess as she led us to a candle lit table by the window. Alex grinned when my face lit up. The waitress brought over a high chair, and I placed Cara securely in the seat. I gave her baby cookies to keep her occupied, though she probably didn't need any. Her attention was captured by the hustle and bustle of the restaurant.

"She really is adorable." Alex pointed out.

I smiled as I took the compliment for her. "She is."

"You look beautiful tonight."

I gave him a lopsided grin. "Thank you."

He shook his head. "You don't see it, do you?"

His gaze was too much for me. I slid my eyes to the melting candles. "I don't know what you're talking about."

"I won't push it." He reached across the table and linked his fingers in mine.

The evening was a wonderful surprise. I couldn't remember the last time I had felt so content. Just as were finishing up, Cara started to yawn. Her head eventually went limp as she dozed off. Alex lowered his voice. "I guess she's had just about enough excitement for one day."

I looked at her affectionately. "I think so."

I grabbed my purse, and began fishing for my wallet. Alex held out his hand in protest. "Oh no, I don't think so. I told you, this was my treat. Sit back, and enjoy."

"Are you sure?" I asked skeptically.

"Positive."

We arrived back at Alex's, and I noticed the car in Jack's driveway. Cara used my shoulder as a pillow as I gently shifted her. "Well what do you know, look who came back."

Alex looked across the street. "I don't like you over there with her," he protested.

I smiled reassuringly. "I'll be okay."

"Abby, you're a strong girl, but I….I don't know how much more you can take. Look, I know you don't like me stepping into personal matters, so I'm telling you now. My window will be unlocked. The options out in the open. Any time you need to find me, I will be there."

I studied him thoughtfully. "I have never met anyone quite like you before, Alex James. Thank you. I will keep that in mind. I better get Cara to bed."

"Be careful."

"Always."

I quietly stepped inside the house and kicked off my shoes. I tiptoed up the steps and placed Cara undisturbed in her crib. I gave a triumphant smile. I let my hair unravel down my back and ambled to my bedroom. Alison stepped in front of me. She looked at ease and perfectly polished, the way I was used to seeing her; it was the way she liked the world to see her.

She raised a manicured eyebrow. "Where have you been all this time with my daughter?"

I should try to take the highroad. "We went out for dinner, excuse me."

I stepped to the left, she followed. "That's not exactly an answer. Who do you think you are? Are you trying to impress Daddy?"

My heart raced. I bit my tongue and gently pushed past her. She grabbed my arm hard, and swung me around to face her.

"I see right through you, Abby. You may have everyone fooled, but I know what you're trying to do, take Jack away from me. I won't let you."

I closed my eyes briefly before reopening them. I glared in her direction. "Are you kidding me, Alison? What do you think you're doing? You can't just abandon your child, and husband for that matter, and expect everyone to take care of your responsibilities. Life doesn't work that way."

I yanked my arm back from her and continued. "You need to grow up."

Alison's face turned red. "You better watch your mouth. Jack will be calling soon. He will ask how things are going, and he will believe whatever I tell him. Face it, Abby, you are always going to be second with him."

The sting of tears burned my eyes, and I turned away from her. "Tell him whatever you want, Alison, you know that you will anyways."

I marched to the safety of my bedroom door when Alison called out. "Don't accuse me of child abandonment, Abby. Have you asked Jack about the letters?"

I stopped abruptly, and turned toward Alison as the color drained from my face.

"W—What letters?"

Alison smirked, she knew she hit a nerve. "Oh please, don't give me that. You know what I'm talking about. You wrote to him for a nearly a year almost every day, isn't that right?"

My eyes grew wide, showing my every thought. "How do you know about the letters?" I breathed.

Alison laughed. "He let me read them too. We have been together for a long time."

I stepped back and turned away as the tears made their escape. So, my father had received my letters. He never once bothered to answer them. My chest tightened. I had poured so much of my heart into those letters. They had been a cry for help and he chose to ignore them. Not only that, but he had showed them to *her*. I shut the door gently and sat on my bed. I glanced at the night table and stared at the picture of my mother, Mark and me. Smiles lit our faces, and we held an outrageous pose, together, as a family. I almost heard laughter from the still image. In that moment, my heart broke. Why had I given my family up for this? The telephone rang, and it fell silent after the second ring. My better judgment told me to stay in my room, but curiosity always got the best of me. I tiptoed out in the hall and sat on the top step, listening.

"I don't know Jack, she's out of control. She has been out with that boy most likely all day. She seems to have forgotten her household responsibilities! And the lip she's been giving me…I think we need to discuss her future very soon."

I sat up quickly, I didn't want to hear anymore. I slipped into Cara's room and quietly packed her bag for the next morning with Janie. I went back into my room, shoved an outfit for tomorrow in my bag, and slid my homework inside. I pulled on a sweater, picked up the bags and tiptoed downstairs. I paused at the bottom stair, waiting until I saw Alison go into the kitchen. I ran as fast and as quietly as I could to the coat room. I found my shoes and shoved them on. I opened the front door and held my breath as the door let out a squeak. I strained my ears to listen for Alison, I heard her chatting in the living room, her voice was growing closer. I shot out the door, and closed it tight. The porch light flew on, and a yelp escaped my lips. I ran and ducked behind my truck, and stole a glance at the house. Alison was still on the phone, scanning the driveway haphazardly. My heart pounded frantically, I feared it was going to burst out of my chest.

Once the light went off, I counted to ten and ran for Alex's window. His lights were off. I clasped my hands together nervously and paced back and forth. He had told me to come over any time I needed him. The concerned look and tone of his voice had sounded convincing. On the other hand, I knew he hated to be woken up. I looked around the neighborhood, I could sleep in my truck, but I'd freeze to death. Or, there was always the option to drive somewhere else, but I didn't want to be so far from Cara. Alison seemed severely unstable.

I couldn't stay out here all night, I'd be blue in half an hour tops. I stared at the window. I did not want to crawl inside unannounced; the window was directly above his bed, I would probably fall on his head. Even when Alex had helped me through the window, it hadn't been a very graceful production. I grabbed my hair in frustration and knelt down. I tapped the window lightly with one finger and waited. Nothing. I stood up and let out a large breath. I knelt down once more and tapped again, this time a little louder. I placed my ear up against the window and listened for movement. I prayed that none of the other neighbors could see this, I probably looked like a crazy person. I released the breath I had been unconsciously holding when I heard something move in his room. The curtain shot back and I stood face to face with Alex. He looked tired, but extremely alluring with his disheveled hair. His hand reached up and he opened the window.

"Come on, grab my hand."

I did as told and strapped the bags on securely. Once I was in, I let the bags fall to the ground softly. I apologized quickly. "I'm sorry, go back to sleep."

Alex leaned over and turned on the lamp. His face looked worried, his eyes glanced from myself to the bags. "What happened? You look white as a ghost."

"It's cold outside." I smiled weakly.

"Abby, please talk to me...let me in."

I stood in the middle of his room and wrapped my arms around myself. "I can't."

Alex got off the bed and stood in front of me. He reached down and wrapped me in a tight hug. I didn't release the grip I held myself in. I gave a tired sigh, as my defenses fell. I slowly began to tell him the evening's events.

"She can't treat you like that! You're the one who has been holding things together." Alex fumed. He studied my face. "You're tired, come on let's get some sleep." I allowed Alex to drag me to the bed where I settled neatly onto his chest. He ran his fingers through my hair and hummed softly. I fell asleep feeling safe, and wanted.

The alarm on my cell phone woke me as I had hoped. I groggily sat up. I glanced at Alex, who appeared to be in a deep slumber. I smiled, and pushed back a lock of hair from his eyes as I leaned down to kiss his lips softly. A new dilemma had arisen in my mind. Where was I going to get ready? The last time I was here, the upstairs bathroom was out of service, and I didn't want to risk running into Mary again. That would be beyond awkward. As I let my thoughts take over, I didn't hear Alex wake up. He placed one arm around me, and tugged me backwards. I fell gently into him.

"Now that's the way I like to be woken up," he shot me my favorite smile.

I ruined the moment by my determination to get ready. "Where can I get dressed?"

He smiled in a way that made me blush. "Here's fine."

"Alex!"

"You can't blame a guy for trying," he muttered. "If this was my dream, you would've jumped at the chance."

I rolled my eyes at him and my thoughts drifted to Cara. Had she woken up in the middle of the night? Was she up now? Did Alison ignore her? My face twisted into a mask of despair. Alex saw it, and made sure the coast was clear to the bathroom. He came in with a thumbs up. I grabbed a fresh change of clothes and ran to the washroom. Once I was dressed, I jogged back to Alex's room, and tossed the bags over my shoulder. Before heading out, I stood on my tiptoes to give Alex a kiss.

"Thanks for everything. But I have to check on Cara and get her out of there."

"Keep your cell on, call me if you need me," he reminded gently.

I ran for my truck, and tossed the bags inside. I carefully made my way to the front door and let myself in. I didn't hear any movement in the house. I entered the kitchen and grabbed a bottle of formula for Cara; she would have to make do with an on the go breakfast until she got to Janie's. I grabbed myself a granola bar, and scribbled a note to Alison. *Took Cara to Janie's. I'll pick her up after school. Enjoy the day to yourself. Abby.* That shouldn't anger her. I had tried to make it sound as non-threatening as possible. I strode to Cara's room and she was asleep. That would work for me. I cradled her gently, grabbed any last minute items, and headed to the truck. We arrived at Janie's a little earlier than normal, but as per usual, Janie greeted us warmly.

"Sorry we're early, it was an odd morning. Do you mind if I change Cara and get her ready for breakfast?"

"Not at all. But that's what I'm here for," Janie said with a chuckle.

"I know, it's just that I'm here earlier than usual, and I have some time to kill…"

"Of course. I'll be in the living room when you're done."

After Cara was ready, I placed her in a high chair, munching on Cheerios. I found Janie. "She's all yours."

Janie stood with a warm smile. "Great, thanks. Abby?"

"Yes?"

Janie's voice grew soft. "I hope I'm not overstepping my boundaries here…but is this morning going to become part of the routine?"

My heart quickened. "I'm sorry if we're too early. I can try and bring her later in the morning." I bit my lip and thought how I could make that work.

"No, no, this time from now on will be fine." Janie looked at me seriously. "Are things okay at home? Word has been traveling a little bit. Is it true that Alison left yesterday?"

"Things are fine." I said quickly and flashed a smile.

Janie looked skeptical. "If you need anything, anything at all, you know my number."

"Thanks, I'll see you later."

After the final bell of the day rang, Ali and I walked to our vehicles. "What are you doing after school today?"

"Not much, picking up Cara was all I had planned."

"Great. I'm supposed to meet Jordan at Alex's. Do you want to hang out with us? You can bring Cara too."

"Sure, sounds like a plan. It's much better than being stuck in that house. I'll meet you guys there after I get Cara." We waved a quick goodbye and went our separate ways.

⌘

Cara was in my arms, and we were ready to leave the daycare when Janie spoke up. "Abby, before you go, I think you should be aware Alison stopped by and wanted to take Cara away early."

I finished strapping Cara in the car seat when I turned to face Janie. My face fell. "You didn't let Alison take her?"

"No. We have a policy here that whoever drops off, picks up, unless we hear otherwise. Also, I didn't like the way she behaved."

Fear made its way through me, how was Alison going to react to this one? Surely it would all be my fault. "Thanks for letting me know, see you tomorrow."

I hopped into my truck and drove home slowly. I was in no hurry at all to witness Alison's reaction. I drove past Alex's house, and gave a feeble wave to my friends who waited outside.

I pulled into the driveway and barely had time to shut my door when Alison stormed out. "How dare you! How could you do this to me? Do you think I'm not good enough to be trusted with my own child? People are talking!"

The tone in her voice frightened me. "Calm down, Alis—"

Before I could finish, her hand struck against my face. The impact caught me off guard. "Unbelievable, who do you think you are, Abby?" her voice soared.

I winced as the stinging sensation pulsated through my face. I pressed a cool hand against my throbbing cheek. Footsteps rushed our way quickly.

Alison groaned, and Ali stood beside me in an instant. "Oh my gosh, are you okay?"

Alex and Jordan stepped in front of us protectively. I noticed Jordan kept a firm grasp on Alex's arm, and I could see why. His face twisted in anger, and his hands trembled. I didn't want a huge confrontation, I was afraid of what Alex might do if he was prodded any further.

I quickly stepped in front of him and placed my hands on his chest. "Alex, don't lose it on me. Alex, look at me."

He did. His anger slowly faded, then turned to pity. "Abby, are you okay? Has she done this before?" he accused angrily.

The anger was back in full force, and he stepped forward to Alison. I pushed him back. "No, this hasn't happened before. Please, let it go. Alex, I am begging you. She's not worth it."

He took a deep controlled breath. "Fine. But if this ever happens again, you can't expect me to stand here like this."

Alison cleared her throat. "My daughter, Abby. Now." Her glare darkened as I hesitated.

"Maybe you should calm down first." I suggested meekly.

"If you don't give me my daughter, I will call the cops. A wild out of control teenager with a child doesn't sound too appealing, does it?"

I was torn. I slowly made my way to Cara and held the precious bundle. Alison tore her from my grip and I winced. Cara started to shift uncomfortably and began to whimper.

"Loosen your grip, you're hurting her!" I shouted.

"Don't tell me what to do with *my child.*"

I watched helplessly as Alison stormed into the house. Alex reached for my hand and squeezed it reassuringly. I looked at my friends helplessly. "I'm sorry, I can't go. I need to watch her…"

Ali nodded, clearly horrified by the events. Alex stopped me. "I can't let you go in with her alone, she's crazy!"

I tried to take my hand away from his. "You have to let me go, please."

Alex released me reluctantly. I ignored my instinct to run and stepped inside, shutting the door quietly behind me.

Chapter Fourteen: Enough

The days following our face off were downright ugly. Alison's temper raged, and I hadn't slept decently in over two weeks. Cara felt the tension in the house and her sleeping pattern had been thrown off completely. I missed quite a bit of school due to lack of sleep from Cara's wails throughout the night and Alison's growing demands. Today was Wednesday, and I needed to go to school to catch up. I looked in the mirror and groaned, silently thankful I had refused to see Alex since that horrible afternoon. Our visits were strictly limited to phone calls only. Lack of sleep had made my skin dull and tired. Dark circles formed under my eyes, making me look like I had taken up boxing, and lost harshly. My eyes were swollen and tired, even my hair lost some of its shine. I let out a disgusted sigh, and wondered how I let myself get this bad.

I wandered into the kitchen and looked around for food to pack for lunch. Nothing intrigued me, which wasn't a surprise. My appetite had faded lately, the best I could manage was to choke down some crackers, and even they seemed to make me ill. I said a silent prayer, hoping Cara would be all right with Alison. I got into my truck and drove to school. As I walked down the halls of the school, it made me think back to my first day when everyone had stared at me. Only then, they had stared with curiosity and excitement; now, they watched me with horrified expressions.

When Ali and Laura saw me, their faces drained of all color. "Oh my god Abby, what happened to you?"

I bit back a cry. "Nothing, just busy."

"Busy doing what? Locked in a basement in chains?" Laura snapped.

I didn't answer. Ali shoved her and whispered. "Take it easy on her, Laura, look at her!"

I wordlessly opened my locker and grabbed my books. I was too tired to speak anyways. Ali looked at me seriously. "Has Alex seen you lately? He's been going crazy. He thinks something's wrong, he's not sure why you won't let him see you…"

Ali's gaze held a silent accusation. *I wouldn't let him see me looking like that either.* I shook my head to acknowledge that I heard her.

"Abby, if things are that bad, you can always stay with me, or Alex…" Ali trailed off.

"I can't Ali." I groaned helplessly. "Cara needs me, and if I leave, who knows what Alison will tell Jack…" My biggest fear was Jack would believe her. "If I leave now, I might not be allowed to come back." I bit off a cry.

"All Jack needs to do is take one look at you, and he will know that something's up. You don't even look like the same girl! You look like a zombie!"

Ali's eyes continued scrutinizing me. "How much weight have you lost?"

"I don't know, ten pounds or so."

Ali's eyes opened wide. "You don't look healthy."

I closed my eyes and rubbed my temples in irritation. Lack of sleep made my temper extremely short. "Ali, I know you're worried, just drop it okay? Drop everything. I'll see you at lunch."

Dealing with my peers had been bad, but seeing my teacher's was far worse. They looked just as horrified as the students; only they had pulled me aside and asked if I needed any help. I shrugged off their concerns and grew more and more irritated as I was forced to sit through the same worried lecture with each teacher. I took my seat wearily and found their words began to fade as I drifted off to sleep. During lunch break, I decided to avoid the crowd. I silently slipped away from Laura and headed to my truck. I hopped inside and made a bed in the front seat. It didn't take long for me to be out. A knock on my window stirred my dreams. I tried to block it out, feeling annoyed. The knock sounded again, only this time it was louder. I sat up and looked outside.

When Alex saw me, his face drained, and he dropped his mouth. He opened my door immediately. His voice was hard when he spoke. "Get out of the truck, Abby." I slid out, and stood in front of him feeling very small. His face looked pained. "When Ali called and told me what you looked like..." he ran a hand through his hair. "I thought she was over exaggerating. Hell. Abby, you look like death warmed over, I barely recognize you! Have you seen yourself lately?"

"Of course I have." I snapped. "Why aren't you in school?"

His voice hardened. "That's all you have to say? I'm worried about you. I have been worrying about you now for almost two weeks! You haven't left the house. I-" He blew out a breath and took my head between his hands and looked at me sadly. "The spark is gone from those beautiful eyes. You can't keep doing this, baby. You are going to kill yourself."

He spoke the words so softly. Tears began to roll down my face. He gently wiped them away. "Come on, you need sleep."

"What about my truck?"

"I will get Jordan to pick it up later."

I sat in his car and closed my eyes. I never wanted to open them ever again.

⌘

The smell of soup caused me to stir. I gently opened my eyes and looked around. At first, I didn't know where I was. I stiffened in fear. My brain began to click on at the familiar scent of Alex's cologne. I pulled the blanket closer and shifted onto my side. Alex sat at his computer desk, scribbling down notes. His eyes fell to me, and he looked relieved.

"You're up." He put his book down, and walked over to me. "How do you feel?"

"A little better....pretty weak still actually." I lifted one arm experimenting with myself, and it took a great deal of effort, my muscles quivered in protest.

He studied me carefully. "You need food."

I wrinkled my nose. "I don't think I can eat."

"Please Abby. You're wasting away on me here."

Something in his tone made me feel guilty. I propped myself against a pillow and nodded. "Sure, I'll try."

"Good, thank you….here." I took the bowl of soup, but the smell made my stomach turn. Alex watched me anxiously so I took a bite. I could only manage five spoonful's before I set it aside. Alex's face creased with worry. He looked at me and managed a weak smile. My head began to spin almost violently. With a groan, I slid beneath the covers and drifted off to sleep. When I awoke, I felt groggy and slow. The room was dark and there was no sign of Alex. I hoped he went to school, I felt guilty keeping him with me. I laid in bed unmoving, when the door gently creaked open.

"Good evening, Abby. It's nice to see you awake." It was Mary. I studied her as she got closer. She didn't seem annoyed with me, she simply looked concerned. I tried to sit up and look alert. The effort made me nauseous.

Mary spoke gently. "Take it easy. How do you feel?"

"I think I'm okay. I'm still pretty tired." I admitted.

"Do you want something to eat?"

"No thanks. I am kind of thirsty."

"All right, would you like me to bring you some tea?"

"Actually, would it be okay if I drank it upstairs? I think I need to move, I feel stiff."

Mary nodded briefly. "Of course, come with me then."

Mary helped me out of bed. I was slightly embarrassed when I began to sway, the dizziness had returned. Mary spoke gently, and I was grateful to her for keeping me upright. I focused on her words and pretended that she wasn't here with me, treating me like an invalid.

"I sent Alex upstairs to try and eat something. I don't need another person wilting away. He's been so worried about you."

I glanced at Mary. "I'm so sorry. I didn't mean to drag anyone else into this."

"Don't be silly. That's what we're here for."

We entered the kitchen and Alex shot up, his arms replaced Mary's. I was uncomfortable with all the attention, and was relieved when I could sit down. Alex slowly released his grip, watching me closely.

"I'm okay Alex, really." I shooed him away.

He pushed his chair next to mine and watched me suspiciously. Mary placed a steaming cup in front of me. "Drink carefully, it's quite hot."

I gripped the warm mug and sighed, the heat felt good. I glanced at the time; it was 6:30 p.m. I smiled. "Wow, I slept for almost seven hours."

Mary and Alex exchanged a look. Alex cleared his throat. "It's Friday," he said quietly.

I looked at him in shock. "Friday? I slept for two days!" I gasped horrified.

Alex's face went pale. "You were almost unconscious, Abby. I couldn't wake you."

My face twisted. "Cara! She's been alone for two days!" I stood and gripped the chair for support as I began to waver.

"Abby, calm down, you need to get better, relax." Alex's patience was forced.

Mary's tone was much smoother. "Alex is right. Stay here for the night and we will see how you feel in the morning."

I looked around helplessly, knowing I would never make it across the street in my current state. I sat down defeated. Mary placed soup and breadsticks in front of me. I took a few unenthusiastic bites and ignored the looks of worry hovering over me.

I spoke firmly. "Alex, you need to go to school, I'll be okay, I promise."

"I don't know, if something happened to you while I was gone I would never forgive myself."

"What could possibly happen? I can barely manoeuvre myself!" I said frustrated.

Alex's eyes looked sad as he reached out for my hand, and gave a reassuring squeeze. "You just need to rest. You will be okay."

The phone rang and Mary rose to answer. "Alex, it's for you."

Alex gave me a look of doubt, and I gently shoved him away. "Go, I'll be fine."

Alex rose reluctantly to get the phone. Now that I felt a little more aware of myself, I really wanted a shower. I tapped my fingers restlessly against the table and bit my lip. Mary sat down next to me. "What's wrong, dear?"

My cheeks flared red. "I could really use a shower…" my voice trailed off as I thought of the effort it would take for me to stand that long. A bath would be safer. "Maybe a bath would be a better idea…" I said quietly.

Mary nodded. "I'll draw you one, stay here."

Before I could protest, she was gone. Minutes later I sat amongst a swirl of bubbles. I sighed contentedly as the warmth of the water soothed my aching body. A light tap sounded on the door. I quickly glanced down, checking to see that the bubbles covered me strategically. "Come in."

Alex crept in quietly. He looked nervous as he made his way to me. "If Mary knew I was in here, she'd have my head."

I laughed uneasily and turned my attention to the bubbles, hoping they wouldn't shift and expose me. I sat perfectly still and took measured breaths. Alex and I talked for awhile. I noticed he had trouble holding eye contact. His eyes lingered over the bubbles longer than necessary; he would catch himself and force his eyes to meet mine. I found it to be almost amusing.

Alex spoke reluctantly. "I better go. Mary should be stopping in soon."

I watched him leave quietly, and moments later Mary came in with clean clothes. "Thank you so much!" The scent of fresh clothes breathed some life into me.

Mary smiled. "You're welcome. Do you need help getting out?"

I was horrified at the thought. "No, I should be okay."

Mary looked at me skeptically. "Okay, if you need anything just holler."

She shut the door behind her and I attempted to get up. My arms trembled in protest as I tried desperately to hoist myself up. *No.* This could not be happening to me. I tried a few more times, and slipped on the last attempt. I swallowed my pride and called out gently for Mary.

She entered in one second flat. She must have been waiting outside of the door. She grabbed a large towel and swiftly, but gently, helped me up. She wrapped the towel around me quickly, I kept my eyes on the ceiling the entire time.

Mary's voice was soft. "There we go. Can you manage the rest okay?"

I nodded. "Yes, thank you."

⌘

As I lied next to Alex, he pulled me in closer. "Do you have enough blanket?"

"Yes, thanks."

"Where's your head at these days?"

I sighed and placed my head against his chest. "I'm sorry for everything that I have put you through lately. I don't know what I would have done without you or Mary for that matter."

Alex gave me a kiss on the top of my head. "I told you, I'll always be here when you need me."

We sat in companionable silence until Alex blew out a frustrated breath. "I have to go away for a week."

"Oh?" I asked with curiosity.

"It's a school thing, they're sending us out on practicum's."

"That's great!" I said, hoping I sounded enthusiastic.

He shot me a look. "Yeah, I guess. A week is a long time to be away from you."

A smile twisted on my mouth. "Yeah," I said softly. "So we better make tonight count. Plus, there's always the phone."

He nodded grimly. "I can't monitor you over the phone."

I laughed at his serious face. "Alex, it's not your job to worry about me, okay? Have fun." My eyes began to grow heavy, and my vision dimmed. I tried to fight back a yawn but lost.

Alex noticed. He traced his lips softly against my forehead, along my cheekbone, and then met my lips. "You should get some sleep."

I nodded and managed to mumble. "Sweet dreams."

The light seeped in through the blinds and caused me to stir. I slowly blinked. Alex zipped up his bag and noticed I was awake. "Good morning, Sleeping Beauty."

He positioned himself next to me and gave me a lingering kiss. He pulled back for a moment before diving in for another. His lips found mine with more of an intensity this time. I wrapped my arms around his neck, drawing him closer. He intertwined his fingers with mine, and with a sigh he slowly sat up.

"What was that for?" I asked breathlessly.

"I had to make it last."

I felt my voice drop. "Right, you're leaving today, aren't you?"

He frowned. "Unfortunately."

I tried to make my voice light. "Good luck, and remember to relax. I'll be fine. Mary picked up all of my homework, I have lot's to keep me busy."

"Yeah, I know." He sighed and stood. "I have to go. Promise me you will be careful."

I held out my hands and he helped me to my feet. I pulled my arms around his neck and gazed into his warm green eyes. "I promise."

He held me for a moment, then gently let go. "If I don't leave now, I never will." He muttered.

"Drive safe."

Alex gave me a gleaming grin. "Promise."

I watched him walk away and listened for his car until I could no longer hear his tires crunch over the snow. It didn't take long for loneliness to settle in around me. I made my way upstairs and felt out of place. I was the only one home. I was pleased I didn't feel the same dizziness as yesterday. I stepped into the bathroom and grimaced. I really did look sick. A few days of sleep had brightened up my complexion, but I was still nowhere near looking how I used too. I forced myself to eat a bowl of cereal, and decided it was time to go home. I wrote Mary a thank you note and pinned it on the fridge. I shut and locked the door behind me and was glad to see Jordan had brought my truck home. I walked across the street, opened up the front door, and stepped inside. I sighed when I saw the mess was back. I heard shuffling from the living room, and I followed the noise.

"Cara! What are you doing?"

I strode over to Cara and picked her off the floor; she had been left alone to wander the living room all by herself. I quickly gave her a once over and sighed in relief when I found no gaping wounds. She had a few superficial scratches but nothing major. I gently carried Cara to her room, and placed her on the changing table.

"Unbelievable, your diapers on backwards. Let's just start fresh shall we? Another bath for you, my dear," I mumbled.

After freshening Cara up, I took her downstairs and fed her breakfast and began tidying up. I started with the dishes, picked up the wrappers scattered amongst the floor, and took out the garbage. I began a load of laundry that barely dented the mountainous pile scattered about. I freshened Cara's crib and cleaned off some of her toys.

I stopped outside of Alison's door, fuming. What a joke she was. I burst open her door. "Nice job taking care of your girl!"

Alison opened her eyes and sat up. "Excuse me? What do you think you're doing in here?"

"Were you aware that you left Cara roaming around loose, all by herself downstairs?"

Alison waved a hand carelessly in the air. "That's what this is all about? She's fine, it keeps her quiet."

I was beyond furious. How could she act like this was no big deal? "What the hell is wrong with you? Did you fall down and smack your head on the pavement? She's not a dog. She's a baby! She needs to be watched."

Alison snarled. "Get out of my room before I throw you out." She plopped back under her covers and called out sleepily. "Oh, while you're up and home finally, we need groceries."

While I was out buying food, Alison had taken off again. I was relieved to come home and see that her car was gone. I finally had the house looking back the way it should. I sent Alex a quick text, letting him know everything was fine, just fine.

⌘

It was only 9:30 p.m. but I was ready for bed. I entered a dreamless sleep when the front door slammed shut. The noise must have woken Cara because she started to cry. I groaned and waited to see if she would quiet down on her own. My eyes were still shut when my door burst open. I gasped as a cold impact met my skin. Icy water began to drip down my face and onto my clothes.

"Get up, Cara's crying. I'm tired, I need my sleep." Alison snapped impatiently.

I sat up at once, and immediately glanced around the room for my baseball bat. She was lucky it wasn't with me, I couldn't be held responsible for what I would have done if I had found it. Before I even made it inside Cara's room, she stopped crying on her own. I shuffled back to my room, changed my sheets, and slipped into a pair of dry pajama's. I slept with one eye open that night. The next morning I slept through my alarm and didn't care. Mary had grabbed all the homework I missed from the days before and she had brought home enough to keep me caught up on for the next week and a half.

I slowly walked downstairs when I heard Alison's voice. "She left us Jack, and she's been getting wildly out of control. I don't trust her with Cara."

I stormed into the kitchen. "Alison, you are so full of sh-" I stopped mid-sentence, as Jack sat next to her. Alison gently dabbed her eyes with a Kleenex and sniffled loudly. Jack rubbed her back reassuringly.

Jack's anger faded as he took in my appearance. "Abby, what happened to you?"

This was my chance to make him see and I took it. "I'm tired, Jack. I am sick and tired of cleaning up after her messes! She has no sense of responsibility; she just ups and leaves whenever she feels like it. And when I'm gone, I come home only to find the house is a disaster! Not only that, but Cara is left to sit in disgusting diapers and she wanders the house alone!"

Jack's eyebrows rose and he looked at Alison. "Is this true?"

For the first time, I felt a glimmer of hope Jack would take my side. Until Alison began to sob. "Do you see? Do you see what she's doing Jack? Look around you! Does this house look like a disaster? Do you honestly think I would leave our daughter all alone downstairs, roaming free as if she were a dog? I can't do this anymore Jack, I can't live like this!"

Jack's face went soft. "No, of course I believe you. You have always kept a good house. I should've known this may happen…"

"Don't believe her, Jack, please! If you want tears, I can give them to you too!" I shouted desperately, all the while glaring at Alison.

"Abby, that's enough!" Jack broke the gaze, and threw his hands in the air. "Why, Abby? Why do you always go back to that? Are you deliberately trying to drive a wedge in this family?"

"Of course not! You don't see it, do you? How can you always take her side without even listening to me? You should know after all the time you have spent with me I could never do the things she's accusing me of!" Tears blurred my vision and I spoke quietly. "I just need to hear you say that you want me here."

"I don't know the answer to that right now."

"It shouldn't be hard to answer. I am your daughter, it should be simple."

"I think you may have found the answer." Jack looked at me with such disappointment I almost believed I had done something wrong. He stared at me for a moment before he spoke quietly. "Are you happy now? I have never seen Alison this upset before."

Sadness fell heavy over me. "Look at me, Jack. Really look at me. Do you think I look healthy? Do you think I look happy?" I raised my voice. "Now look at her! There is a huge difference—"

"What am I supposed to think, Abby? She's my wife."

I glared at him. But I was his daughter, shouldn't that count for something? I could feel a sentence burning the back of my throat. I knew I should hold the words back, but really, what was the point? We had already reached the point of no return.

"You know, this was really hard for me to come out here; stepping into a world I had no clue about. Do you know how many years I have hated you for now? I thought maybe by me coming here, we could salvage something of a relationship, but now I think I was right all those years ago; hating you."

I took another shaky breath. There was no stopping my words. "You are a coward, Jack. Going back to a selfish woman who left you and your baby girl without a second thought. And then you jump back to her the first chance you get? What about Mom? You left us for that witch of a woman, and you have never even said you're sorry. How could you have left us? How could you possibly sleep at night knowing you broke our hearts?"

"I was four years old and wondering when my daddy would come back home. I hate you. I have always hated you. And I loathe the bitch." My voice broke and I felt sick as I thought back to all those years; losing the house, barely having enough food to eat, the tears from my mother and me. My glare grew darker as Alison smirked. A rage rose in me that I had never before felt.

Jack's face went bright red. "Get out, Abby."

"So that's it then, Jack? Again, choosing her over me? What a man you are. You must feel so goddamn proud."

Alison walked to Jack's side. "You heard your father, get your things. I think you have put our family through enough."

I wanted so badly to knock her down to the ground. Instead, I took a deep breath and silently counted to three. "I will have my things gone. And you," my eyes glowered at Alison, "are a sorry excuse for a human being. You have nothing on my mother. You have no class, and not an ounce of a clue on how to behave like a responsible adult. I have never felt such hatred for another human being as I do for you. I truly hope that you get what's coming to you."

Jack's face marred in anger and his voice shook. "That's enough, Abigail. Get your things, and get out."

I went upstairs and quickly packed my belongings. I marched past the angry adults and tossed the bags in my truck. I went back upstairs to Cara's room and sighed. She slept peacefully on her back, arms spread out above her head. The tears started to flow then.

I gently covered her back up. "I'm so sorry, kiddo. I tried to be strong. I will be back, I'll figure something out."

I forced myself out of the room and stopped to face Jack. "You better take care of Cara," my eyes settled on Alison. "If I find out that she has been hurt, you will be sorry."

"You've overstayed you're welcome." Alison said, slightly uncomfortably.

I wasn't done. "I hope you're extremely proud of yourself, Jack, and just in case you want to test my theory, talk to my teachers, or even Janie; she didn't feel it was safe enough to hand Cara over to her own mother."

I blew out a frustrated breath. "This is me, Jack. This is who I am. I tried to be the bigger person here. I truly hope you can see that, and remember how much I have helped you out." I lowered my voice and paused for a brief moment. "Was I really that hard to live with?"

Jack avoided my eyes and I continued on. "What about the letters, Jack? I know you got them. Why did you never write me back? I begged you, I waited so long for my dad to come home! You promised you would come back for me, but you never did! How could you leave?"

"Life was always easier without you, Abby." Jack's tone was barely audible.

I didn't expect those words. They caught me off guard and they hurt. I took a moment to gather myself. "Well then, I hope you two will make one big happy family." I forced the words out. "I'm proud of who I have become. I'm sorry you won't be there to see me grow up; from this point on, you have proved to me once and for all that you don't deserve to be a part of my life."

I slammed the door shut behind me and hopped into my truck with a very heavy heart. I sped onto the freeway and toyed with the idea of stopping in to see Alex once more. I didn't have the fight in me to look my new friends in the eyes to say my goodbye. So, instead I sent a text message. I would see most of them again when I started college in the fall. Alex was another matter. I didn't know what to tell him. He deserved so much more than an electronic message, but I didn't have enough strength in me to see him. I needed to see my mother, I was on the verge of falling apart. It was now clear my father didn't love me. He didn't want me. He never even bothered to fight for me. Instead, for the second time in my life, my father had chosen Alison over me, and this time I was live and up front to see it happen. Once I pulled onto my old neighborhood, my spirits lifted slightly. I was pretty sure I had no more tears left in me. My head throbbed, my eyes were heavy, and my heart was shattered into a million tiny pieces, and it hurt so much. I never did call Mom or Mark to tell them I was on my way home. I knew I wouldn't need to, they were always there for me, and would welcome me with open arms. That's what a family was for. My mother ran outside when she heard my truck. My heart instantly felt warm as I saw her, the dull aching thud momentarily disappeared. She ran to the door and opened it before I cut the engine.

I jumped out and my mother's arms flew around me. "Honey, you have no idea how much I have missed you!"

She squeezed harder before her eyes met mine critically. "You feel a lot smaller than I remember." She took in my appearance slowly, carefully and she looked upset."Abby, what happened?"

Mark stood in the doorway and I gave him a smile. He marched purposefully beside me, and wrapped me up in a bear hug. "It looks like you could use some food, let's get you inside and you can fill us in on everything."

⌘

It was now just after 8:30 p.m. and I tried to ignore my mother's angry voice as she reamed Jack out on the other end of the phone. I heard her demand to speak to Alison, and by the sounds of things, Jack wasn't letting her. Probably the only smart move he would ever make. My parents had been sympathetic and understanding when I told them the events that led me back home, but near the end of my story they couldn't hide their anger. It felt nice to have someone on my side, but at the same time, I wished I had never told them any of it. The recent events which had transpired in my life felt like my own personal shame, I didn't want to burden anyone else with them.

I stretched out onto my stomach and stared at my cell phone. I read Alex's text for the hundredth time.

"Five more days to go here and I can come home. I hope things are remaining uneventful. Looking forward to holding you again. Hope your dreams have been peaceful. Can't wait to see you smile."

Tears filled my eyes, he had no idea I was gone. I couldn't think of anything to say to him so I put my phone away and tried to get some sleep, and hoped things would be clearer in the morning. For the next week, I spent some quality time with my parents and kept myself busy by catching up on homework. Mark had called my school, and for the mean time we arranged that I could do my schoolwork through distance education so I wouldn't fall behind. I was grateful the school was being so co-operative, but they were well aware of my situation. I was a very good student, but I knew it helped Mary was on my side.

I spent my afternoon's lazing away and catching up on the latest gossip with Sarah, who was still with Greg, and they seemed to be doing well. Watching the two of them together was hard. My heart ached for Alex. He called once he found out I was gone. I couldn't answer the phone. I had no idea what to tell him, what could I possibly say? I wasn't sure what I was doing and so, I avoided the one person who I missed beyond words. I closed my eyes and tried to think of something positive. In the short time I had been home, my complexion was back to its bright and healthy glow, the dark circles had faded, my hair had gotten back it's luster, and I was back to a healthy weight. It felt good to be loved and welcomed into a household again. Despite everything, I still felt restless and I knew it all boiled down to Alex and my worry for Cara.

I flopped down on my bed, and stared at the ceiling. My mom walked in. She plopped next to me. "How are you doing, kiddo?"

"Fine, I guess." I smiled.

"No you're not. You miss him, don't you?"

"Jack? No, not even a little bit."

My mom let out her twinkling laugh. "No, I believe his name is Alex?"

I sighed, the sound of his name tugged at my heart. "Yes."

"Honey, I know how careful you are with your heart. This boy must be something very special if you let him in. Are you considering going back?"

I sat up and looked at my mom wide eyed. "Are you kidding me, go back there? Do you not want me here?" I asked quietly.

"Of course I do, I will always want you here. But I can see that you're restless. Your heart may not be here anymore. Abby, you are growing up and falling in love."

I bit my lip, fearing she was right. "What do I do?"

A smile crossed my mom's lips. "Let yourself fall. Sometimes the best things in life are the ones that push us out of our comfort zone. I think deep down, you have made your decision." My mom continued. "I see you're worried about Cara. Don't forget, my daughter, I know you very well." My mom paused. "I'm not sure I can see you being happy here anymore."

I bit my lip and spoke quietly. "I don't know if I'm ready to go back, Mom. The things he said to me, the things I said to him…"

She threw her arms around me. "You've been through a lot lately. Nobody would blame you for taking a breather. As for what you said to your father, he deserved a good wake up call."

Mom smiled. "Your friends have been calling. It sounds like they miss you."

I smiled sadly. I missed them, too. While it was great to see my old friends again, I knew that I had changed. I had been through so much in the last little while, and the new friends I had made saw me through the worst of it. We had forged a tight bond.

"You don't have to stay with Jack. I'd be willing to bet one of your friends would be more than happy to have you."

I bit my lip, thinking things over. I needed to see Cara. I needed to see Alex. I lifted my blue eyes to my mother's and she nodded. She knew. She leaned in once more and wrapped me in a warm embrace. "I'm going to miss you. I am so proud of the woman you're becoming."

Chapter Fifteen: Reverse

I kept in touch with Ali and Laura while I was away; we spoke almost every day. They were extremely excited to hear of my return. Over my absence, I had grown closer to Ali than Laura. Ali listened without passing any judgment on my decisions, and she was always ready to give me valuable advice. She also kept me merely updated on Alex, whom I had yet to face. Ali had spoken to her parents and they agreed to let me stay with them until I could figure things out. Saying goodbye once more to my friends, my mother and Mark felt like déjà vu, but at least this time I had somewhere to go where I could feel at home. I made good time, the roads were clear and I was now familiar with the route.

 Before going to Ali's, I decided to see Alex first. Butterflies grew fiercely in the depths of my stomach. In an effort to keep them controlled I turned up the music, hoping it would drown out my thoughts. I pulled in behind Alex's car, Mary's was nowhere in sight. I stepped out of the drivers seat and glanced toward Jack's house. The lights were on. I hesitated ever so slightly. I didn't have it in me to face both issues today. Cara would have to wait just a little longer. I walked carefully up the slick steps to the large door. The sun began to set, turning the sky a brilliant shade of pink. I rasped my knuckles against the door and waited, hoping Alex would answer. I let out the breath I had been holding and watched as it floated away in a puff of white. Footsteps sounded, and the door swung open.

 Alex stood there, mouth slightly agape. His expression surprised. "Abby?"

My words came out in a rush. "Alex, I never meant to hurt you. It was such a horrible day. I really needed to get away from it all. I needed to go somewhere where I could breathe." I held up my hands in a helpless gesture.

"I understand." His voice dropped. "But you could have come to me." Alex wrapped his arms around himself, trying to keep the cold at bay. "I thought I was worth something to you."

I squeezed my eyes shut briefly. "You mean everything to me, Alex." I forced myself to meet his gaze.

"Well you have a hell of a way of showing it."

"I'm not good at this." I said weakly.

"I didn't think you would ever come back." Alex shook his head. "I thought I would never see you again…" His voice grew hoarse and he stopped.

I took a small step closer to him. I yearned to touch him. I had missed him so much, and standing here next to him now, I would have never believed that someone like him could have ever wanted me. There was a distinct loneliness amongst his gaze. He smiled weakly, but it never even came close to reaching his eyes. I knew in that moment I how much I had hurt him.

"You were the first person I wanted to run too." I added quietly. "I just…I got lost."

He nodded stiffly. I wasn't sure what to say next. Perhaps my actions could be stronger than any words I had to say. I moved in closely, carefully. His green eyes were cautious, but he did not move. I placed my hands on his chest and pressed my lips against his. He closed his eyes and sighed. He ran his hand gently through my hair, softly stroking my cheek.

"You never said goodbye," he mumbled quickly. He pulled me in close, and wrapped me in a warm hug. I fit neatly against him and let out a deep sigh, his arms felt like home.

"I can't Abby," he said suddenly.

I released him and gazed up at his face, he looked torn and lost. He shook his head sadly. "I am glad that you're okay." A half smile played on the corner of his lips. "The sparks back in those beautiful eyes."

Alex hesitated and moved back, sadness running heavy in his features. "Have a good night, Abby." I watched wordlessly as he gently shut the door in my face.

⌘

Ali and Laura had the door open before I was out of my truck. "You're here! You're really here!"

I smiled and braced myself for the warm hugs I was about to receive. "It's good to be back. I missed you girls so much!"

"She's here, Laura! She's really back!" The girls squealed and I laughed. "Come on, let's bring your stuff inside. It's freezing out here."

Once we were inside, we made ourselves warm drinks, and settled in Ali's bedroom. I filled them in on Alex, and my visit home. They gave me a quick recap on school and the town gossip. I, of course, was the hot topic, and to my dismay Alison was a close second. Alison's maternal duties were now being watched very closely. Apparently she wasn't the picture perfect model she made herself out to be. My absence had been noticed. The thought made me feel nauseous. This wouldn't help matters at their home very well at all. Sure, Jack and Alison may now finally realize how much of a help I had been, but Alison would not like the thought of so many others comparing her skills to my own. Especially if she was losing.

"Alex has been keeping an eye on them you know."

My trance broke as Laura's voice echoed through the room. "What was that?"

Laura and Ali exchanged a glance. "When Alex found out you left, he had it out with Jack."

"Alex didn't say anything to me…" I trailed off.

Laura shook her head. "He wouldn't."

I bit my lip, chewing thoughtfully. "Everything turned out okay?"

Ali chimed in. "Yes. Words were exchanged more than anything. Mary stepped in before Alex had a chance to do anything he may have regretted."

I buried my face amongst my hands. "What a mess this has turned out to be."

"I wouldn't say all is lost," Ali began. "Mary has been going over to check on Cara a lot lately. She's keeping an eye on things. Secretly, I think Jack's relieved to have someone competent in his corner."

Laura sat down beside me. "Are you going to see Cara?"

I nodded. "Yes, tomorrow."

Ali stood. "I wish you all the luck in the world."

Chapter Sixteen: The Meeting

Monday morning came, and the day was bright and cold. I should have been going to school but I needed to see my sister. I got dressed and drove to Janie's, praying that Cara still attended daycare. I approached the steps hesitantly and knocked on the door. Janie answered.

"Hi, Janie." I gave a quick wave. "I'm sorry to put you in this position but-"

Janie grabbed me and wrapped me in a hug. "Thank goodness you're here! Cara's missed you something terrible, and so have I! Come in, come in!"

My stomach dropped with worry. "Is she okay?"

"Physically, yes, she's fine. Emotionally, I'm not sure what to think. She's been cranky, her appetite's off, and she's not as social as she usually is. I think she's been looking for you. It's not my place to say, but that Alison woman has no mothering skills, and I don't think she cares to acquire them."

"I was afraid this might happen." I groaned. "Do they bring her to you often?"

"Oh yes, they are regular clients."

"Can I see her now?"

"Of course, she's right over there."

I followed Janie into the playroom and saw Cara. She normally took such an interest in the other children; laughing and giggling, or staring wide eyed at them with wonder. It would entertain her for hours. But not today. Cara sat in the corner and stared dully at a toy, unmoving.

I gasped. "Is she always like this?"

Janie looked upset. "Some days are better than others."

I gingerly stepped toward her. "Cara?" I called softly.

She twitched slightly. I knelt down in front of her. "Cara, baby, it's me. How's my little munchkin doing?"

Her eyes studied me for a moment. I stood perfectly still and waited for some sort of a response. After what felt like forever, her eyes lit up, and she let out a delighted little squeal.

Janie sighed in the background. "Thank goodness!"

I smiled and gently picked her up to give her a big hug. She wriggled with excitement. "I think we should play with some of your toys, what do you say, little girl?"

I spent the majority of my day with Cara. I promised Janie I would try to visit on my lunch breaks. I left with a heavy heart. Cara had grown up so much since I left. She was starting to talk, nothing major, but she could say a few words here and there. Cara had even begun to walk on her own. I had missed her first steps. I hoped that someone captured the moment so I could relive it. Cara's sad little image was locked in my head. Near the end of our visit, she was back to being the happy girl I held in my memory, but I worried about her heart. I knew I couldn't stay away. She needed me around. It was time to call Jack.

⌘

I rubbed my hands together in a furious manner in an effort to keep myself warm. My feet took on a life of their own as I began pacing the snow-dusted walkway. I called Jack early in the morning. I had expected him to hang up on me, but was pleasantly surprised when he agreed to meet with me. We decided the lake would be the most comfortable place to gather. A tall figure began to walk in my direction. It was Jack. I strode over to him in what I hoped radiated confidence. My feet came to a screeching halt when I realized that Alison was with him. *Oh no. Is this a trap?* The click clacking of Alison's heels echoed amongst the frozen landscape. She was dressed in a stylish ensemble, with large sunglasses on. I looked around in slight panic.

"Hello." I said cautiously.

Alison merely nodded. She clutched onto Jack's arm like a lifeline. Her body language made it clear that she wanted to be anywhere but here. Jack didn't seem to notice. He cleared his throat. "I know you saw Cara today."

I braced myself, ready for an attack. "Yes, I did. I've missed her."

Jack's hard exterior broke, and he looked distraught. "She hasn't been sleeping well and her appetite isn't what it used to be. Nothing I do or anyone else does can crack a smile out of her. I think she needs you."

My smile grew so wide that my cheeks ached in protest. "I know we may not see eye to eye, but I would like to be there for Cara in anyway I can."

"Jack, honey, I don't think that would be such a good idea." Alison protested quietly.

Jack snapped. "None of us are sleeping, Alison. I'm starting to get worried about our daughter, and you should be too." Alison was taken aback. Jack had never, ever went against her before.

I took my chance. "I would love to see her. When would be a good time to visit?"

Jack shook his head. "Abby, can I speak to you privately?"

I looked at him in astonishment. "Sure."

Alison cleared her throat. "I should go with you two."

Jack kept his voice low and somewhat threatening. "Stay here. This is between Abby and me."

I stood unmoving and watched as Alison pursed her lips, shooting me a dark sidelong glare.

Jack moved past me hastily and motioned for me to follow. I stepped next to him. Jack heard me approach and he cleared his throat. "Words were exchanged that I should have never said to you that day, Abigail."

I winced at my full name. "It's Abby," I corrected quietly.

I watched Jack, he stared out at the lake lost in thought. His breath came out in large white puffs like a dragons snort. I had never heard him apologize before. He never said the word "sorry" directly but I knew he meant it.

Jack cleared his throat again, this time it was louder, and his words were carefully chosen. "I know this is probably very inappropriate but I would like you to come back and stay with Cara and me."

My head began to swim as Jack faced me, waiting for my response. I choked. "What about Alison?"

"She will never admit it, but she needs help with Cara. This isn't easy for her." He cleared his throat. "I have quite a bit of traveling ahead of me, and I would sleep easier at night knowing Cara has someone who will look out for her."

My brain kicked into overdrive. Living in that house would not be easy, I would only be asking for heartache. Jack continued almost hesitantly. "I never realized just how happy you kept Cara until you were no longer there. She's a completely different child now, and it's beginning to concern me."

Jack's face grew grim with concern and my chest ached. I couldn't help but wonder in the moment if he had ever been worried about me that way. My words came out before my brain had time to process anything. "Okay. I can be there tomorrow morning."

Jack slumped his shoulders in relief. "Thank you."

He turned on his heel and headed to Alison when I called out. "Jack, you really love Cara, don't you?"

"Of course I do." I heard the surprise in his voice.

I struggled to keep my voice polite. "And Alison?"

"Yes, very much," he answered without any hesitation at all.

I nodded, that's all I needed to know. Jack's voice cut through the crisp air. "Before you left you said you were proud of who you've become. Your mother raised you well." He continued on. "We are like strangers, you and I. That's probably my fault. I'm not sure if we can ever repair what's been broken but I am glad I got to see how you turned out."

I turned to look at him but he was gone.

⌘

After the emotions of the day had leveled themselves out, Ali and Laura decided it was time to celebrate. Jordan was having friends over for the evening, and we were invited to go along. The girls piled into my truck and away we went to find the campus. I pulled into a vacant spot and we jumped out. Ali lead the way with familiarity.

Laura playfully jabbed her in the ribs. "Look at our innocent little Ali. I get the feeling you come here often."

Ali went red and shoved Laura into me. "Oh, hush."

I followed silently, taking in the lively campus around me. Students were bundled up and laughing. Relief seemed to be heavy in the air as another school week came to an end. White twinkling lights were draped around the bare trees, providing the campus with a warm glow. A thrill of excitement coursed through my bones. Next fall this would be us. I looked toward my friends as they laughed brightly and I smiled. I couldn't ask for a better group of people to embark on a new chapter of our lives. Ali swung open a large carved door to one of the student living buildings. We linked arms as we made our way through the crowded but lively hall. Ali danced with excitement as she knocked loudly on a door marked with automotive posters.

Jordan answered. His strong face lit up when he saw Ali. "Hey, babe. Glad you could make it." He leaned in to give her a kiss. Jordan's mischievous eyes looked up and he motioned for us to come inside.

Laura gripped my arm in wonder. "Oh my. Oh my, my, my," she muttered under her breath. "Mm. College is going to be fun."

I nodded in agreement. The place wasn't that big but somehow it managed to hold close to twenty people. Everyone seemed to have a drink in hand, and a smile on their face. Voices rose high in excitement and laughter filled the room. Music played upbeat tunes but no one seemed to pay much attention to it. I looked around and only recognized a few faces from previous gatherings way back when. Jordan towed Ali away and Laura took off on her own personal mission. I was left alone. I made small talk with a few people before I slipped into a quiet corner. I glanced outside the window and watched the snow fall softly under the glow of the streetlights.

"Pretty, isn't it?"

I glanced over my shoulder and Alex towered over me. "Yes, it is." I bit my bottom lip and looked away. I felt uneasy and wasn't sure what to say anymore. Lately, it seemed that whatever I said would only make things worse.

"Did you want to go for a walk with me?"

I looked back in surprise. "Sure, that would be nice."

Alex placed his hand on the small of my back and led me through the crowd. We bundled up and I followed him outside. We walked in silence, the only sound coming from the crunching snow beneath our boots.

"So, this is your school," I began lamely.

"It is. Soon it will be yours too I take it."

"Yes, I can't wait."

"You'll like it here. I'm sure you will meet a lot of people."

I nodded wordlessly, not entirely liking the tone of his comment. "I suppose so."

"So," he began. "I hear that you're moving back home?"

"Word travels fast. I am."

"Are you sure that's a good idea?"

"No, but Cara needs me."

Alex let out a heavy sigh. "I admire your dedication, I really do. But you need to have fun too, Abby. You're just a kid."

I balked at the comment. "A kid? Just a kid? You are only three years older than I am. You don't have the right to talk down to me."

Alex stopped, grabbed my arm, and swung me in the opposite direction. "That's not what I meant. I just mean you're putting too much pressure on yourself. You need to enjoy life while you can before the world asks too much of you."

I met his eyes and swallowed hard before moving closer to his lips. He pulled away quickly, creating a large gap. I looked down at my feet, kicking the snow. "Alex, I need to know something. Please be honest with me. You always have been before, so I'm counting on you."

His eyes deepened. "Shoot."

"Is there something wrong with me? Am I….am I…hard to love?"

His face looked shocked and his voice fell heavy. "Is that what you think? No, you're not hard to love at all. That's part of the problem."

He let out a loud sigh. "Trying to keep my distance, now that is proving to be difficult."

"Is that what you're trying to do, Alex? Leave?"

"Listen, Abby…"

I interrupted him. "I always planned on coming back, Alex, for you. I was so lost that day. I needed to run. Sometimes the way Jack looks at me makes me feel like I'm a gaping disappointment. And now, I can see the same doubt in your eyes."

The tears began to well as I whispered the next sentence. "I feel like I have lost my best friend. You don't even look at me the same way anymore." I braved a glance at Alex. His face paled, it looked like someone had just knocked the breath out of him. I didn't want to know his thoughts.

"Abby, I don't know if I can go down this road again." His voice remained unsteady.

My body stiffened. I should have kept my mouth shut. I sat down on a cold bench and watched the snow swirl from the sky. It was over. My face drained of color as a thought burst through my head. "I'm just like him. I ran away, I left you behind."

Alex knelt down. "You're nothing like him. You came back. I know why you left, I knew you had to go…"

Tears began to trickle down my face. I tore my face away from his. "Alex, I am begging you. I can't cry in front of you. You don't need to see that. My heart can't take anymore. Please, I am begging you. Just go."

Alex stood slowly and began to create distance. He never did push me beyond my limits. When he was no longer in my view I buried my face into my hands and began to cry.

⌘

The morning sun warmed my face. I blinked open my eyes and stared at the ceiling. Today I would be moving back to Jack's home. My gut twisted in an uneasy flop. I looked around the bedroom and was grateful packing up would be easy; most of my things were still in boxes. Ali and I ate breakfast together and she helped me load up my truck. Once everything was in the bed of the truck, I embraced Ali in a warm hug, thanking her and her parents for giving me a place to lay my head at night. I climbed in the drivers seat and made my way back to a place I was sure I would never go back.

Chapter Seventeen: Home Sweet Home

The familiar street was lined with cars and the driveway was full. I had to park four houses down. I began hauling my things inside, and forced my way through the crowded house. Not one person offered to help.

I neared my last load when I dropped a box. Heads turned toward me with faint curiosity. "It's all right folks, I've got it, don't worry about me." I called out in a sarcastic tone, knowing no one would come to my aid.

"Abby, when did you get here?" Alex reached down for the box immediately.

"About twenty minutes ago."

He shot one eyebrow up. "And you've been unloading these by yourself?" Alex glanced outside. "Where did you park?"

I smiled grimly. "A few houses down."

Alex's eyes gave me a once over. "Huh, and it appears you haven't taken any spills. I'm impressed."

I smiled. This felt more like it, the way things used to be. "Believe it or not wise guy, I can actually remain upright at times." We bantered back and forth until the last of the boxes was brought into my room.

Alex turned to me and looked at me seriously. "This is really big of you, coming back here. I'm not sure whether it's brave or extremely stupid. Maybe a bit of both."

I tugged my arms around myself securely. "I'm not doing this for them. I'm doing this for Cara."

"I know."

"Do you know what's going on here? I don't recognize a lot of these people."

Alex rubbed the back of his neck. "I guess Jack got a promotion of sorts. A lot of his coworkers are here. I think Alison arranged it."

"Sounds like something she would do." I glanced down at my outfit hesitantly. I was under dressed for the occasion.

"You look fine."

I snapped my head up. "Oh…um, thank you. But I think I should change. I don't need another reason to feel like the odd one out."

Alex nodded. "I'll see you downstairs then?"

"Okay."

I closed the door and began rummaging through my belongings. I slipped into a pair of black slacks with a pretty blue long sleeve shirt. The arms were delicate with lace detailing. My fingers worked quickly to pull my hair into a loose side braid. I looked into the mirror with satisfaction; at least it looked like I belonged. I went downstairs and made small talk with the some of the guests. From across the room, I saw Mary was here as well. Our eyes met and her face brightened.

Mary's step was filled with determination as her arms pulled me into a fierce hug. "I am so glad to see your pretty face. Let me have a look at you." I stepped back and Mary took me in happily. "It's nice to see you looking so healthy."

A warm heat moved its way across my cheeks as I remembered Mary helping me from the confines of the bathtub. "Thank you, I feel really good."

"This house missed you, whether they realize it or not." With a wink she walked off to talk to a nearby group.

Alex stood nearby, and he did a double take my way. His eyes landed on me and I couldn't help but notice his lingering look. I smiled shyly. I half heartily listened to a dull conversation about some new medical procedure when I spotted Cara. I pushed my way through the crowd until I was next to her. She sat in her high chair, looking curiously at the crowd.

"Hi, little girl!" I cheered.

Cara jumped and let out a high-pitched gurgle. I clapped my hands and picked her up gently, bouncing her lightly on my hip. I smiled down at Cara, it was nice to see her blue eyes bright with happiness.

"I knew she missed you. That's the first time I've seen her smile in weeks." I brightened at Jack's tone, which was heavy in relief.

I turned to him, and gave him a small smile. "Would you mind if I took Cara out this afternoon?"

Jack rubbed his chin and looked around. "I don't see why not. This isn't exactly a place for a baby at the moment anyways. Take her car seat out of my truck."

"Thanks, Jack."

I changed the car seat easily and we were on our way to the lake. Once we arrived, I lugged the stroller out from the back and placed Cara inside. With a quick adjustment of her toque I took my time walking around, admiring the glistening water, and watched the ducks frolic. I found a clean, dry bench where I sat down, gently pushing the stroller back and forth until Cara was asleep. I pulled my knees up to my chest and sat there lost in thought. With a quick glance from my phone, I realized I had been gone close to two hours. I decided to head back home. I was relieved to see that the cars were gone. I was able to pull up on the side of the road next to our driveway. I slipped into the house and lay Cara in her crib.

A cold voice sounded behind me. "So you really are back. That's a bold move isn't it?" Alison sneered.

I was taken aback by her tone. "Guess so, but I heard you needed the help, so here I am." I held my arms out in a gesture of helplessness. Alison's face fell.

I turned at the sudden footsteps as Jack entered the room. "Cara's sleeping?"

I spoke quickly. "The fresh air must have gotten to her."

Jack shook his head. "I wouldn't be so sure. We tried taking her outside, nothing worked. It's you. She feels settled again."

I was honored by his words. It was a foreign reaction, feeling proud of something Jack had said. His words usually held the opposite effect. Jack continued, his eyes taking us all in. "Well, a house full of women. This ought to be fun. Alison, can you help me with something?"

I watched as the two of them walked hand in hand through the door. I stepped into my bedroom and began unpacking my things. Once all my clothes were hung, and the drawers were full, I didn't know what to do with myself. The house was astonishingly clean and Cara was fast asleep. I curled up in the bay window and watched the world outside. Alex caught my eye. He worked on Mary's car in a determined manner. Even under the hood of a vehicle, he possessed a quiet confident way of carrying himself. It was hard to miss. I rested my head in my hand, and hoped that I hadn't lost him forever.

⌘

"Things are going to be different around here." Jack spoke with a determined authority.

Alison and I sat at the kitchen table, listening as Jack discussed how we would share responsibilities around the house. Since Jack would be traveling more often, he wanted to ensure that we could cohabitate in peace. The adult members in the house would now have rotating chore duties. I was liked the idea, and hoped it would run smoothly. It would be nice to not have to take on the brunt of the jobs. However, glancing at Alison and her wrinkled nose I wasn't holding my breath. Tonight I was on dishes duty. Alison had been placed in charge of making dinner and she had made more dishes than necessary. I was elbow deep in dish soap, scrubbing away furiously at the stack of pots and pans. Once the task was complete, I headed up to my room and Alison sidled next to me.

As she glanced at me, a sly smile lit her features. "Are you done, Abby?"

"Yes, finally." I glanced down at my hands; they were pruned from the water. I grimaced, I was much too young for dishpan hands already.

"Hold on just a minute." Alison called out. She came back with an armload of dirty dishes. "Here you go," she wore a big smile. "I knew it was your day, so I saved up. I know how you like to keep busy."

I gritted my teeth, and watched her walk away. Once I was done, round two, I gave Cara a bath and put her down for the night. Jack had the night shift; it was just Alison and me. The house was eerily quiet, and it left me unsettled. I was outstretched on the couch with a book, when she caught me glancing over at Alex's house.

Alison looked rather amused. "He is a cute one. But I think you need to set your sights lower, honey." Alison clumsily walked over and leaned heavily against the window frame. She burned her eyes into mine. I shot off the couch, feeling vulnerable. One glance at the cup she held told me it wasn't water she pounded back.

⌘

"Get up!" I groaned and lazily waved my hand in the air.

"Get up!" The light flicked on, nearly blinding my sleepy eyes. I sat up with a start, looking around in confusion. Alison stood in my doorway. I glanced out the window and the world was still dark.

"What time is it? What's wrong?" I mumbled, clumsily tearing off my quilt.

Alison came forward at an alarming speed. With one swift motion, she took hold of my hair and began to drag me down the hallway. She abruptly released her grasp once we were in the kitchen.

"What did you do with it?" She screamed.

"Do with what? I don't know what you're talking about, I—"

Alison rifled through the cupboard and held an empty bottle of vodka. "It's empty! What did you do with it you little monster!"

Fear began to claw at me. "Nothing, Alison. I think you may have drank it."

Alison let out a frustrated yowl and picked up a pot that was left to drip dry on the counter. She gripped the handle and threw it blindly. The pot landed with a loud clang, barely missing my head. The noise woke Cara and she began to cry.

"Make the noise stop or I will." Alison glowered.

I ran to Cara's room as quickly as I could. She stood in her crib, her face red from her cries. I picked her up and bounced her comfortingly. "It's okay little one, it's okay. I've got you."

I sat down in the rocking chair and she began to quiet. I listened intently. I heard no more movement in the house. With a sinking feeling, I knew I would be facing a new monster this time around.

The week had been hard. I spoke to Jack about my concerns but he was in denial. He began to make excuses for her; she was overworked and tired, it was just the stress getting to her. On a Thursday night, I finally had a free evening. I met up with the girls for dinner and a movie. I pulled into the driveway shortly after midnight. Friday was a study day, so I would be able to sleep in. As I walked past Alison's car, something looked out of place. I peered into the drivers door and was taken aback. Alison was inside, draped over both of the seats.

"Dammit." I muttered. I tapped at her window. No reaction. I pulled the door open and nudged her.

"Go away."

"Come on, Alison. I can't leave you out here." I reached inside and pulled her out.

Alison was unsteady on her feet and used the car for support. I looked at her tall slender frame and compared it to my petite one. This would not be easy. I placed Alison's arm around my neck and began to head to the house. I was glad Cara was with her aunt for the night.

Once Alison realized it was me who assisted her, she began to thrash. "I don't need any help from you. You're the reason I'm in this mess in the first place!"

With her anger propelling her, Alison gave a hard shove my way. I felt myself go down. Alison went with me and she came down heavy. The left side of my face slammed into the cold pavement. The tearing of skin burned against the cold. I scrambled to get upright and planned to leave her outside in the snow. I dug my hands into the cold and pulled myself up. Alison had somehow managed to get herself steady first.

"You!" Her hands clawed the air and grasped me. I shoved her off, and this time, only she went down. She landed stomach first and began to shout profanities. I winced as the silent night was violated. Lights came on in the neighboring homes. I looked at the dark sky above and cursed. *Damn woman is going to be the death of me.* With a groan I knew I had to get her inside. I struggled with her for what felt like forever.

"Abby? Hold on, honey." Amongst the chaos I thought I heard Mary's voice. I didn't have time to tear my eyes off of the drunken woman flailing about.

Mary's voice tore through the darkness. "Alex! Alex we need help out here."

At the sound of his name I stopped and turned. It was a mistake. Alison tackled me like a football player on the field. I spit out a mouthful of snow and shoved her off. Alex ran toward us, and in one quick swoop, he plucked Alison off me like she was nothing more than a feather. He brought her inside the house. Mary hurried over to me and helped me up.

"Are you all right, honey? Are you hurt?"

"N-no. I'm fine."

Mary placed her arms around me and led me across the street to the safety of her house. I looked back at Jack's house with concern. "What about Alex? He's still in there."

"He'll be done soon. Come on, you're staying over tonight, okay?"

I nodded and allowed myself to be led away. Mary cleaned up what scratches I had and called Jack, who would be leaving work early to come home. Alex was still with Alison. He had been there for almost an hour now. I began to pace Mary's kitchen nervously. I thought of Alex and the terrible memories this would surely bring to life of his drunken uncle. Mary sat and waited with me for her nephew to come home. Alex entered the room suddenly, causing us both to jump. My heart ached as I took in his appearance. He looked tired and broken. His eyes moved slowly and landed on me. His features twisted into an expression that I couldn't quite read.

With one long step he was in front of me. "Are you okay?"

"I'm fine. How are you?"

Another set of footsteps creaked in the kitchen. Jack stepped in, looking upset. Alex excused himself from the room. Jack studied me and cleared his throat. "Are you all right, Abigail?"

"Yes."

Jack looked at Mary apologetically. "I'm so sorry to bring this on you. Alison is on a new medication and she can't mix it with alcohol. One drink with those pills can cause rapid personality changes. Chances are, she won't remember a thing in the morning. She's asleep now."

Mary began to scold him and Jack interrupted. "I promise this won't happen again. I'll see to that."

Mary tsked. "You are lucky your little one wasn't home this evening. I think it's a good idea that Abby stays here tonight."

Jack nodded wearily. "I think so too. Tell Alex thank you for me, please."

"I will."

Mary set me up in the guest bedroom. She looked exhausted as she said her goodnights. Mary was beginning to feel less and less like my teacher, and more like family. I tossed and turned, trying to get comfortable. It was no use. Alex was on my mind and the tortured expression he wore. My bare feet touched the cold wooden floor. I creaked the door open and waited for any sign that Mary was up. I heard nothing. I ran quietly down the hall and went downstairs. A dim light shone through the creases in Alex's doorframe, he was still awake. I knocked at the door lightly.

"Come in."

I stepped inside, shutting the door behind me. Alex sat on the edge of his bed, face buried in his hands. As I stepped closer, I could see he trembled slightly. My hands reached out for him and he looked up. I sat next to him, waiting for him to speak.

"How long?" His voice was hoarse.

"Not long at all, maybe a week."

"Dammit Abby!" He stood abruptly. "You can't deal with crap like this on your own. Trust me, I know." His voice cracked and he slammed his mouth shut.

I stepped in front of him and cradled my hands against the sides of his face. "It's okay, Alex, everything is okay."

He shivered at my touch, and I held my delicate frame tightly against his strong one. I drew him closer, running my fingers through his hair. We remained locked in each other's grasp until Alex stopped shaking.

Alex pulled back, locking his eyes within mine. "Please don't keep things from me. You work so hard to keep me at a safe distance. When will you see that I've always been here for you? I *will always* be here for you."

I pressed my lips against his. "I promise. You see all the ugly parts of my life and yet you still look at me like I'm worth having."

"You are worth having, Abby. Anyone who makes you feel any differently doesn't deserve you."

"You're where I feel safe." I whispered.

"I will never let anyone hurt you." Alex traced a fingertip across my collarbone. I quivered at his touch. His mouth pressed against my neck softly, carefully, before finding my lips. Alex pressed himself against me with an eagerness I had yet to experience. My hands traced down his backside and I pulled him against me firmly. His hands gripped my waist as he led me backwards, pressing my back against the wall. He pulled back, breathless.

"I'm sorry," he breathed.

I pushed a lock of dark hair from his eyes and touched my lips to his. "Don't be." I held his stare eagerly. I didn't want him to stop.

"Are you sure?" he asked quietly.

I nodded. My knees began to shake as the longing over took his eyes. He caught my trembling hands and gently interlaced his fingers within mine. "Hold on tight," he whispered against my ear.

I looked at him questioningly. He smiled and pulled my legs around his waist. He walked to the bed with ease, laying me down as he pressed his warm body against mine. The wall I had been building came crashing down and I let it fall. I gave into his warm touch and soft lips. Tonight, I was letting go.

Chapter Eighteen: Uninvited

"Good morning."

My lips twitched into a smile as I huddled deeper into the warmth of Alex's body. I still tingled at the memory of his touch. I shifted onto my side to face him. "My toes are still curling from last night."

Alex smiled, brushing a lock of hair from my eyes. He leaned over and gave me a tender kiss. "Are you okay?"

"Never better."

Alex's kind gaze lingered over the scratches where my face hit the ground. He traced them gently. "My poor girl. Never again, I promise."

I draped my arms around his neck, pulling him closer. The sound of footsteps upstairs pulled our attention away from each other. "Mary's awake," he muttered. His eyes twinkled. "How are we going to explain this?"

I pressed my lips together in a thoughtful expression. "Hmm. It looks like we may have gotten ourselves into a situation."

Alex chuckled. "I blame you. Damn girl crawls into my bed at night. What was I supposed to do?"

I swatted him lightly. A light knock sounded at the door. We froze. "Alex? Is Abby in there?"

I raised a hand to my forehead in dismay and shut my eyes. Alex let out a small groan and dropped his head to my chest. "She is."

A long pause followed. "Breakfast is ready."

We ate in silence. Mary exchanged looks of disapproval our way but did not say one word about the thoughts that so clearly ran through her mind. Despite the uncomfortable tension in the room, I felt content, warm. Alex sent teasing gazes my way until Mary cleared her throat loudly. I tore my eyes away and focused them onto the plate before me. A loud knock broke the silence.

Mary wiped her mouth with a napkin before getting up. "Abby. Jack is here."

Alex stiffened next to me and took my hand in his. Jack noticed his guard and stepped forward slowly. I squeezed Alex's hand in a reassuring matter. "It's okay," I whispered.

Jack looked around the room in clear discomfort. "I want to thank all of you for last night. I'm so sorry things got out of hand. I can assure you, it will never happen again."

Jack's tired eyes looked my way. "Do you think you will be coming back home?"

I bit my lip. Alison had never been particularly kind to me in the past. But after last nights events, I felt all the more uneasy. "Are you sure this won't happen again? I don't know if I can deal with that…" I let my voice trail off.

Jack stepped closer next to me. "I promise you, Abby. I know my word doesn't mean much, but it will not happen again. I've gone through her medicine cabinet, andI know what works and what doesn't. It is taken care of."

Alex gave a hard sigh. I could tell from the way he held himself he was not happy about my decision to back. He also knew that once my mind was made up, he couldn't do much to change it. He whispered in my ear. "You can come over here anytime. My door is always open."

"Thank you." I sent a curt nod to Jack. "Okay. I'm ready."

⌘

Jack opened the front door and I followed quietly behind. "Would you like to join me for coffee? Alison is still asleep."

Jack had never invited me along for much of anything. Even though I didn't care for coffee, I accepted his invite. I followed him into the kitchen and sat at the table and we waited for the coffee pot to brew. He placed a steaming mug in front of me.

"Thank you." I said rather quietly as I scooped an unholy amount of sugar into the black liquid. "Jack?"

He looked up. "Yes?"

I bit my lip and closed my eyes as I spoke. "Can I talk to you? About Alison?" I slowly opened my eyes and saw he had put down his paper. I had his full attention now. Now that I had it, I didn't want it, but the question was out in the open.

Jack kept his voice low and steady. "What would you like to know about Alison?"

Again, I bit my lip. I would have to word this just right. "Has she..." I began slowly. "Ever had a history of abuse or anger before?"

Jack's jaw set. "What are you getting at, Abby?"

I winced at his tone. It was accusing and hard. "She seems to have a lot of pent up anger, especially toward me. I was just wondering if that's well...normal I guess? For her?"

Jack's face set into an unreadable mask. "She had a rough go while you were away. Things will get back to normal soon enough."

I stared at him wordlessly, he hadn't really answered my question. I didn't know Jack well enough to pry, especially on such a sensitive issue. Luckily for me, Jack wasn't done. His eyes continued to scrutinize me. "I'm sorry you had to see her like that. It hasn't happened in a very long time. She won't hurt Cara, you don't have to worry about that. She loves her, in her own way. I will talk to her and make sure she understands you are here to help."

"Thanks, Jack. I don't mean to cause any trouble..."

Jack looked up. "Anymore questions?"

Yes, say yes. "No."

Jack picked up his paper once more, and went back to reading. His body language said this conversation was over.

"Thanks for the talk, Jack." I muttered under my breath.

⌘

Cara was asleep with her little arms sprawled over her head. Alex and I had taken her out for a long walk in the morning and the fresh air did its job well. Jack had gone to work and I was left alone with Alison. Her usual polished look was not in effect today. Her bare face made her look worn out. I left the comfort of my bedroom for a glass of water in hopes I could slip back to my room without being noticed.

Alison sat on the couch where she beckoned for me to come over. "Abby? Come here."

I froze and hesitantly made my way into the living room. Alison raised a thin brow. "Well are you going to stand there all day? Sit."

"How are you feeling?" I asked tentatively.

"How do you think I'm feeling? I feel awful," her eyes narrowed. "Jack mentioned I shook you up last night. He's now watching me like a child. I just wanted to thank you for that."

Her tone turned icy. "I think you over reacted, but I shall let it slide. You are just a child after all." Alison suddenly looked bored and began to inspect her nails.

I stared blankly, not too sure how to respond. There was a part of me, a rather large part of me that had begun to fear her. Still, I didn't want to let her know. "I wouldn't say I'm just a child." I protested quietly.

Alison perked up. Her superior stare bore down. "No," she mused. "Perhaps you're not as innocent as everyone thinks." She barked with laughter.

"What is that supposed to mean?"

"I'm not blind, my dear *child*. I have my eye on you. You know," she paused to purse her lips slightly. "I watched you and that neighbor boy when he dropped you off. Something's changed there."

I shivered at the thought of her knowing. "I'm not sure what you're talking about."

"Oh my girl, I think that you know exactly what I'm talking about. I won't lie to you, I am impressed you managed to land that one."

The color drained from my face only to be replaced by a warm heat. Alison gave a sickly sweet smile. "Don't worry, your secret is safe with me."

With that, she strode away.

Mary called late in the afternoon to invite Cara and myself over for dinner. Mary, Alex, and I had a relaxing evening for the most part, when we weren't chasing after Cara. Now that she had found out what her feet and legs could do, she ran with them, literally. After dinner Alex walked me home. He held Cara safely within his arms as she drifted into a happy slumber, his free hand enclosed around mine.

"I can take her from here." I whispered.

He nodded and gently handed Cara over. Her head snuggled into my shoulder with a sleepy gurgle. "I had fun tonight," he glanced up at the house. "Will you be okay here for the night?"

"I think so. I got the impression from Alison that Jack had some serious words with her. I think she'll be okay."

"I hope so." Alex rubbed the back of his neck and frowned slightly. "I don't like you being here."

I squeezed his hand. "I'll be okay, I promise." I smiled teasingly. "Besides, I happen to know a boy who's window is always open for a late night visitor…"

Alex chuckled and wrapped his arm around my waist pulling me into him. "Sweet dreams my tease."

With a quick kiss goodnight, I stepped into the warm house. I peeked into the living room and Alison was passed out on the couch. I tiptoed up the stairs and put Cara down for the night. I closed my door gently and got ready for bed. A sudden thud at my window caused me to jump. I pulled back my curtains and Alex stood below my window dusting snow off his hands.

"What are you doing?" I called down as quietly as I could.

"Is Jack working tonight?"

"He is, why?"

"Where's the warden at?"

I couldn't help but smile. "Asleep on the couch."

"Good. Can you let me in?"

"Here?"

"Yes, why else would I be standing out here freezing?"

I hesitated, but only for a second. "I'll meet you at the back door."

A short moment later I opened up the kitchen door. Alex wore a cheeky grin andI pulled him inside, leading him to my bedroom. "This is pushing it." I muttered.

Alex kicked his boots off and pulled me into his arms. "I don't trust her alone with you. Just for tonight, let me stay. I won't be able to sleep otherwise. I need to know you and Cara will be safe."

Only a fool would argue, and I was no fool. "Deal."

Chapter Nineteen: Run

A knock at my bedroom door sent me jumping out of bed. I quickly looked down and let out a sigh of relief. Alex was gone. I spent the night in his warm embrace and he had set the alarm early and snuck out before the sun rose. I threw on my bathrobe and begrudgingly went to open the door.

Jack greeted me. "Are you feeling okay? You don't normally sleep in."

"I'm fine, thanks."

Jack rubbed his neck, looking rather uncomfortable. "The fridge looks empty. Would you like to join me for a trip to the grocery store?"

"Okay…" I left the sentence hanging. I wasn't used to being included so often.

"Good, are you ready to leave now?"

"I just need to get dressed."

"Okay. I'll wait for you downstairs."

The grocery trip wasn't much of a bonding experience, but it was a start. I couldn't hide my smile. Jack had asked me to go somewhere with him; me, his very own daughter. I peeked over at him, wondering what had brought this on. I knew asking me to join him wasn't particularly easy for Jack, but it sparked hope from within. He was making an effort, no matter how small it was a start. For the remainder of the day, Jack and I had actually gotten along. We even managed to have a few decent conversations. Alison did not appreciate any of it. Her glare darkened as the day went on, and I felt the anger radiating off of her. I began to keep a close eye on her and tried to avoid having my back to her. I was probably over reacting, but somewhere deep inside a silent warning was going off.

After dinner, Cara was fussy so I took over. She offered me an escape for almost two hours. I took her in my room to entertain her for awhile. She tired herself out by eight-thirty, and putting her to bed for the night had been easy. Jack was going over to Mary's for a visit, and lucky for me, he dragged an unenthusiastic Alison with him. I settled onto my bed to finish the last of my homework when I was interrupted by the phone ringing.

"Hello?"

Alex's lively voice filled my ear. "How's my girl doing?"

"I'm doing good. How about you?"

"Pretty good, I suppose. I'm hiding down in my room. I'm pretty sure Mary knows I spent the night with you last night. That woman has the eyes of a hawk."

I couldn't help but laugh. "I'm sorry. However, I did appreciate the company last night."

"So did I." Alex paused. "Abby? Are you sure you're okay over there?"

"Yes, why?"

"It's nothing really…I just worry is all."

At the sound of his concern, uneasiness settled over my chest and held on tightly. I tried to shake it off. Today had been a good day, for the first time since being back in this house I could see the light amongst the darkness. So why did I feel like a storm was brewing?

"Abby, you still there?"

Alex's voice brought me back. "I'm here. Sorry, I was just focused on my homework. I forgot to do it earlier this weekend."

"Ah okay, I'll let you get back to it then. Are we still on for after school tomorrow?"

"Definitely. Goodnight."

"Night, sweet dreams."

Once my essay was out of the way, I turned out my light and tried to fall asleep. It didn't go well. Frustrated, I kicked off my quilt and went downstairs to get a glass of water. Out of the corner of my eye, I noticed Jack's office door was open. I peeked around the house and all was still. Curiosity got the best of me as I inched closer. Jack never left his office open, ever. When I first moved in I was given strict instructions to never set foot in the room. Before I lost my nerve I opened the door wider and stepped inside. The room was dark, and I couldn't see anything. I ran my hands against the wall until my fingers grasped a light switch. I quickly flicked it on. The office was surprisingly neat. A large oak desk held his computer, a lamp, and some files that were neatly stacked to the right. Pictures of his friends and family, other than myself, hung on the wall next to Jack's degrees. My eyes settled onto a small wooden chest that was tucked under the filing cabinet. I sat on the floor and pulled out the handcrafted chest. It had the word *Abby* scribbled neatly in large black letters. I looked around once more, feeling as though I would be caught at any moment.

I carefully pried open the lid. My heart caught in my throat. The chest was filled with pictures of me that my mother had sent over the years. Tears filled my eyes as I wondered why he felt the need to hide them. I rifled through the chest, and his hidden possessions consisted of a set of my baby shoes, my favorite hair scrunchy, and a stack of envelopes. I gently picked up the envelopes and loosened the tie that held them together. My throat swelled as I realized what they were; my letters. I slowly opened one envelope and stared down at my messy writing from so long ago.

> *Where are you Daddy? It's so cold again here tonight. I miss you. Mommy misses you. We can't stop crying and my heart hurts. Was I bad? I don't know what I did, I'm sorry Daddy, so sorry. Please come back. Please, I love you.*

I slid the note quickly back inside. I wasn't ready to read the rest. They hurt too much. A shaky breath escaped my lips. I wondered if the letters affected Jack at all. Surely, they had too. He wasn't made of stone. I pulled my attention away from the letters and began to sift through the photos.

I jumped when Jack's startled voice shot through the quiet. "What are you doing?"

I stood quickly. "Oh, Jack…" I looked down at the open box. It was fairly obvious why I was in here. "Why am I in a box Jack? Why do you keep me locked away?"

Jack looked furious as he marched past me. He slowly knelt down and his eyes looked at the envelopes. He held them so delicately, like they could break at any moment. Jack let out a large sigh. "It's not an easy thing for me to do, reading these letters, and knowing they came from you. You were a little girl…they tore me open."

The room suddenly felt very cold. "I waited for a response, Jack. I waited for so long." I looked at his walls once more. "Why aren't there any photos of me on your walls?"

"Because, I couldn't look at you, Abby. It hurt too much, it still hurts. I ran out on you and your mother, it was my choice. I know that." He turned to face me then. "Do you know what the worst part was? Do you?"

I stepped back from the intensity he exuded. "No."

Jack closed his eyes. "I didn't feel bad about what I had done. It felt good to leave, to be free."

My hand clasped over my heart. "How could leaving us feel good?" I whispered.

"The pain came later…about the time when your letters started coming. I couldn't respond, I didn't know what to say anymore."

Jack lowered his voice. "I still can't look at those pictures of you, they hurt me. Even now, I can barely look at you."

I stared at him, unmoving. I was close to feeling completely numb at this point. Jack rubbed the back of his neck. "I got called in tonight. Alison's still at Mary's. I think Mary's trying to set her straight." Jack turned his back to me. "I'll see you tomorrow."

I watched Jack leave the room. Everything about the way he carried himself told me he was ashamed. I cried myself to sleep that night, and my slumber was an eventful one. In my dream, I heard crying, softly at first. I stood alone in a strange hallway that I'd never seen before. Pictures of me growing up haphazardly hung on a cracked wall; most had begun to fade. The crying started to get louder, and more desperate. I recognized who the cries belonged to, Cara. I began searching the dark rooms, looking for her. Each room I entered was empty. I started calling her name desperately when all of a sudden there she was. Her tiny body looked frail and beaten. Her eyes were puffy from crying. I reached down to pick her up when my arms went limp. She fell to the ground with a dull thud. Her eyes looked up at me wide and frightened, and then she was gone.

I awoke with a start and felt ill at the thought of dropping Cara, even if it was only a dream. A cold sweat trickled down my spine, causing me to shiver. I wandered into the bathroom and splashed cold water on my face. I quietly tiptoed into Cara's room and went weak with relief to see she slept soundly. I quietly shut her door behind me and crawled into my bed, closing my eyes softly. The bedroom floor creaked but I decided to ignore it, I was too tired to move. I turned over onto my back where I was met with a sharp blow against my face. I opened my eyes with a start, and briefly wondered if I was dreaming. A force knocked me from my bed onto the cold hard floor. A searing pain tore through the back of my head as I collided with the night stand. I looked around the room wildly, trying to see what was going on. A warm trickle of blood ran down my face. I tenderly touched my head to investigate the damage. My hair felt sticky and damp from the blood. I stood up quickly, panicking now, blood made me nervous. I ran to the door and then I saw her. I froze in fear. Alison stood in a corner of my room, looking wild and angry. I tried to speak, but no words came out.

She took a step forward and stopped. "Where's Jack?" I managed to say, but my voice was no more than a squeak.

"He's not here. It's just you and me." Her glare darkened. "Do you know whatI had to go through this evening? That silly twit of a neighbor spoke to me like I was an invalid," she gritted her teeth. "I don't like the direction in which this household is heading. I told you to stay out of my way and you chose to ignore me. I think the message needs to be made crystal clear."

I edged back to my bed, and glanced around fiercely for my cell phone. I couldn't see it, I must have knocked it over when I fell. I glanced at Alison once more. She looked calm and collected. I took a step back and something cold brushed against my foot. I looked down, and there it was, my phone.

Alison watched me in interest, and I was cautious not to make any sudden movements. I silently counted to three before making the move for my phone. Alison's eyes widened in rage and she leapt towards me, grabbing my hair. I tried to shove her off of me, but she was strong, and much taller than I was. She slammed me into the wall, but I kept a firm grip on the phone.

"Give it to me!" she shrieked.

I thrashed wildly and managed to grab a chunk of Alison's hair. I shoved her as hard as I could. She fell with a thud to the floor. I ran into the hall and dialed Alex's number. My mind was going a million different directions at once. Should I take Cara out somewhere? My earlier nightmare suddenly flashed through my head. I had never seen Alison this angry before. What if I was holding Cara and she made me drop her? I decided to run for help and come back for Cara, praying it was the right decision. I took the stairs two at a time, and I heard Alison storm behind me. Alex's sleepy voice came into my ear and I faltered slightly.

"Alex! Alex, please help, she's gone craz—" the phone flew out of my hand as Alison clutched my arm.

I twisted to get free when I lost my footing. The ground came up fast and I fell with a sickening crack. Dots clouded my vision and the room began to spin. I screamed out in sudden pain as I tried to sit up. I clutched my left side and crawled instinctively toward my phone. Cara began to cry. I looked around rapidly for Alison. She was nowhere to be seen and that frightened me. I cursed under my breath, I should have called the emergency line first. Panic began to take over my body. My breath came out in short gasps, and my heartbeat was almost deafening. I made one more lunge for the phone but my legs gave out on me. I let out a frustrated sob as my vision began to fade away. Amongst the sound of my thumping heart and the blood coursing in my ears, I heard Alex's voice. I closed my eyes tightly and that's when the darkness took me.

Chapter Twenty: Leave A Memory

I awoke to a steady beep and throbbing pain. I opened my eyes and the room was very bright and slightly out of focus. I blinked a few more times until I could see clearly. It took me a moment to recognize I was in the hospital. I shifted slightly and a sharp pain tore through my side, I let out a quick gasp.

"Hey, take it easy, it's all right now, I'm here." I followed the concerned voice, itwas Alex. He took my hand gently and scooted closer. I smiled weakly. His handsome features were shadowed with concern and fear.

"Where's Cara?" I whispered.

"She's with Mary."

I nodded weakly. "And Jack?"

"He's here, working. He knows you're here. He's come in to check on you a few times already."

I shifted again, only to be met by more painful jabs. I winced. "What's the damage?"

Alex's mouth tightened again. "You broke two ribs and you hit your head pretty good. There was so much blood…" Alex paled considerably. He locked his eyes with mine and they looked shaken. "I thought you were dead when I walked in."

His voice broke and he tore his gaze away to study the ceiling. I squeezed his hand reassuringly. "I'm okay Alex. It's all right. I'm so sorry I called you. I dialed your number purely from instinct."

Alex looked at me quickly. "No, don't be sorry. I'm just glad you're okay."

He gently cradled my face between his hands.

"Can I come in?" Jack stood just outside the door. He looked relieved to see I was up.

"How are you feeling, kiddo?"

I winced. "Uncomfortable."

He nodded. "That was quite the spill you took. Alison was so worried."

I looked from Alex back to Jack in confusion. "She was worried?" My voice startled me, it sounded like I was on the verge of hysterics. "Where is she? Is she here? I don't want her here, I—"

Alex leaned forward to calm me down and Jack looked confused. I looked at Alex wildly. "Where's Alison?"

"I think she's in the waiting room…"

Alex's face looked pained. Jack looked serious. "What's going on?" I demanded.

Jack spoke softly. "Alison tried to calm you down. She said you were upset about something. She didn't know what set you off. She tried to stop you, but when you fell…it really scared her."

"And you believe her? She did this to me, Jack! She—" I winced and hunched over, I had made to many sudden movements too fast.

Alex glared at Jack and muttered a curse. Jack tried to remain composed, but I could tell I had hit a nerve. "Abby, you just had a serious fall. You may not be remembering things clearly. I know you and Alison have had your disagreements but if what you're saying is true, that is a very serious accusation." His eyes grew hard.

I glared at the ceiling, how could he not believe me? What was I going to do now? Would I be safe to go home? My eyes wandered to my wrists. They were bruised with the faintest impression of fingerprints.

I held my wrist up to him. "What about this Jack? She grabbed me and threw me against a wall!" My expression darkened as I saw the hardness fill his features.

"Aren't you trained to spot things like this, signs of abuse? Why won't you believe me?" My voice cracked as I pleaded.

Alex's grip tightened over my right hand, I glanced at him quickly. He glared at Jack. Alex stood over me in a protective stance. I knew if I wasn't in between them, Alex would have lunged. I cleared my throat and tried to wiggle my hand out of Alex's tight grasp, he wasn't aware he was hurting me. "Alex," I whispered, "my hand." He looked down and his face dropped. He released my hand quickly and paled once more.

Jack cleared his throat. "Alison's very distraught right now, she thought you were dead. She grabbed your wrists to stop you from falling."

I let out a sob. "No, that's not what happened."

Jack shook his head and quickly got up, leaving the room swiftly. I stared after him feeling helpless and hurt. Alex's gaze burned into me, I turned to him, feeling a little uneasy.

"Do you believe me?" I whispered.

"Of course I do. When I answered my phone and heard your voice…you sounded terrified. And when I walked in and saw you and her, I knew. It took every ounce of my strength and self-control to not lay a hand on her."

I relaxed slightly, and then sat up quickly. "Has anyone called my mom?"

Alex shook his head. "Not that I know of."

I breathed a sigh of relief. "Okay, good. I don't want her to know, she would go crazy."

Alex and I talked for awhile and somewhere in between I dozed off. It was a peaceful sleep until a shadow crossed my face, blocking the distant light. Cold hands wrapped around my neck. I looked up and saw Alison smile. I tried to squirm but she held me down. My breath was tight but I managed to let out one last curdling scream.

Strong hands gripped onto my shoulders, and shook me gently. My eyes flew open to meet Alex's worried stare. "It was just a dream." I muttered. "It was just a dream."

My hospital stay was short, only a day and a half before I got to go home. Jack picked me up and we drove home in silence. As we pulled into the driveway, he stopped me from getting out of the car. "Just a minute, Abby."

I sat back and waited.

"Don't go in there and start anything. Alison hasn't quite been herself since your accident. She's been going to see a counselor, I think it's helping her."

I glared and got out of the car, slamming the door shut. My little 'accident' was caused by his deranged wife. I walked in and was greeted by Cara who took a few unsteady steps to me. I smiled and slowly knelt down, and Cara threw her little arms around me in a hug.

"I can't believe she's going to be a year old next week." Jack shook his head in disbelief. "She sure did miss you."

Time had sped by. I had been living out here for five months now. "I missed her too." I offered.

"I need to run out and pick up a few things, will you be fine here?"

I nodded stiffly. "Sure."

I felt alone once the front door slammed shut behind me. I stepped into the living room with Cara following at my heels. I plopped down wearily and stiffened when footsteps sounded behind me.

"It's good to see you up and about, Abby."

Alison stood behind me. She made her way over and sat down across from me. "I didn't mean for things to go this far. Truly. I am sorry but the message was received, was it not?"

I nodded curtly.

"Good. I think we will get along just fine from now on."

I stared at her calm appearance and my fear faded into anger. "If you ever lay a hand on me again, you will wish you hadn't."

Alison rose an eyebrow. "I see. Tell me something though. I'm just curious, how does it feel to know your father didn't believe you when you needed him the most? You were scared, were you not?"

I tried to sound steady and sure of myself. "I have someone else on my side."

Alison nodded. "You don't need to worry about me, Abigail. I have made my point crystal clear." She stood and leaned forward. I flinched slightly. She placed a hand gently on the top of my head and stroked my hair. She gave a small smile and glided away.

While Jack was out, I went back into his office. I passed the time looking through old photos when I came across a memory I held close to my heart. I clutched the photo tightly to my chest. I had a copy of this very picture; it stood on my night table after all these years. I set the image aside gently on his desk and scribbled a note to go along with it.

> *Jack,*
> *Don't box up this memory. It was the only picture of you I didn't destroy. It was the only memory left of my father, and it's been kept close to my heart ever since. I hope that it does you some good....don't box it up, don't lock it away. Look at it Jack...look. Let it see the light of day.*

I slipped out of his office and never entered the room again. Once Jack got home, he went straight to his office, and he stayed in there for over an hour. Our paths crossed later in the day and he gave me a strained look. I had hit another nerve.

Alison found me sitting outside on the front steps awhile later. "What did you do to him?"

I looked up in surprise. "Do what to who?"

"To your father! Do you think it's fun to play with people's emotions?"

I stared forward, watching the cars go by. "I don't know what you're talking about."

Alison reefed me up. "Look at me when I'm talking to you!"

Anxiety took over my body. I glared up at her and tore my arm away. "Don't you touch me." I threatened.

I took a step back. Alison didn't notice, she was too busy fuming at the sky. "I don't know what you're trying to do, Abby, but your father's been through enough!"

A shouting match broke out between us. Jack came out holding the picture I had left on his desk. Alison and I stopped shouting as Jack stormed forward. His eyes were red and slightly swollen like he had been crying. Jack looked from Alison to me. "Enough. Alison, go inside. This isn't your concern."

Alison opened her mouth to speak but decided against it. She went inside quickly. In the moment, I felt exposed. I had never seen Jack let his guard down before, it was very unnerving.

"Abby," Jack began wearily. "Alison is all I have, don't you go putting her through this."

"She isn't the only thing you have."

He looked pained. "Yes, she is. Don't you see? If I leave her, if things fall apart here, it makes what I did to you and your mother so much worse. It would have been all for nothing." Jack held up the picture. "Why would you give me this?"

I hesitantly looked his way. "I thought—"

Jack's voice grew angry. "No! You didn't think, that's your problem. You don't think, you just act! I don't want it. I told you, Abigail, I can't look at these things! This photo belongs in the past. I left it all behind me long ago."

I focused my eyes on the ground. "It wasn't an easy thing for me to keep around, Jack."

Jack took a step forward and roughly shoved the picture at me. "Here. Take it. I don't ever want to see things like that again."

"But, Jack…"

"No, Abby. It's a memory I don't want to have. Leave it alone and let me forget."

He slammed the front door shut. I sat down on the porch steps and clutched the picture tightly. "I don't want you to forget…I don't want you to forget me." My voice got lost in the cold winter wind. I studied the picture quietly before setting free a heartbreaking sob.

Chapter Twenty-One: A Beginning And An Ending

I slept somewhat soundly when a whimper woke me. I sat up and clicked on my lamp. Cara stood at my door. "Cara, what are you doing up, what's wrong?" I rose quickly out of bed and scooped her up.

"Bad," she sniffled.

"Aw, kiddo. I'm sorry."

Listening quietly, I heard Jack and Alison arguing again from downstairs. I tried to drown it out. The sounds of their heated voices brought me back to my childhood, and I didn't want Cara to have the same memories. Ever since I had given Jack that picture, the two of them seemed to argue non-stop. Guilt washed over me. Again, I had caused another disturbance in the household.

Cara wriggled and I looked down at her. "How did you get out of bed?"

"Climb-duhed."

I smiled a little. "You sure are a determined little thing. Should we put you back to bed?"

Cara looked up at me teary eyed and shook her head.

"I could read you a story?"

Again, Cara shook her head, this time with more force. I sighed. "All right, do you want to sleep with me tonight?"

Cara nodded her head with a little smile. "Teddy!"

I laughed quietly. "All right, kiddo. C'mon, let's get Teddy." A few moments later we both snuggled in bed, and Cara fell asleep clutching onto her stuffed bear tightly.

⌘

I made it one month longer in the house. Almost every night my sleep was plagued with horrible nightmares and I woke up screaming. I couldn't take it anymore, and I tried hard. The tension in the house grew worse with each passing day. I was jumpy and flighty. My lack of sleep made me snippy and irritable. Jack never did let me bring up "my accident" again, or the picture incident, he didn't want to hear about it. Any of it.

The final straw for my decision to leave came early on a Saturday morning. I suffered from lack of sleep, as per usual, when I decided to go to Alex's. Everyone in the household was up, and Cara saw me getting ready and wanted to come along. I smiled weakly and nodded. She walked with full force now and could almost put together whole sentences. I smiled at the thought; my name had been her first word. It was now early spring and the weather began to show the promise of warmth and new life. A light long sleeve shirt was all that was needed to stay warm these days. Cara and I walked hand in hand. She was a bundle of energy, I on the other hand could barely keep my eyes open. I hoped the fresh air would help clear my foggy haze, but to my dismay, it did no such thing. I looked across the street and Alex waited for us outside. He was going to take us out for breakfast. Cara saw him and squealed with excitement. A wide grin crossed Alex's face and Cara hopped for joy. We met up with him, and he quickly scooped Cara up in his arms for a warm greeting.

He glanced at me and his face fell. "I thought you were going to get some sleep last night," he spoke quietly.

I glared at him, this was becoming a regular argument between us. I tried not to snap at him, but I was so overtired it didn't take much to set me off. Instead I shot him a strained look. "Not now, Alex. And I tried to sleep. Believe me, I did."

He pursed his lips and shot me a look, promising we would discuss this later. Alex set Cara in the car seat, and to my dismay I realized I had forgotten my wallet. "Shoot, I'll be right back."

Alex didn't have time to respond. I turned and began walking away. I studied the ground absently, wondering where I had placed my wallet. I was halfway across the street when Alex began to call my name frantically. I stopped to look at him and he ran toward me. His voice finally registered within my ears. "Truck." It all happened so quickly; I turned in horror as a pickup headed my way. The driver must have slammed on the breaks for a horrible squealing sound erupted beneath the trucks tires. The truck skidded sideways, and it stopped inches away from me. I stood there frozen, unable to move until Alex yanked me out of the way. The driver cursed at me and took off.

Alex turned me around, his face was pale but he was angry. "Dammit Abby! What the hell were you thinking? Are you trying to get yourself killed?"

I looked up at him, shaking wildly. "N-No. I..I didn't see it."

Alex stared at me in disbelief and released me. He turned around and started running a stream of words that made me wince. I had told him the truth; I hadn't seen the truck. I looked over at Alex's car and Cara's little head peeked out. I felt ill. What if Cara had been with me at the time? I would have never forgiven myself if anything happened to her, especially if it was my fault.

Alex stared at me, rage sparking in his green eyes. "How much longer are you going to keep this up? I can't stand by anymore and watch you do this to yourself."

I wound my hands in my hair and held them there. I still saw the blue truck speeding my way. "I didn't see the truck," I whispered.

Alex sighed and brought me close to him. His arms fell over me like a security blanket until I broke free. "I don't know what to do anymore."

His eyes took in the house. "How are things in there?"

I shook my head. "Horrible," I muttered. "Ever since the accident the air has been so thick, it's stifling. I was making such progress with Jack but now he watches my every move like I'm going to have some sort of breakdown. And the way he talks to me…it's as though he's waiting for me to set his world on fire."

I broke off and looked at the house. A heavy sadness fell over me that almost swept me off my feet. "I don't like who I'm becoming. I'm tired, cranky, and just overall miserable. I don't know how you've put up with me for so long."

Alex smiled weakly. "I'm stronger than I thought."

I broke a small grin at that and shoved him playfully. Alex studied me before he spoke. "How do they treat Cara?"

I frowned thoughtfully. "Jack's good with her. And Alison…" I smiled suddenly, "Cara doesn't like her much, even Jack sees that."

Alex laughed. "The kid's got good taste."

I nodded. "Still…Alison wouldn't hurt her. She likes to show her off when she takes her out, for appearance's and all."

Alex nodded thoughtfully. He took my hands in his and met my gaze softly. "I have been wanting to say this for quite some time, but you were never ready. Ready, or not, I'm going to say it now. Abby, move in with me and Mary."

I looked at Alex wide eyed. "Are you kidding me?"

"Nope."

"I don't know. Are you sure? We would see each other a lot…"

Alex's grin widened. "I know. Every day, that's kind of what I'm going for."

I bit my lip thoughtfully. "How would Mary feel about that?"

"She loves you. To be honest, I think she'd sleep a helluva lot better knowing you're safe. So would I," he paused. "It wouldn't be forever. Once I'm done with school we can get our own place."

I thought out loud. "I would still be close to Cara…" I looked up at Alex, pondering my options. Alex waited patiently, as he always had with me. He was my safe place, he was always my safe place. He was my home. "Okay. Let's do it."

⌘

Four months later I sat in the back row with Ali. We were dawned in our graduation gowns amongst a slew of excited students. This was it, the ending of a chapter, and the beginning of the rest of our lives. Once the final speech was given, we all tossed our hats into the air and cheered. Afterwards, I forced my way through the crowd and found my mom, who smiled proudly as tears ran down her face. Mark was there and he held her comfortingly. Alex sat next to them smiling proudly, he was the first to grab me in a congratulatory hug, followed by many others.

Jack was there as well. He had brought Cara along who was dressed up in a cute blue dress with a matching bow in her hair. She pushed her way past the others and jumped up to give me a hug. I turned to Jack and he extended his hand. His face wore a pained smile. I stared down at his hand and took it gently. He gave me a quick handshake. "Congratulations."

I thanked him politely and gave him silent props for sitting so close to my mother. I looked at my mom and gave Mark a silent thank you. He had done a great job of keeping her reigned in. For most of the ceremony it looked like she wanted to pick up a chair and slam Jack with it. The evening was filled with a festive party for all the graduates and their parents. The event was hosted by Laura's parents. Near the end of the evening, I sat in a quiet spot reflecting on the past year. I still couldn't believe I had survived everything that had been thrown my way, and now it was all over. Alex's offer had been a blessing. I felt safe in his house and was able to sleep. The nightmares faded away after the first few months. As my luck would have it, I was able to be apart of Cara's daily routine. I was granted access to get her up in the mornings and tuck her in at night. It was a fight for me to get in the house at first, but after the first week of Alison banning me completely, she was forced to change her mind when Cara became sullen and depressed, that's when Jack had laid down the law. And so began my routine. If I was lucky, I was able to have Cara over for Friday night sleepovers.

My mom found me quickly and sat beside me. "How does it feel, honey?"

I stretched out my arms. "Amazing. It's like this huge weight has been lifted off of me."

She gave me a quick hug. "I'm so proud of you! I can't believe how grown up you are already." Mom looked teary eyed and her voice was thick in emotions.

"Please don't cry, Mom. I don't want to start up again!" I gave my mom a half smile. "And thanks for behaving yourself."

She gave me a stern look. "You're welcome. It wasn't easy," she frowned. "If he had brought that woman along with him, I'm afraid all bets would have been off the table."

My mother's voice grew serious. "I'm sorry Jack's been such a disappointment to you. But you know, he really is proud of you."

I nodded slightly. "I saw it in his eyes today."

Mom frowned again. "Typical Jack, he only realized how wonderful you were once you left. And that little girl of his, she sure is cute, and boy, does she loves you."

I smiled. "I know."

My mother's voice turned taunting. "Speaking of love…Alex sure is a nice young man. I really like him."

I blushed. "Yes, he is. He's been my life saver."

"He loves you, you know."

"Mom…"

"I'm serious, Abby. The way that boy looks at you, that's something special." She smiled and held out her hand. "Come on, let's join the party!"

I followed my mom and Alex found me. He wore a playful grin on his face and he grabbed me, hauling me onto the dance floor. I spent the rest of the evening dancing in his arms.

⌘

Summer past in a blur. Alex and I had taken Cara on several camping trips. Alex graduated from University and received a job offer in the city. We spent the next few weeks looking at houses and we managed to find a cute place in a friendly neighborhood, still close to the college. That summer, our lives changed. Alex and I moved out of Mary's place and I worked most of the summer to save up for school. Time passed quickly, I was already half way through my first year of college. With each passing day, Jack and I grew more and more distant; any relations that we had forged were being erased quickly. I remained close to Cara, often picking her up after daycare. We settled into a routine that allowed me to spend a few hours with her before I had to bring her home. We had worked out a system for Cara's sake; every other weekend she would come and stay with Alex and me.

A few weekends ago, we decorated one of the spare rooms, one that Cara could call her own. The memory made me grow content as I remembered leading Cara into her new bedroom. I watched her brilliant blue eyes light up like a Christmas tree. That was a good day. It was now Friday afternoon, and it wasn't going so well. I was in a foul mood all morning, Jack had begun to play games with me. Jack was late…again. This had started to become a habit with him. The plan was simple. In order to salvage some sort of a relationship with Jack, I had come up with the idea that he would drop Cara off at the coffee shop where we would have a quick cup of coffee and attempt to have a civil conversation before he went on his way. The plan had worked well for the first two weekends, but lately the plan came to a halt. Sometimes Jack would be up to two hours late, other times he wouldn't show up at all. It was always the same. I would call him, frustrated, and he would claim he forgot, or he would tell me to pick up Cara myself. Today was one of those days. He was over an hour late and I waited for him like a fool, yet again. I grabbed my cell phone and dialed his number impatiently.

"Hello?"

"Jack, this is Abby, where are you?"

"Oh, I'm—"

I jumped slightly when a loud crash shot through the background. A female's voice hissed. Jack spit out an impatient remark, and then he cleared his throat. "Abby, we're having some delays here. Do you think you can pick Cara up? And possibly even keep her for a week or so?"

My anger faded and quickly turned into concern. "Sure, is everything okay?"

Jack sighed loudly. "It's fine. Alison and I just need some freedom for awhile."

"I'm on my way."

I didn't want Cara to feel the same way I felt about Jack, if one of his daughters could have a decent relationship with him, then I would consider it a win. As I headed to Jack's house, worry began to gnaw at me. He better not leave her. He said he simply needed some freedom. What kind of freedom? How long, and how far would that freedom take him? Is that what he said before he left my mom and me?

I pulled up in front of Jack's house and knocked at the door. Jack answered it and Cara bounced behind him. "Abby!" she squealed and ran at me to give my leg a fierce hug.

"Hey, munchkin, ready for some fun?"

Cara smiled. "Yup!"

I nodded for Jack to follow me. He didn't. I growled silently and helped Cara into her car seat. "I'll be right back, okay?"

Cara nodded, and I went back and knocked loudly on the front door. Jack opened it up looking wary. "Yes?"

"What's going on, Jack? You are coming back for her, aren't you?"

Jack's wary look quickly turned into anger. "Of course I am!" He snapped. "Do you really think I would leave her?"

I raised my eyebrows. "You haven't given me any reason to think differently."

Jack rubbed the back of his neck. "Knock it off, Abby. I won't leave her, ever."

I nodded slowly. "Fine. Call me when you're ready for her again."

I walked back to my car when I heard Jack call out. "You've done good for yourself, right?"

I turned around to face him. "Yes, we have." I lowered my voice wearily. "I've been trying to keep in touch with you, but you have made that near impossible."

Jack nodded. "I know. I think it's best this way."

I straightened up. "Would it honestly hurt for you to acknowledge I'm your daughter too?"

Jack stepped back. "I think it's best if we don't get to know each other."

"Why? What would be so wrong with getting to know me?"

"Too much time has passed between us. Cara's my second chance at being a father. I don't know how to do this with you. I don't know if I can." He met my eyes for a split second. "Drive safe."

I stood alone in the driveway and watched him walk inside. He closed the door quietly behind him. So, that was it. That was how he chose to end things. I turned slowly and walked back to the truck. Cara peered out at me. Her little feet bounced excitedly as she clutched her teddy bear with a secure grasp. I smiled, if that couldn't brighten my day a little, then nothing could.

I hopped inside and turned to face her. "Alrighty kiddo, let's go home."

⌘

"So that's it, that's all he said to you?" Alex sat next to me his face in disbelief.

"Are you really that surprised?"

Alex sighed and drew me closer to him. "I guess not. I had hoped he would wake up. I'm sorry that's how it went down, babe. It's his loss." He kissed me lightly on the top of my forehead. I snuggled deeper under the covers while Alex stretched beside me.

"Tomorrow will be a better day," he whispered in my ear.

I hummed softly, hoping he was right. One week later Jack called saying they wanted Cara back home. I held a mixture of feelings on the subject; one was relief they were in fact coming back for her, and the other was sadness. I really enjoyed having Cara around. Alex and I sat next to Cara on her bedroom floor. We helped her gather her things together and she wasn't happy about it. She had her lower lip pushed out in a pout.

"What's wrong Cara?"

"Stay here," she whimpered.

Alex smiled a little, but his eyes looked sad. "You want to stay here?"

Cara nodded and plopped down on her carpet with a thud. "We love having you here, Cara, but your mom and dad want to see you too."

Cara shook her head fiercely. "No, don't like her."

Alex and I exchanged a look. "Don't like who?"

"Her!" Cara almost growled the word. "Bad."

Alex shot me a concerned look and whispered. "Did you check her for bruises?"

Panic shot through me, but I relaxed quickly. "I have never seen any on her."

I studied Cara. "Cara? Alison's bad?" Cara opened her eyes wide and nodded 'yes.'

"Can you tell me why she is bad?" I prodded gently.

Cara held her arms wide. "Angry, grrr."

I smiled a little, Alison was a very angry woman, even a two year old could see that.

"Okay," I said reluctantly. "It's time to go."

Cara's face was torn, and she pouted. "No!"

My voice was pained. "Come on, Cara, let's go."

Cara stood and shook her head. "Stay, please!"

I looked at Alex helplessly. He nodded and scooped her up. Cara started to cry. Alex soothed her while I quickly collected her things and followed them out to the car. Alex hopped in the driver's seat and I slid into the passenger side. Cara screamed and cried for the whole ride. Once we pulled in Jack's driveway, I quickly unbuckled Cara and carried her to the front door, Alex followed. I gave him a silent look of gratitude. He was always there when I needed him.

Jack opened the door and looked surprised. "What's wrong with her?"

"She didn't want to come back." I had to nearly shout over Cara's cries.

Jack's eyebrows furrowed. "I see. Here, let me take her."

I hesitated and reluctantly handed her to Jack. Alison stood close by, and she scooped her out of Jack's arms.

"No! Down!" Cara started to squirm. Alison tried soothing her, but it didn't work. Cara held out her hands in a desperate attempt toward me. "No! Abby! Down, now!"

Alison glared at me and walked away with a still screaming Cara. I looked at Jack wide eyed. "I've never seen her act that way before!"

Jack looked sullen. "Yeah, well we see it quite often." His face turned grim. "How about that? I see her every day and already she's tired of me."

I felt pity for him then, but it didn't last long. I had hoped that maybe his heart would ache in the moment like mine had for the majority of my life.

I cleared my throat. "She said Alison was 'bad.' Do you know anything about that?"

Jack glared. "That's not really your concern."

Alex squeezed my hand reassuringly. "Actually, it is our concern."

Jack leaned against the doorway. "Mothering doesn't come naturally to Alison. You took over on that part, Abby. You have been there for Cara since was seven months old. She's chosen to bond to you I suppose."

I nodded slowly. "That sort of makes sense, but why would Cara call her bad?"

Jack smiled. "Alison doesn't know how to play the games right."

"What games?"

"The ones you and Cara made up together. Look, Alison has me to help her out, we'll be all right."

Something didn't feel right to me. "What about when Alison's alone with her?"

"She can't be alone with her," Jack snapped.

His reaction did nothing to soothe my concern. "Why not?"

"Because she can't handle it, that's why. Are you happy now? Go on, feel free to pry into our private lives some more."

"That's enough, Jack." Alex snapped. "Abby's done nothing but try and help you since she's arrived. She's just trying to understand what's going on here."

"Well, now you know. Please leave."

I nodded and snuck a peek inside the house. It looked tidy. "Fine, but if you need help, you know my number."

Jack rose his voice. "Wait."

I turned and waited. Jack looked clearly confused. "Why do you do it, Abby? Why won't you quit? Why do you keep coming back?"

I took a step forward. "It's simple. Until you acknowledge the fact that I'm your daughter, I will always try. And I need to know that my little sister is safe."

Jack managed a half grin. "You are persistent, aren't you?"

"I like to think of it as a quiet confidence. Kind of like yours."

Jack's eyes opened wide, and he stepped back. "No, you didn't get anything from me," he mumbled under his breath.

I didn't say a word. I stared at him accusingly, it was just one hit after another. Alex's hand slipped into mine and he led me gently to the car. "Hey," he tipped my chin up. "I see you."

I smiled. "I see you too."

⌘

It was very early in the morning when a loud pounding noise on the door woke us. Alex mumbled. "Stay here, I'll get it."

I sat in bed for about five seconds, then followed after him. I was surprised to see Jack at the door with Cara and some of her belongings.

"What are you doing here?" I asked in surprise.

Jack looked at me apologetically. "I need to take care of some important things today. I thought Cara would be better off here for the day."

Alex took Cara's hand gently. "I'll take her to her room."

"Thanks." I whispered as he gently slipped past. I invited Jack inside, and he accepted reluctantly. I crossed my arms. "Don't worry, I won't bite."

He smiled a little at that. "I've brought some of her things."

"Okay, thanks." I looked at the items he had brought, there was much more than usual.

Jack spoke a little harsher than necessary. "Alison and I are going out tonight, you don't mind if Cara stays the night, do you?"

"Of course not."

His posture relaxed. "Thanks, I'll pick her up tomorrow."

"Okay, see you later."

I watched Jack walk out to his truck. He hesitated before turning back to me. He looked nervous and unsure of himself. I should have enjoyed watching him squirm, but apart of me felt like I needed to throw him a lifeline, and so, I met him halfway. The closer I got to Jack, the more nervous I began to feel myself. He looked completely vulnerable but he gazed back at me with slight wonder.

"How do you do it?" He asked mystified.

I studied him curiously. "Do what?"

"This!" he gestured with his arms. "You keep giving me chance after chance, aren't you tired yet?"

"Exhausted." I smiled.

Jack looked away and then his eyes bore into mine. "You have my eyes."

His words surprised me. It got hard to breath. Jack finally saw me, my own father finally looked back at me, acknowledging me in his own way. My heart held a strange tug, something I had never felt before. Self-consciously I placed a hand over my chest, letting it act as a shield. Jack took a step closer, really studying me now. He nodded as if to himself, and then he held out his hand. I looked down at it. He wanted to settle this on a handshake? No, that wouldn't do. I took a step closer and threw my arms around him. He stiffened in shock, surprise, or disgust, I wasn't sure. I let him go and took a step back pleased to see his eyes were strangely bright. I knew in that moment, he would never say the words I longed to hear, but in our own silent way, it was a start, a small gesture towards moving past the hurt.

"It's just a hug, Jack." He nodded stiffly and I smiled. "It's never too late, as long as you're willing to fight."

I decided to leave it at that, and walked inside. Alex greeted me with a grin on his face. "Did you see?" I nearly squealed.

He returned the smile and he pulled me against him. "I saw the whole thing. You're relentless. Congratulations, babe."

"Thank you!" I said happily.

The day passed quickly and I was full of hope. I found I got ahead of myself, I began to imagine a full house for Christmas. Cara was in good spirits and we had tuckered her out for bed by playing hide and go seek. I fell asleep feeling light and happy; things were coming together. It had taken awhile, but it was finally happening. I settled into a pleasant dream when strange lights flickered through the bedroom. I woke up to find that I was the only one in bed. Voices floated up from downstairs. I rolled over to check the time. It was two-thirty in the morning. The blue and red lights flickered against the wall like a candle burning out. It left me with an eerie feeling. I got up and threw on a sweater, and headed downstairs. I followed the voices into the living room and found Alex sitting down. He looked pale and upset. My eyes flashed to the two police officers who stood before him. My glance met Alex and he saw me before anyone else noticed I was there. He got up abruptly and walked over to me with forced speed. I felt cold and panic began to stir.

"Abby, come sit with me, okay?" He glanced down and squeezed me reassuringly. "I've got you. We're going to get through this."

I didn't argue, I let him take me. I eyed the officers who looked at me solemnly. Get through what? Whatever news was about to come my way wasn't going to be good.

"Are you Abigail Taylor?" One of the officers asked gently.

"Yes," I choked out.

"I am so sorry to tell you this, but there was an accident tonight involving Jack Halett, your father?"

Alex nodded for me when I gave no response. I gripped his hand tightly. My eyes fell to the window outside. I was confused, the weather was clear, the roads should be fine.

"Miss Taylor?" I looked at them helplessly and waited for them to tell me something I could grasp on too. "I'm sorry, but there was a fatality." The officer lowered his voice. "Mr. Halett was pronounced dead upon our arrival. There was another passenger, with him, Alison Halett."

The officer stopped and waited for a reaction. When there was none, he continued slowly. "Mrs. Halett has sustained serious injuries, but at this point it looks like she's going to pull through. From what we can gather at this time, it appears the other driver was intoxicated. He ran a red light and—"

I stared up at the officers blankly. I could see their mouth's moving, but I heard no sound. I let go of Alex's hand and stared out the window, hypnotized by the flashing lights. Alex's eyes were glued to me and he squeezed me gently. I turned to him and stared blankly. His mouth moved as well. As hard as I tried, I couldn't make out what he said. I slowly turned back to the officers and pretended to listen. I knew everything I needed to know; Jack was dead.

Chapter Twenty-Two: The Funeral

After the officers left, I sat in shock for a few hours. When the sun rose, I left to go to the hospital. Alex drove me and when we arrived I found out which room Alison was in. I didn't know why I was here, but for some reason, I needed to see her.

Alex held my arm. "Are you sure you want to do this?" His green eyes looked worried and upset.

I shook my head slowly. "Yes. I need to do this. Please keep an eye on Cara."

He nodded and turned his attention back to Cara who sleepily leaned against his right shoulder. Alex wrapped one arm around her and sat deeper in his seat. I hesitated outside of Alison's door. I studied her lying in the bed, she appeared to have taken quite the beating. I stepped inside the room.

Alison looked at me slowly. "What do you want?"

My eyes quietly assessed her. The right side of her face was bruised and swollen, she had a large gash on the top of her forehead, and her right arm was in a cast that went up to her shoulder. Her hair was tousled and her eyes looked puffy. She pulled her brows together. "What do you want?" she repeated.

"I—I don't know." I whispered.

Alison let out a single laugh. "Did you come here to pay your respects? Or did you come here to place your pity on me?"

I wrapped my arms around myself. "Do you remember what happened?"

Alison's face fell and she looked away. She took a shuddery breath. "I remember his screams. It was so loud. The truck came out of nowhere. Once I saw it, I started to yell at Jack to do something. He tried—" her voice broke but she continued. "I felt the impact. Glass was everywhere. Jack didn't scream long after that. When he grew silent I knew…"

Tears slipped out of the corner of my eyes as the reality of it all settled in. "I'm so sorry."

Alison looked at me harshly. "He's gone and you never even got to know him. Or should I say he never got to know you? It's too late now, Abby, you missed your chance. What do you have to say about that?"

Her words felt like a cold hard slap against my face. I took a deep breath and shook my head backing away from her. I was almost out the door when she called out. "He put pictures of you up in his office. He said it was time for you to see the light."

I stopped in my tracks and turned around slowly. "What?"

Alison looked bitter. "After you left, he spent a lot of time in that office. I peeked inside one day and found him rummaging through a box with all of your things inside. He said he kept you locked away for so long that it was time for you to break free."

My jaw dropped as I took it all in. Alison's face turned over. "That doesn't mean he loved you, Abby. He said he was tired of running from the memories so he thought it was about time he faced them. He said those pictures haunted him for so long, they found him in his dreams…"

Alison locked her eyes with mine and began to sob. "That doesn't mean he loved you."

⌘

It was now my fourth day in bed. I curled up in pajama's and my hair was pulled into a messy pony tail. The morning I had received the horrible news about Jack, Alex and I decided we should tell Cara. She didn't quite understand what we meant, all she could grasp was that I was upset, and that upset her. We decided not to push the issue further and I slipped into a debilitating mourning. Alex took time off work to support and watch over me. News spread fast of Jack's passing and Mary was the first one on our doorstep. Alex invited her to stay with us for a few days to help out. In my silent grief, I had never given a single thought as to what Alex was surely going through himself. It was such a strange feeling knowing someone you had just touched, just spoken to was gone forever. A selfish part of me was so angry that Alison was still around. Why her? What did she have to offer the world that Jack couldn't?

For the next few days the phone wouldn't stop ringing. On the other end of the line it was always the same; emotional voices telling us how sorry they were. Every time I heard the phone ring I shuddered in annoyance, it was a constant reminder of why people were calling in the first place. Next came the unexpected visitors who showed up to bring casseroles. It was meant to be a gesture of kindness, but I never understood it, who could eat in a time like this anyways. I brought my knees to my chest and tried to turn off my brain. I didn't know why I was so upset, I had spent most of my life hating Jack. Ever since I moved out here, our relationship had been rocky. It wasn't until the very end there seemed to be hope. Maybe I wasn't mourning Jack at all. Perhaps I was grieving the loss of things that could have been.

The bedroom door creaked open and Alex stepped inside. He peeled the covers off of me. "Come on, Abby, time to get up. You need to eat something."

I sat up and shot him a look, and tore the covers back. Alex sighed, and this time he ripped the covers off and dropped them to the floor. "Abby, you need to eat something."

"I'm not hungry."

Alex sat next to me and he softened his tone. I turned my back to him. He leaned down and stroked my hair. "I know how hard this is for you. I can't even imagine the emotions that must be going on in your head. But trust me, you can't let yourself get lost in the grief. Don't hold on to it, let it go."

I knew why he was worried. I wasn't sleeping, or eating for that matter. But what made him nervous was the fact that I hadn't cried or even spoke about it. Alex continued. "When my uncle Robbie died it was the hardest thing I had ever gone through in my entire life. I still remember the empty pain."

"I thought my life was never going to move again, everything stood still. I was in a dark haze and at the time, it almost felt good; easier, like if I didn't deal with it, or if I stayed mad at the world the pain wouldn't find me. But Abby, holding on to all of that pain nearly destroyed me. I won't let it happen to you. I love you too much to watch you go through that. I'm here for you. We will get through this, together. You are not alone."

The tears began to well now. I remembered the horrible way in which Alex's uncle was taken from the world, and I couldn't even imagine having to deal with that. Alex and his uncle were close, almost like father and son, while my father and I were merely strangers. I slowly sat up, facing Alex as he rose with me. I avoided his eyes, I couldn't look at him, not yet. He didn't rush me, but then again, he never did. Instead, he traced the line of my jaw softly with his fingertip, and tucked a flyaway hair behind my ear. I raised my eyes to his and saw the sadness and despair buried within.

"He's really gone....I had just spoken to him Alex. We were right outside on the driveway. We were going to fix things. He finally looked at me! For the first time, he really looked at me…"

Alex didn't say anything, he just waited. I winced, and grabbed at my chest. "It hurts so much. It won't stop, I can't make it go away."

The tears started then and I couldn't stop them. Alex held me in the safety of his arms as sobs racked my body. Once my tears quieted, Alex left me alone in bed. My eyes felt heavy from the tears I let escape. I pulled the blanket tightly over my head, I didn't want to see anything. A sound from the bedroom caught my attention. I listened and heard whispers coming from my room. I pulled the blanket lower and peeked out. Alex crouched in front of Cara and they looked deep in conversation. Even from this distance I could see Cara's big eyes were wide and full of concern.

"Sleeping?" Cara whispered loudly.

Alex nodded. "She's not feeling too good, sweetie."

Cara looked back at me with an almost horrified look. I giggled at that, and sat up a little. "Hi, Cara."

Cara bounced, sending her little curls bouncing. My eyes wandered to a large piece of paper that she clutched tightly. "What do you have there?"

Cara looked from Alex to myself with a large smile. "Card!"

Alex smiled and elaborated. "She wanted to make you a get well card."

My heart tightened with emotion as I imagined Cara and Alex working on a project together. "Let's see it. Come on up." I moved over and patted to an empty spot next to me.

Alex swooped her up and placed her on the bed. Cara crawled and plopped next to me and handed over the card proudly. I took it and smiled, admiring the colorful image. "It's beautiful, thank you, Cara." I gave her a kiss on the top of her head.

Cara turned to me seriously. "Better now?"

I laughed. "Better now."

Alex smiled in relief as he flopped down next to us. "How are you doing today?"

I shrugged my shoulders. "I feel pretty drained."

Alex smiled sadly. "And your heart, how does it feel?"

I took a cautious breath. "It's still torn."

He grabbed my hand and held it protectively. I glanced down at Cara who stretched out comfortably next to me. I suddenly wondered what was going to happen to her.

⌘

I couldn't hide forever. Cara was my motivation to get up. After I showered and dressed in a clean outfit, I found Alex. Mary was still here and she had offered to take Cara out for a walk, who was beyond thrilled at the idea. She wanted to pick some pretty flowers.

I looked at Alex hesitantly. "Have you heard how Alison's doing?"

"She's still in the hospital. She broke her arm and hit her head pretty good, but it sounds like she's going to pull through."

"I see."

Alex stroked my arm reassuringly. I sat down and put my hands in my hair. "What about Cara? What's going to happen to her? I don't know if I can just hand her over to Alison." I pursed my lips as I remembered Cara's latest reaction to her.

Alex spoke gently. "Jack's lawyer has been trying to reach you. He wants to discuss a few things."

"Oh." My eyes widened. "Well, that's good I guess."

Alex nodded. "It's better than nothing, right? Do you want me to make the arrangements?"

"Sure." Something about what Alex said didn't sit right with me, what was it? *Arrangements.* "Alex....who's in charge of Jack's funeral?"

Alex stiffened and turned to me. "No one's offered yet."

I was horrified. "He's been gone for five days now! Where is he, just lying on a slab somewhere? Oh no, Alex—"

Alex strode over to me and held my shoulders. "Hey. Look at me, Abby. Remember to breathe. He's safe. It's not your fault, don't even go there."

"I need to make arrangements, don't I?" I asked quietly, a new set of tears forming.

"You don't have to do anything."

I bit my lip, if I didn't who would? Jack was a well respected man. He was good to his neighbors and patients. People admired him. He deserved to be remembered. The question was, why was no one else stepping in? Were they waiting for a family member to take over? Were they waiting for Alison to get better? Was I strong enough to handle this, bringing people together to remember a man I barely knew?

Mary solved that problem for me. While Alex was setting up a meeting with Jack's lawyer, Mary and Cara came in. Cara hopped around like a bunny with a handful of colorful flowers. I smiled at the way Mary gazed down at Cara, her eyes filled with affection.

"Abby! Look, pretty!" Cara thrust her tiny hand in the air and clutched tightly to the colourful bouquet.

I smiled, knelt down, and took a sniff of the vibrant bundle. "Very pretty, they smell good too! Should we put them in some water?"

Cara nodded excitedly and followed me with a bounce in her step. As I filled up the vase, I watched Cara out of the corner of my eye. I wondered how she could be so happy. When she finally understood what happened, would she shed a tear? Would her little heart break? I dropped the flowers neatly into the vase and put them on the kitchen table. Cara climbed up onto a chair and plopped down to admire her flowers. I smiled and gave her some coloring items, she wanted to draw her latest infatuation.

A gentle pressure gripped my arm and I looked to see Mary beside me. "Can we talk somewhere quiet?"

"Of course."

I led Mary into the living room and sat down next to her. She looked at me seriously. "How are you doing, dear?"

I thought I was okay until I tried to answer. My words failed me and the tears once again blinded my vision. I sniffed them back in frustration. "I'm sorry, I don't know why I keep doing this!" I said exasperated.

Mary patted my hand. "It's all right. You have suffered a large loss, let them out if you need too."

"You sound like Alex." I mumbled.

Mary smiled and spoke sadly. "He'll be good for you. He will get you out of the dark tunnel."

"I know he will." I whispered.

Mary watched me thoughtfully. "This isn't easy but I've known Jack for many years, he was a good friend." Mary studied me. "I didn't always agree with his choices, but he was a good man with a large heart."

Her face drifted at some faraway memory only she could see. Tears welled behind my eyes as Mary let her tears fall freely. I clasped her hand in a comforting manner, and waited for her to finish. She cleared her throat and continued. "If you wouldn't mind, I would like to handle the funeral arrangements. I feel it's the only way I can pay him back for all that he has done for me."

I nodded unable to speak. Mary squeezed my hand a little harder, drawing my attention back to her. Mary's eyes were warm and bright as she continued. "I know Jack never made things easy on you, but he loved you in his own way. You brought great pride into his world, and I'm honored you are a part of Alex's life, mine too for that matter."

I looked at her speechless. She smiled softly as her hand rose up to her chest. I knew the gesture well these days. I leaned in to hug her, she returned the embrace, and let her silent sobs break free. They sent fresh pain ripping through my already shattered heart.

⌘

Alex and I sat hand in hand in the lawyer's office. My heart pounded as I studied the elderly gentleman in a black suit, his face and eyes offered no hints of what was to come.

"Alison will keep the house and vehicles, as well as the furniture. And you Miss Taylor," the man lowered his glasses and looked at me in somewhat disbelief. "Will serve as the legal guardian for Cara Halett."

My body went limp from relief. Alex wore a proud grin. The man cleared his throat. "Jack came to see me on Cara's first birthday. He was dead set on appointing you as her legal guardian." The man's eyes narrowed. "It was against my advice."

Alex glared at the man as he continued. "You are free to go to the house and collect Cara's things. You will receive monthly sums to help out with her care. Alison will have the right to visit her, of course, but the majority of her time will be spent with you."

The man rifled through his paperwork and held out his hand. "This is also for you."

I leaned forward and took the envelope out of his hand. He looked at us with cold eyes. "That's all."

We thanked him and left his office. As soon as we were out, I threw my arms around Alex and he picked me up briefly. "She gets to stay with us!" I nearly squealed.

"It's where she belongs."

I didn't read my letter until two days after I had received it; the day of Jack's funeral. My mother arrived, without Mark. She felt the need to pay her respects alone, as she joked all the memories she and Jack shared weren't all bad. The morning of the funeral I sat in my closet wearing a black dress. I stared at the letter, not knowing what it would contain. I stroked the font softly and tore open the top of the envelope and delicately unfolded the paper. I took a deep, controlled breath before I let my eyes wander to the words scribbled neatly.

Abigail:

If you're reading this; then I am no longer here; that might be a good thing for you. After a lot of thought, I have decided to leave Cara in your care. You have always had a way with her, and the way I see her look at you...I don't want to be responsible for taking that away. I have already taken too much from you.

This letter will also serve as my apology. I am sorry I could never say it to your face. When I left your mother, I also left you. I never did go back, and I don't know why. But looking at you over the past year it does my heart good to know you are apart of me; the better half, no doubt. You have more courage than anyone I have ever known. You will go far in this world, Abby. I need you to know one more thing; I did see you; I always have.

-Jack Halett; your father.

I folded the letter up and carefully placed it in my drawer. I went to the washroom and stared at my reflection. I could see Jack's eyes staring back at me, and it was then that I crumpled over and let the sobs escape loudly. As I made my way downstairs, my heart felt hollow and my head felt light. I stepped into the foyer and my family wore a sea of black. Alex was dressed in a black suit, my mother wore a black dress and she had her hair down the way Jack had always liked it. Cara was also in a little black dress with a bow in her hair, she insisted on that part.

We walked out to the car silently and got in without a word. Cara was uncharacteristically quiet. She didn't quite understand what was going on, but she knew it was serious. Cara knew that today was the day we would say goodbye to Jack. She understood he was sleeping and would never wake up. We pulled into the church and walked inside. I held onto Cara's hand tightly as she followed with a sad expression on her face. Once we were inside, I gasped slightly; the whole town had shown up. Sad eyes looked my way and weeping people filled the room. I tried to ignore the sounds of sniffles and escaped sobs. We found our seats near the front row and sat down quietly. Cara crawled into my lap and I hugged on to her tightly. She placed her teddy bear in her lap and looked around with wide eyes.

Alison sat in the next row over. Her face was still bruised. She looked my way and her features went cold. I knew what that look was. A part of her mourned Jack, while the other part was furious at him. Jack had left me with the most precious thing of them all; Cara, for she held a piece of Jack and he left it to me. Despite my feelings toward Alison, I decided to give Cara a choice. I looked down at her and spoke softly. "Cara, do you want to go see your mom?"

Cara looked up at me with worry. She clung to me tightly and shook her head. "Stay here, Abby!"

I nodded, selfishly pleased by her reaction. "Okay, we'll stay here."

The church was alive with random pictures of Jack. In some, he wore his uniform, others, he was on fishing trips or laughing with friends and family. My heart nearly stopped as two pictures stood out amongst the rest. The first one was black and white. Jack held me in his arms. I was three years old and a proud smile was perched upon his face. I remembered that day well. It was one of my last happy moments with him. We were camping, and he had spent the majority of the day carrying me proudly on his shoulders. He had told me that the world needed to see me, and though I was small, I would always rise above the crowd. I was his little princess that day. My eyes glistened over as I remembered his laughter.

The other picture was much more recent. I glanced at Mary and she pretended not to notice. It was a picture taken from the first night Mary had invited us over. In the photo, Jack and I studied each other. I remembered that moment fondly, it was a rare occasion, one where he was actually relaxed around me. It was real. The conversation hadn't been forced, it came easily and the laughter was free; it was the laughter of relief.

I held Cara securely as I listened to those who went up and paid their respects. I couldn't find the strength in myself to go up there, but I realized I didn't have too. I had given Jack much more than any speech would give him, I offered him forgiveness. It was a simple gesture but only he had known how much that took from me. The years of anger and hatred, the wall I had built so carefully, I had taken it down in front of him and finally let him in. I had given him something he had been trying to do on his own for awhile.

After the ceremony was over, I studied Cara. She made conversation with anyone who would listen. I smiled warmly at her. I owed her a lot. She would never know how much of an impact she had on the relationship between Jack and I. She brought us together. In the moments where Jack and I had nothing to say, nothing to offer each other, Cara would reach out. She saved us, she was the link that tied us together, she was our family tie. As I watched her jabber on, I knew I would be tucking her in every night and telling her stories of a man who loved her more than anything in this world. With each story, I hoped she would think the world of Jack. I wanted her to look at pictures and say his name with love, I wanted her to know she had a father who would have done anything for her. I wanted her to know she was his world, even if I was never truly a part of his.

It was ironic; though we were both a father's daughter, I had refused to say his name throughout my young years. His name had brought pain and anger. Now I would be speaking it for Cara, and it would be spoken with admiration. My hope for her was simple; to know her father loved her, and would always love her.

My thoughts were interrupted by Cara tugging at my dress. I knelt down to be level with her. "Abby? Daddy's sleeping?"

"Yes, honey, he is."

Cara's face fell slightly. "He won't wake up."

I smiled sadly. "No, baby, he won't wake up."

Cara nodded sternly and focused her gaze on her smiling teddy bear.

Alex found us. "How are you holding up?"

I shrugged. "I'm okay…I'm ready to go."

Alex held my hand and Cara reached out so we could each hold onto her. Her blue eyes lit up in concentration. "Daddy story?"

I smiled warmly. "Of course." My voice took on a story like tone. "He was a great man and he loved you so much.…"

And so, it begins.

Made in the USA
Columbia, SC
11 May 2018